The Whispers Within

The Whispers Within

Will Whispers Be Enough?

Nilsa L. Cleland

To order additional copies of this book, contact:
Xlibris Corporation
1-888-795-4274
www.Xlibris.com
Orders@Xlibris.com
124366

I would like to thank my husband Daryl, and daughter Christina, many family and friends, in particular Kimbo for their unrelenting support of my desire to finish this project of 11 years.

Additionally, I would like to thank the Colorado Coalition Against Domestic Violence, police officers, prevention of domestic violence and sexual assault advocates who help victims find new lives.

Should you find be in an unhealthy or violent relationship or assault, please contact your local police department or call the Prevention of Domestic Violence, 1-800-799-SAFE.

I heard him staggering down the hallway, banging into the banister, sloshing his drink of choice, most likely a gin and tonic, along the way. As he reached for my door, I felt my airways constrict and the walls of the room close in around me. My body stiffened, and my senses numbed, as I listened for the faint squeak of my bedroom door to open softly.

I am seventeen-year-old aristocratic-born Candace Spencer, and I quickly recognized the monster that prowled the darkness of my sanctuary. My breath faded as the muscular figure slithered into my room and onto my body. My nightmare only lasted a few minutes several times a week, but I lost a part of my soul a little bit more during each horrific moment. I closed my eyes and lived one more death as he devoured me, but tonight, I vowed it would end. The prominent and respected businessman revered by the community would not return to my bedroom again. Never again!

I had no idea how long it had been away; a Spiritual Guide's time was measured very differently compared to human lifetime. Was it a day later, or had one or twenty years passed? Right now, I had my first assignment in my new form, Mari Santiago, a sixteen-year-old teenager struggling to survive her family's domestic violence and sexual assaults in the tough streets of New York.

The Whispers Within reveals the parallel of two dissimilar lives between two teenagers: one alive and the other dead. Mari comes to know Candace in a manner she would have never dreamt. Candace, having lived life at the opposite economic strata from the inner-city life Mari was accustomed to, is only equipped with whispers of encouragement to defeat Mari's demons.

How will Candace handle returning to earth as a spirit when she did not deal with her own nemesis while alive? Will Mari be consumed by the demons that surround her, or will Candace pave a way for Mari to flee them? Will they both come to know each other's demons? Will Candace's whispers be enough for Mari to conquer her demons while building a new life?

Whispers

I whisper to you soothing words when pleas resound within the canyons of your mind,
I whisper to you when outstretched arms embrace barren air,
I whisper to you when rivers of tears flow and no one is near,
I whisper yet desire to scream.

—*Nilsa L. Cleland*

CHAPTER 1

The sliver of light seeping under my bedroom door immediately woke me from my restless slumber. I, Candace Spencer, heard his attempt to glide suavely through the corridor while slurping each drop of his drink, all the while heading toward his trophy room. As my doorknob turned slowly, it opened invading the sanctity of my bedroom while I lay still as if in a deep sleep although my senses were fully awake. My heart's rapid beating stopped as though on command, while my internal clock woke me before I felt his hand clamp down tightly around my mouth. His sweaty hand and putrid smell of alcohol would gag me instantly when one hand would clamp on my mouth and his other hand slipped off my bedcovers. He would click off the soft glow of the lamp standing on my nightstand next to her bed. His free hand would then slip under my nightgown and pull my panties off in one swift move. He would bear down on me with hunger. My soul died with every second of my punishment. After several forward lurches, he would stiffen, quickly heave himself off, and disappear out the same door he had used to invade my sanctuary. Though my immobile body would simply lie there a few minutes after my offender would finish his deed, my heart hardened increasingly. Through my closed eyes, I imagined the intruder's tall, athletic, well-built body slide out the shadows of my room. There was no need to open my eyes. I knew the figure that had lurked in the dark for many years. In the early years of my intruder's entrance, I would try to lift myself to yell for help, but I knew that would not help me. My mother was out because of her sleeping pills, and I knew of no one that would come to my rescue. I knew who my night creeper was all too well, even though during the day my offender's physique did not seem as muscular and overpowering as the monster that glided into my bedroom at night. During the day, he was simply my father.

Normally, I would rush into my bathroom for a scalding hot shower in an attempt to wash away all traces of dirt, shame, and disgust my young body endured—not tonight. I walked very slowly to my bedroom closet. My legs felt like lead. Tortured by my father's vicious grip, I always felt his imprints on my thighs hours, days, and even weeks later. Tonight, I slowly and quietly opened my closet doors so they would not creak to alert anyone else in the house. Why do the doors refuse to shut out the nightmares and their locks not work against the wickedness of the shadow?

"Fat chance anyone will wake," I thought. "Mother has already knocked herself out with her sleeping pills; our housekeepers and cook have left for the day, and Father has gotten his fill of me," I somberly mused.

I pulled out numerous shoes from the right side of the closet, and then I swiftly pulled up the carpet, revealing the secret hiding place for my most cherished possession. I pried up a loose board, so I could reach inside to retrieve a deep-burgundy-colored large velvet satchel. I quickly unlatched the button from the loop to reveal a pink diary covered with medieval pictures of Cinderella and her sweet prince. I had written in my diary, since the age of twelve, all of my innermost feelings and I did not feel comfortable sharing with anyone what was hidden in the pages that lay within my diary. As my eyes filled with tears, I softly muttered to myself, "Father, I don't understand why you did those horrible things to me. I kept quiet when you told me to shut up so you could listen to the news about financial stuff after you got home, while drinking your gin and tonic. I remembered how to make your drink—one fourth tonic, three parts gin, and one cocktail onion. I put the drink on your end table by the sitting chair every day when you got home from work. No matter what I was doing, I stopped just for you. I got your first drink every night so you could relax, while in reality, it just brought me night terrors. My father would command, "Candace, I need a gin and tonic, so I can relax now and sleep well tonight. I want to forget my day. Now, go get it! That's it, Candace," her father would say after he had a taste of the drink to ensure it was up to his standards. He would then lean in real close to me, as long as no one could see, and tell me, "It tastes just like you do, Candace. Just like you." In a wicked whisper, Mr. Spencer would snicker at me.

As I wrote my brokenhearted words in my diary, I found I could barely breathe. I glanced toward my dresser that held a photo of my mother looking up in surprise as my father had clicked a photo of her brushing my hair. I had forgotten about that photo even though it stared back at me every day. I struggled to write, "Mother, these words are for you. I never understood why you never helped me when I needed you the most. I don't think your society friends would know about our family if you had simply packed up your things and taken us away from here. You could have told everyone later you had an emergency. I know you married Father because you were forced to do so by your parents. I was born out of wedlock and all of your plans went out of the window. Your parents sent you to live with your grandparents and were miserable until I was at least three months old. It was not my fault, but you have always treated me as a stranger. Perhaps that is why Father took advantage of me and you did nothing. We could have gone to Aunt Debbie's house. Remember, she was your favorite sister? She would have stood by your side. Why did you hide behind those pills? Didn't you love me, Mother? Mother . . . Mom, I needed you! How will you feel in the morning when you discover I am gone? How will you feel when those pompous and highly paid doctors tell you that your daughter's life was ended with the same pills you used to block out your daughter's night terrors? Yes, Mother, my terror will be ended once and for all with the same tool you used to push yourself away from me and life."

With that, I fixed my bed so it would be neat and tidy the next morning. I placed my diary gently into the burgundy satchel that held my heart. I quietly slipped into my bathroom and raised the toilet tank lid. I extracted a plastic baggie full of sleeping pills. I had been going into my mother's medicine cabinet every week for the last couple of months and stolen pills for exactly this night. I replaced the lid on the toilet tank quietly and filled my pink glass.

"No turning back!" I thought. I brought the baggie filled with pills, and the pink glass, with me back into my bedroom and sat down on my bed. I opened my baggie and spilled all the pills onto my hands. I looked into my room one last time. In the morning, I would not see the shiny medieval clock that would strike seven to remind me it was time to wake so I could get ready for school.

"I cannot believe I am doing this," I thought. "This is the first time I have ever taken pills. I just can't handle this anymore. I'm so very sorry," I softly said as I held my diary tight to my chest. My diary was the first to hear about all my adventures and tortures, and now it will be the last to hear my final thoughts.

With that, I downed all forty pills with large gulps of water from my pink glass. I meticulously smoothed out my sleeping gown, placed my burgundy velvet satchel on my chest, and closed my eyes. I then placed my hand on my only best friend— my diary. I needed to feel my one best friend by my side as I departed into what I hoped would be a peaceful journey.

Now I would no longer be an object of pathetic sexual fulfillment for my father. I endured because I had to. No more. I could not breathe, and I shook like I had never shaken before. It was over. No more monsters to bear. No more silence to bear. Finally, it was peace for me, or was it?

I whisper to you soothing words when pleas resound within the canyons of your mind,
I whisper to you when outstretched arms embrace barren air,
I whisper to you when rivers of tears flow and no one is near,
I whisper yet desire to scream.
I beseech you, I beseech you come unto my side.
Don't lie down and ignore my cry.

CHAPTER 2

Where am I? How long has it been since I died? All I know is that I had been placed in the one spot where no one ever bothered me. I guess prayers are heard and answered. There really is a God!

This is the only place I would come to feel safe with my thoughts among the tranquility of nature. I could see the rippling waves softly crash against the colored stones lying peacefully in the brook while green rays appeared as the sunlight pierced through tinted leaves from nearby trees. Yes, it seems my favorite season, autumn, had commenced. Listening to the serene sounds of the flowing stream, my spirit was calmly soothed. I remembered writing pages and pages in my diary at this very spot, fantasizing about the moment I would surprise my soul mate. My prince would sense my presence while he stood at the edge of the spring water, waiting for his horse to finish drinking. He would be a fearless warrior who would keep all evil away from the treasured palace where I lived. My prince would capture and keep my heart because of his courage and love. My prince would transport me away in his sparkling gem-covered carriage to a world filled with glee, just he and I. We would be far from the reality of my real home.

As I looked around my sacred area, I remembered it was far enough from home that I could breathe and feel alive yet close enough I could run back to meet my dysfunctional family for dinner when my time away would come to an end. The ends of my lips involuntarily curved upward as every muscle relaxed deeper and deeper into the puffy cushions of my lounge chair. It smelled so fresh as the aroma of pine and lilac burst into the air. As I lazily glanced up, I saw a scatter of fluffy white clouds that dotted the clear blue sky, similar to the clouds on my childhood bedroom walls. Walls that sought to occupy the room of a young child but instead occupied the soul of a much-worn older person. A child who longed to break out of the weary shell she was forced to cocoon within. A child who simply sought to enjoy the mischief youngsters get into, youngsters who wanted a chance to play volleyball, soccer, basketball, share fantasies with a best friend, or simply exist peacefully without care of what the day or night would bring. To be young and be alive again, plus fortunate enough to enjoy it, would be a different life unlike the one I had known.

As I looked down at my new body, I noticed I was petite in stature. I showcased a slim build with voluptuous breasts and a nice round butt. Woo-hoo, I finally had boobs! If I had to come back in a body different from my old one, this one was rather tasteful. My hair was a beautiful shade of auburn that flowed fully and gracefully onto the middle of my back. I sat up confidently and strolled leisurely to take a closer look at the stream as it flowed downward to the open mouth of the lake several miles ahead. When I arrived, I stared onto my reflection in the stream. I could see my eyes were emerald green with eyelashes the fashion world could only dream of having. "Wouldn't my old girls at my school be jealous of Candace?" I thought. After a few moments, I went back to my lounge chair, so I could resume my quiet relaxation allowing the hungry folds of my chair to consume my weary body. Returning to the world of the living was not an easy task. I'd like to think that things on earth would be different this time around.

As I lie back in the lounge chair, I allow my mind to drift to the bleached white picket fence speckled with the miniature red rose bush that circled the house I once lived in until my early teens. Flickers of daisies and pansies in a patch nestled between two wooden logs had brought my thoughts to my suburban Victorian home. My house, which was painstakingly designed to ensure all its furnishings, wall colorings, paintings, and figurines were coordinated with the same motif and would always be the talk of the town after every dinner party. I recalled certain toys I was allowed to play with. These were toys specially designed for me, so I couldn't disrupt the look created for my fairy-tale room after I played with them. If I placed the toys in the wrong place, my mother would reprimand me so I would know how to respect the fact she had searched high and low with a designer from France for toys and furnishings that would fit the room created just for me. *Do I not understand how exhausting it was for her to fly to France for a quick weekend of shopping specifically for my fairy-tale room, for her little princess? I needed to be more appreciative by placing my special toys back in their proper places when finished!* The only fairy tales in those days were the ones I concocted within the theatre of my mind. The theatre where I gave the actors wonderful scripts they could enjoy and go home happy at the end of the day! Those days were over, and I had to force my thoughts back to the mission at hand.

I found a file with my name on it and the name of my new case subject on top of the end table next to my chair. Hmmm, Mari Santiago. So, Mari, what has brought you to me?

CHAPTER 3

I fell asleep while reading Mari's file and was woken by Mama Lynn, my new instructor in the Intermittent Level, where new Spiritual Guides transfer to from their previous "newbie status / safe zone" transition area. I was startled yet I was quick to get on my feet and be guided into Mama Lynn's class, where all new Spiritual Guides are registered. Mama Lynn's gentle eyes and mannerism made me feel very comfortable as I was led into her new Spiritual Guide's Course 101, where I noticed others were already seated for class. All Guides are comfortably guided into their Safe Zone prior to attending the Spiritual Guide's course. The transition helps in recognizing that new members are recognized as special. The Guide's experience will help in bringing hope into his or her subject's life. Not everyone comes into this special zone. It is reserved for people who have unique qualities that can help in assisting living people get their acts together so they too can eventually become Spiritual Guides helping living souls cope with their unique situations when their time on earth comes to an end. This intervention may mean the difference between life and death. It is all up to the selected subject.

The ability to direct a Spiritual Guide from his or her comfort zone will make it easier to convert the Guide into a classroom environment where the Guides can relax and learn from one another. It is imperative for all Guides to exert his or her knowledge to their new subjects. As Mama Lynn immerses into her class's topics, I was immediately captivated by my new role as a potential Spiritual Guide that will someday obtain wings after I successfully graduate from my first mission. After twenty-seven weeks of education regarding my new case's tasks, I graduate, and meet Pearl. Pearl is to be my new "soul mate" for my new adventures with my subject. Pearl has been doing this a really, really long time, so I feel pretty confident I will be in excellent hands during my first assignment. I am excited to finally go out on my own and prove to Pearl, my supervisor, and the rest of the executive team that I am ready and capable to triumph over my new mission. I am also excited to prove to myself that I can handle this mission while becoming an effective Spiritual Guide. Additionally, Mama Lynn and Pearl, or Pearlie as I decided to call my new supervisor, had mentioned to the graduating class that there was a very big surprise for the Guides when they successfully direct their subjects onto the right paths for them.

This afternoon, I would see for the first time the teenager I was assigned to. I truly did not want this case. Actually, I hated this case before it even started. I felt the nausea working its way up to my throat.

"Ugh! I was taught to handle everything that came my way with dignity and completion until it was finished. I just need to deal with this case. I simply need to remember, mind over matter and do not allow emotions to overpower *you*!" I thought to myself.

"It is over," I continued to contemplate to myself. For the first time in my life, I was chosen to do something important. I thought I knew why I was chosen, yet at the same time, I was terrified I may not be able to complete my task, and my subject's life may be at stake. However, it is time to bring hope and script out a new life to this poor young girl. I may not have been strong enough to fight my demons while I was alive, but I am going to do my best to help end my subject's demons. Hopefully, it isn't too late!

CHAPTER 4

She emerged from a cluster of children. Each child was carrying a set of books, and others were also carrying musical instruments in tattered cases. She walked quickly away from the crowd, looking around as though searching for someone or something. With a slight nod of her head toward a boy who appeared to be about seventeen years old, she crossed the street to where he was waiting.

"OK, that must be her brother," I thought as I looked through the subject's file given to me by my Pearl the day prior. It fits his description. He appeared to be 5'11", dark brown hair, cut short and tight to his head. He sported a slim build and was very neatly dressed for a boy having finished a full day of school. His dark brown puppy-dog eyes acknowledged his sister as she got closer, and he fell into step with her as they both walked home. Five minutes later, they entered a dilapidated five-story brick building that fit right in line with the rest of the adjoining buildings in the run-down inner-city neighborhood. After climbing four flights of stairs, they entered their apartment.

Mari Santiago went straight to her room, closed her door, dropped her handful of books onto her bed, and commenced undressing. Glistening black hair that softly draped her shoulders was swiftly pulled back tightly into a ponytail. As she commenced to change out of her school clothes into a loose pair of jeans and sweatshirt, I immediately noticed how her body reflected that of a much older child. Her breasts were quite full for a sixteen-year-old. Although she was stocky in build, she was well proportioned physically and could easily pass for eighteen years of age. Her skin was full of acne, showing signs of her adolescent years and several years of eating too many unhealthy snacks. She wore black rectangular-rimmed glasses that obscured her beautiful almond-shaped black eyes that could speak to you without words ever leaving her mouth.

"C'mon, Jon. Hurry up! We need to start dinner, and I don't plan on cooking it by myself again," she bellowed out to her brother. Good gosh, he's slow—he still hasn't changed, Mari thought as she started pulling out pots and pans onto the counters of their small kitchen.

"Girl, quit the crap! I'm gonna help. I don't want you whining to Mom and Pop how you didn't get most of your homework done 'cause you had to cook all by your ugly self," Jonathan Santiago yelled back to her from his bedroom.

"*Boys are such jerks!*" she thought as she continued her tasks.

From my vantage point, I observed how the Santiagos' home reflected a tidy and modestly furnished three-bedroom apartment. Their kitchen was painted white. The kitchen window was secured with a middle lock, as well as dual-side locks that screwed into the wall keeping the uninvited out. It was dressed with a frilly blue-and-white curtain displaying a variety of fruits and baskets. All the pots, pans, and utensils were weathered through the years of use, yet they still sparkled and were neatly stacked according to size. My eyes continued to scan their living quarters and fell on the small living room where heavy light blue with dark blue velvet flowered drapes hugged a pair of beige linen curtain sheers. The tan sofa covered with brown, blue, and green flowers with matching chairs were protected under a clear plastic covering. The family television set was medium sized and old in comparison to the newer versions out in the market. Yet the television was neatly decorated with a white doily and a shiny blue ceramic sailboat with white wavy sails. The three bedrooms were minimally decorated except for religious figurines of Jesus Christ, the Virgin Mary, and several saints. Heavy wooden crosses were nailed securely into the walls, portraying a clear view of their beliefs. The white and beige sparkled linoleum floors were spotless and maintained the tidy look the entire apartment possessed. Nothing looked out of place. "My gosh, if I didn't know better, I'd think they have a full-time cleaning staff on the payroll," I thought as I continued to survey their apartment. I learned about this period of time in my Spiritual Guide's Course 101. "Blows me away," I thought as I tried to remember the phrases of these new times and all the slides and videos about the era and location I was returning to for my assignment.

"Hey, Jon, are you gonna come out and help me or are you gonna stay in your room all day?" Mari screeched out angrily.

"Crap, girl. Shut up already. I'll be there in a minute."

"Oooh, I'm gonna tell Mom you cussed at me and I'm gonna laugh my butt off when she smacks you right across your big mouth."

"Yeah, yeah. I don't care," Jon retorted as he slowly walked into the kitchen. "So, what have you done so far?"

"I've already started the rice, and I'm cutting the onions and peppers for the beans. I need you to season the pork chops and start cooking 'em." Mari instructed her brother.

At 5:45 p.m. sharp, Benjamin and Sara Santiago walked through the doors, displaying very weary faces indicating a long and tiring day at the manufacturing plant. Benjamin, known to all as Benjy, was a handsome dark wavy-haired Don Juan—looking man who walked in first dropping his silver thermos, newspaper, and lunch box onto the kitchen table. His crisp short-sleeved tight-fitting uniform accentuated his 5'9" muscular body. Taking his seat at the head of the table, he commenced his daily routine of grabbing a beer out of the refrigerator and reading the Spanish newspaper before dinner.

Sara quickly went to her bedroom, changed into a bright pink floral housedress and pink slippers, and came into the kitchen to add the final touches to her family's evening meal that Jon and Mari had started.

"Jonathan, Mari, do yu have yur school work done?" she asked.

"I just need to finish my math and science homework," Mari answered from her bedroom that was next to the kitchen. She was sprawled out on her bed with her books in front of her, taking up most of the space.

"Jonathan, what about yu?"

"Aye, Mami, I'm almost finished. I only have to do my social studies homework and then I'm done. I had some free time at school today, so I worked on some of my homework there," Jonathan answered from the kitchen table without looking up.

"Jonathan, I need you to finish your homework somewhere else, *hijo*. OK?" Sara said as she put food on the table. Neither Sara nor Benjy called Jonathan "Jon" or any other nickname. They wanted Jonathan and Mari to understand that children needed to be mindful when their parents called them. They were to respond immediately since Sara and Benjy did not want disrespectful children and this was a step taken to help ingrain respect into them.

"Yeah, OK, Ma," Jonathan answered as he picked up his books and left for his room.

After dinner was finished, the children resumed their homework and Sara started cleaning up the kitchen. Although it was Friday and the start of the weekend, the children were not allowed to put their books away until every bit of their homework was completed; then and only then were Mari and Jonathan allowed to relax and watch television or play their video games. As Sara filled the sink with hot sudsy water, she noticed Benjy's dash into the bathroom for what she assumed to be a long shower for the start of an evening out with the boys.

After his shower, he quickly changed into a pair of trousers and a nicely ironed sport shirt, indicating he was definitely not staying in for the evening.

"OK, here we go," I thought as I observed Benjy paying exceptional attention to his hair and how he looked in the mirror. Once satisfied with his appearance, he splashed his face with a handful of aftershave cologne that was sure to get him noticed by the opposite sex. It had worked for him in the past and he expected it will work for him tonight. After he finished in the bathroom, he pulled out a wad of money, counted it, put a portion of it into a small drawer of the spice rack on the wall, and placed the remainder in his wallet.

"*Sara, puse el dinero para el alquiler, utilidades, y para que compres la comida que necesitamos en la gaveta.*" I was bilingual in several languages and Spanish was one of them. Benjy told Sara he put money for their rent, utilities, and groceries in the drawer. Whew, at least a school topic came in to help me out, I thought.

Keeping her eyes on the dishes she was putting away, she simply nodded her head and gave him a curt, "*Maldita sea!* Damn, Benjy, why yu do this? Why yu no stay home wit me and thee kids?"

"*Para donde vas?* Where yu go?" Sara asked, apparently not pleased, and defeated at the same time with the obvious indication Benjy was out for some fun on the town that evening without her or the children. She also wanted to know where he was going.

"*Ah, mujer!* I go shoot pool wit the guys," Benjy answered as he continued to get ready to leave.

"You no tell me not'in' *hasta ahora*! Wha guys are yu go wit?" Sara continued to probe. She had no idea Benjy was going out with the guys until now.

"Sara, the guys from work I always go out wit," Benjy answered, sounding a tad irritated.

"Wha time yu going to be back?"

"I no know. Go to sleep or stay up. I no care!"

"Uh, hmm," murmured Sara.

I noticed Sara's eyes narrow and veins turn to ice as she focused on the dishes to avoid a scene in front of the children.

"So, this is Papa's night out with the boys," I thought as I thumbed through the pages in my file regarding Benjy's history. As I started skimming through his information, I learned he had a Friday-night social ritual, called *viernes social* where he left his family so he could enjoy a night out with the boys. It seemed he not only had a Friday night ritual out but many times in the past, he also had Saturday and Sunday nights out as well. I remembered in my Spiritual Guide's Course 101 when I first left earth, it talked about situations like this, where men and sometimes women too left their homes to experience who they were as individuals. They would just leave to prove that they could to have some "me" time. Not all men and women were like Benjy in that they went out so they could and would exert their control and their power over their wives, husbands, girlfriends, boyfriends, or children. This was a very different scenario from those that went out for a couple of drinks during the weekend or after work to catch up with their friends. What I learned looking through the files was that these weekend drinks did not always end up with in a fun night for Sara and the kids.

A few moments later, Benjy bolted out of his apartment door. Sara went to her bedroom window in hopes she could see the direction her husband would take.

"I wonder if that son of a bitch is playing pool wit the boys or he gonna play pool wit his balls," she said as she pounded her fist with all her might on the window frame. Sara was so tired of this. It was almost twenty-one years of the same things over and over.

Mari walked into her parents' bedroom after seeing her mom's noticeable change and put her arms around her mother's petite waist as she laid her head on the small of her back.

"Mami, do you want to watch TV with me? I'm done with my homework."

"No, no right now, *hija mia*. Tonight I light candles for the saints and pray with my rosary. *Despues*, OK? Later," Sara said in her heavy Spanish accent. Sara turned around and hugged her daughter. With tears streaming down her worn face, she softly murmured, "If no be for yu kids, I no be in this *casa y* be married with Benjy."

"What did you say, Mami?" Mari asked although she was certain of what she heard her mom say. She had heard her mother say those words over and over so many times before. She had heard her mom say she would not be in their house if it were not for her and Jonathan. Ugh, Mari felt so guilty having to be part of what hurt her mom, her very special mami.

"*Nada*, not'in'. Go see TV. No sit close. I no wan yur eyes getting more bad than they are," Sara told her daughter with a gentle tone and shoved Mari lovingly out of her bedroom, but not before Mari gave her mother a peck on both of her cheeks. Mari pivoted on the ball of her foot, giving Sara a quick and stiff salute before she headed straight to the living room to receive her evening dose of the tube.

As I continued to observe Mari as she sat in front of the television, she seemed to be watching TV as images crossed the screen, yet I sensed she was not watching them. I commenced to write notes in her file of my observations to this point. I felt certain Mari's mind was on a different program.

The program Mari was thinking of had scenes that were not the ones she would eagerly want to settle herself into her favorite spot to watch with a bowl of popcorn. Mari was very familiar with the actors. She loved them with all that was instilled in her heart, yet she loathed watching the program since she always knew how it would end. She could hear their lines before they left the actors' mouths. She could anticipate their movements, and the props they would use. This was a channel she could not change. At least not right now. She settled back in her sweats, holding her favorite popcorn and started to watch TV. She blocked everything out of her mind and heart, and stared intensely at the screen and its images. After a couple of hours, she called it a night and went straight to her room, where she bolted the lock for the evening. Mari knew she wouldn't be able to shut out the sounds that would eventually come from the kitchen, living room, or her parents' room but she could be at least secure herself in her own little cave. She went to bed with her sweats and covered herself from head to toe with her bed comforter. She couldn't drown the sounds that sometimes came from the other rooms, no matter how many blankets she would put over her head or how she squeezed her hands to her ears. She was desperately saving her meager weekly allowance for an iPod with headsets like Jonathan had. He went to sleep with his set in his ears listening to the music and not the wild crawling in their home. She firmly believed he didn't always listen to his music because he liked it, but only because that was the only way he could deal with their homelife. Home sweet home, my butt! Maybe, just maybe, she could fall asleep, stay asleep all night long, and wake up to the beautiful warm rays of sunlight that would creep through her window blinds, inviting her to the world of the living. But, she knew better.

I knew better too. As I continued to watch Mari, I could only suspect she slept in her sweats in the event she had to dash out of her room at a moment's notice. Oh yeah, she knew the drill! Except in my case, I was not allowed to wear anything but my nightgown. If I wore some pajamas, my father would smack me for making it difficult for him. If only I could pull her away from this awful place, I thought. Soon, very soon! The time had to be right. Whether I wanted it or not, I would have to be a spectator for a while. To watch a scene I had seen so many times before in my own life and kept hearing about it, as "friends" would gossip about her life to her other "friends" yet did nothing to help. Except in my life, words weren't spoken. Mother would motion me to go to my room; she would then go hide in her room, pop some pills, and drift off to sleep after a tall stiff drink as a nightcap. It was not proper for a woman of her status to raise her voice or even ask her husband where he was going or what he was doing. Even if she considered asking, my father would not bring himself to tell her. It was none of her business. My father provided his family with a very wealthy and comfortable way of life. He worked hard, and he believed in compensating his long hours with pleasant recreational activities that did not include his wife and, least of all, his child. Perhaps the actors, stage, and props were different in Mari's story, but the ending was always the same. Always!

CHAPTER 5

Her hair blew freely in the warm summer air, sometimes covering her face when the wind shifted and threw wisps of it into her eyes. She didn't care. She was having a blast as her stomach tickled when the Ferris wheel dipped and quickly ascended once again for another joyful circle. The sky was a crystal light blue with Pacific blue waves caressing the shoreline as the current peacefully moved the water. The only sounds resonating were the gleeful laughter produced by her mami, papi, brother, and herself as they enjoyed the exciting rides in the amusement park. The park was closed to the public. Mari's family was the only admission in the park this day. It was their private family day! No one was fighting or bickering. All you could hear was laughter. All you could see was her dad hugging her mom, brother, and herself. It was so great! This is real, right? This is what family life should be, so it had to be real.

"Mami, want to go on the merry-go-round? How about you, Papi? Jonathan, I bet I can beat you to the biggest horse on it?" Mari ecstatically said to her family as she bolted to the majestic carousel.

Her dad was the first to respond. "Of course, *nena linda*, my beautiful daughter. We would love to. Come on, Jonathan, let's go have some—" *Crash.* The sound of broken glass startled Mari from her fantasy dream. She was about to put the pillow over her head and curl into her comforting fetal position when she heard her bedroom door reverberate as a kitchen chair slammed into it. Her body started to shake with fright as her eyes bolted open. No, that is not real. My carousel is real!

"Oh sweet Jesus, if you really do exist, please make them stop fighting. How can you let this happen? Moms and dads should be happy. They should hug, kiss, and play with their children. Go to the park with merry-go-rounds," Mari thought as she prayed fervently to the God she believed must have been in another country helping someone else at this very moment. God, how can you do this to my mami and us? You whom I pray to almost every day. Am I praying wrong or are you angry because sometimes I fall asleep and do not pray to you? Do I need to do something really bad to myself so my parents will hug and love each other again? With me being gone, maybe Mami will not have to be here to be hurt by my papi. Do I need to hurt myself really bad so I can see you and talk to you directly and maybe then you will help them?

"Ahh, Mari, please do not think like that. I did hurt myself really bad," I whispered to Mari. "Nothing good happened. My mother ended up hurting herself pretty bad and ended up in a hospital. My father ended up just working and drinking his life away. Please, please just reach out to someone you trust. Let your voice be heard." Whispers continued as I sat down next to a trembling and tearful Mari.

CHAPTER 6

Sara's tear-streaked face was distorted in anguish as she confronted Benjy. The petite, 5'2", 110-pound woman was holding her ground. Her spine-chilling nagging shrieks fell upon deaf ears. Benjy went into their bedroom and commenced undressing, oblivious to his wife's high-pitched cries demanding he tell her whom he was with. *Ay caramba*, all he wanted was a restful sleep in his warm bed. He wanted to lay his head on a soft pillow and have a very quiet house. Perhaps that would erase the throbbing headache he had. Maybe he can have Sara make him some café, nice and black espresso style. That would definitely make his headache go away, but Sara was making it really hard for him to keep his cool.

Well, Benjy is having a good time, I thought as I strolled in to see how things were going. He had such a good time playing pool with Paco, Ramon, and Gregorio. I noticed things really got hopping when, according to Benjy, a sweet-looking babe with the tight ass started giving him the eye. Oh yeah, he knew it would be a hot time tonight when she strolled over and asked if he had a light, so she could puff on her cigarette with those luscious full red lips of hers. Her snug low-cut crimson silk blouse exposed a delicious set of breasts that were difficult not to drool over. When she sat next to him, she discreetly rubbed her shapely legs against his trousers, indicating that she wanted to get to know him a little more intimately. Of course, Benjy had to oblige. *I mean, I gentleman, right? It no be nice of me not to pay attention to her when she come see me and speak wit me? I no only am a gentleman, but I am a man too.*

I had never seen anyone consume as much alcohol before. Even Benjy could not remember how many shots of rum they had before he followed her to her car. She had seen enough and knew how it would all end. In a split second, Benjy and his evening's date hopped into the backseat to explore each other's bodies. "Ay, mami, yu is hot!" Benjy thought. Although he didn't want to leave her before another ride of ecstasy, he knew it was getting really late, and he would have hell to pay when he got home. He gave this hot babe a kiss she would not forget for a very long time as he pulled her out of her backseat and settled her into the front seat of her car. He seductively pulled the seat belt over her bosom. He looked at her with burning eyes, not allowing her glance to move anywhere else.

"Yu be so good, mamacita. I no forget yu," he softly spoke to her, knowing he had already forgotten her name as he moved away from her car. He needed to head home and face the woman he lived with, who would not let him forget he had arrived after midnight.

Benjy was definitely right about the hell he had to pay! The walls of his head were about to explode when Sara started her tantrum like she usually did when he got home after the midnight hour. Crap, crap, he was going to have to get up out of his bed if she wouldn't shut up. And he was going to make sure she knew he wasn't going to put up with her stuff. He was not happy. Papi no happy—nobody happy. That's the way it was in *his* house!

That was the way it was in Father's house, growing up. His father would work long, long hours in the fields dealing with chickens, goats, pigs, horses, cows, and spreading their manure all around the fields so it would help the crops grow. Benjy remembered the 4:30 a.m. hour, when his father would wake his butt up. "*Hijo, levante*, son, get up. Time to work. Put yur clothes on. I be in kitchen," Benjy's father would bellow. After a fifteen-minute breakfast of eggs, bacon, bread, and milk, both father and son would head to the fields before the crow would start its morning song reminding the rest of Puerto Rico it was time to wake up. Benjy's mind drifted to a time when his mother did not have breakfast ready on time. It was 4:35 a.m., and Benjy's father got so angry he broke Benjy's mother's hand so it would help her remember what it was she uses to cook her husband's breakfast with on time. Benjy was yanked by the collar by his father so he could head outside while his mother was left whimpering by the sink as she started to pull out the fixings for lunch to ensure it would be on time for Benjy's father when he returned from the field.

"Benjy, yu see that? Yu show a woman where her place is. Yur woman need to have your food ready on time. Yu go work hard in the field makin' sure yur family have food on the table, and if no food be ready when yu wake out of bed, then yu need to show yur wife tha no good. Oh no, tha no bueno, hijo. My father, yur abuelo, he teach me how it done. He make sure food on table when he got up. Oh yez. We go to work wit full belly. Mama knew her place. Yur mother know her place. If no, her husban teach the woman her place in thee house. Yur mami should know her place. Benjy, yu teach woman yu man of the house. Yu teaches her." Benjy's father would instruct Benjy as to make sure he understood his role as a husband. Benjy would only nod his head since any other response would elicit a smack across his face, and he was going to go see Angelina later that night at her barn. "Oh yeah, Angelina. Sweet Angelina," Benjy thought as he turned in his nice comfortable bed. His father's lunch had been hot and ready by the time they returned from the farm chores.

Right now was not the time to reminisce of old times. It was already 1:15 a.m. It was time to sleep and not have his wife carry on like a pathetic old hag whining about him having some time with his friends. He worked damn hard to make sure she and the kids have a roof over their heads, food for their bellies, and clothes on their back. What the hell more did she want? He brought her over to the United States of America to make sure she and his children would not have wants and be proud of him, Benjy—father and husband. "She no grateful. No grateful of me and my hard work," Benjy said softly as his anger simmered on.

"How come yu be home so late? I am tired of working away so hard wit washing, ironing, and cook food for yu and then all yu do is no respect for me and yur children. Do twenty-one years of marriage mean not'in' to yu? Who tha woman? Is she da woman from tha *bodega* yu look at so much when we go there? We no have to go to tha store to buy tings so much but yu go all thee time. Do yu wan me to put yur clothes in tha street *o la basura,* tha trash? There yu wan to live, like trash *o basura?* Wha kinda example yu setting for yur children? Yu no respect me, yu need respect yur children. If it no be for da children, I go away a long time ago!" Sara barked at him as she wrung her housedress into tight spirals in her hands.

As an encaged lion leaps out to freedom, Benjy flung his bedcovers off and leaped onto the floor. "Oh no, what is he going to do?" I thought in horror as I saw him rocket toward his wife. Even with all that I had been through in my life, I could still feel my body freeze into place and my muscles lock at what I feared I would see. At that very point, I saw Benjy grab Sara by her hair with his left hand and fiercely backhand her across the mouth with the other.

"*Callate, mujer!* Shut up, woman! All I wanna do is sleep. Yu wanna know why I stay out so long? It's because of yur *boca,* yur mouth. Yu no know when to shut up," he shouted at her, inches from her face. With that said, he threw her against the living room wall with the fisted hand that held her hair. She was flung across the room like a rag doll that is broken and is thrown away by a child. The doll no longer fulfills the pleasure of the child.

"Damn it, Sara, get up and call the police," I screamed at Sara, forgetting that my words could not be heard by anyone except Mari. I was not allowed to do anything. Simply observe, listen to their thoughts, evaluate, and whisper words to Mari. Words that I hoped with prayer would bring about acts of courage for that young forgotten teenager. Now Sara needs help and I am unable to provide her with any assistance. Yeah, my gut told me Sara wasn't going to do anything except be a punching bag for her husband. I've seen this before. Different actors, different stages, different props! I remembered how my own mother would mask her black-and-blue puffy eyes with an extra layer of makeup and then put on large sunglasses. She would later go sit in her reading room for the better part of the day with a bottle of aged cognac by her side. She would instruct me to tell her friends that would drop by unannounced that she had taken ill and had retired to her quarters under doctor's strict orders to rest and avoid interruptions that would hinder her recovery. Yes, my mother was quite proper. My mother never reached out and called upon anyone for help. It was private family business. No one was to know. She was fearful of people gossiping among one another when they met for drinks at the country club. No, she would not be the topic of discussion for others to laugh about or raise their eyebrows when she walked across the room. I was left alone to deal with my pain.

I could not talk to my mother because I knew she would not believe me if I had told her everything, even though I knew she had to hear her husband leave their bed to come into mine. Mrs. Spencer would not want anyone to know her husband was a molester of his own flesh and blood.

I could feel the walls of my heart swell as I shifted from my hidden memories and instead watched powerlessly as Sara leaned against the wall in a crouched position with her arms wrapped around her body as she laid her head onto her bent knees. Her eyes were closed, yet tears flowed as though the dam of Niagara Falls had been flung open. She looked so frail and lost.

"Because of tha kids, I let yu hit me wit yur dirty hands. Yu just wait. Yu just wait," she thought as every muscle in her face throbbed.

I wished I could go to Sara and hold her hands so I could also tell her it would be OK. "You don't have to take it anymore, Sara!" I thought. Even so, I could do nothing. I could feel others' emotions and thoughts related to my subject, Mari, but could only communicate to Mari. What a crock! How I wished I could be helping Sara right now, but instead, I sat at the edge of my seat, watching Sara get the crap beat out of her. I couldn't do what I wanted to do when I was the subject of the abuse and now I can't do what I want because I am a Spiritual Guide. How I really needed to talk with my supervisor right now! A nice sturdy baseball bat would come handy in situations like this. We need to get some things looked at more closely about our responsibilities here on earth. I could be the Spiritual Guide with the baseball bat out to help out victims of abuse. Nope, boy, that would not fly! I also came in peace and wanted to be here for Mari.

Mari would be the only one who could sense me and hear my whispers if she wanted. She could not be able to see me. I could not force Mari to do anything since she was free to choose her own path. That was very clear in the contract I had to read and sign before heading on my journey back down to earth. It was under the clause "Free Will." For a minute there, I thought it was something about the movie *Free Willy* or at least something related to it. Dang it, I could be such a dork sometimes! All I could hope for is that I would say the right words to convince Mari to choose wisely. I only spoke the right words at the right times since I understood tough times were coming to her. Hopefully, my words will be the arms that embrace Mari and my words the shoulder that she could lean on when her heart is heavy. Failure was not an option. I would not be like others who failed me when I needed them the most. I was simply a lifeless body that was on a mission to help kick someone's booty when the time came, by whispering what was needed to be said when the time came. It was time for me to do some smooth talking like the actors do when the pinnacle of the show is at hand. Why make it more difficult than it already is for Mari to grow up? Life is difficult as it is without this unnecessary ugly stuff that is affecting her mom and ultimately affecting her and Jonathan. It was up to me to see that nothing went wrong. Mari's life depended on it!

I slipped back into Mari's room. All I could see was the silhouette of a body underneath a blanket. Her body lay rigid in a circular fetal position, with hands cupping her ears. The only movement displaying any sign of life was the faint rise and fall of her blanket against her body. Morning will arrive before long, and it is up to Mari how she molds it. The day will bring you happiness and hope, or you can continue to dwell on the misery that was brought to your mom and now onto you. Either you will let it lure you into pain or lift you onto a new horizon filled with rays of sunshine. It is up to you, Mari. You are stronger than you think. You can be the David that demolishes Goliath. For now, sleep your fears away. Rest, morning will come soon enough, I mused as I simply sat next to her.

With God's help, my whispers would permeate the thick walls surrounding Mari's soul. Mari could etch a new life for herself and her family.

CHAPTER 7

Mari rustled under the bedcovers as the loud clatters of pots and pans announced the morning's breakfast process had commenced. Mari's heavy eyelids slowly opened, taking in the morning's light, acknowledging the reality that the rest of her body did not want to face and bringing to an end the night's escape. She yawned, stretched her tight limbs, and immediately bolted upright, realizing she needed to dress and check out her mom's battle wounds. She quickly changed into loose-fitting navy blue workout sweats and hoodie and rushed into the bathroom. As she glanced toward her mother by the stove, Marie noticed she was wearing sunglasses. Sara kept an extra pair of sunglasses in her nightstand. Mari simply sighed and tried to keep her emotions in check so her mom would not worry about her too.

"Morning, Mami," Mari greeted Sara with a slight hug as she rushed by on her way to the bathroom. Sara merely nodded and continued preparing what seemed to be scrambled eggs and toast, "Yep, breakfast for a champion," I thought as she continued to observe the two interact after such a tough night.

I noticed Sara wore heavy face foundation to conceal the bruises she received the night before. I inched closer to examine her face and noticed her cheeks were red with a purplish shadow. Her right eye was swollen twice its size, barely exposing her eye.

"That lousy, no-good piece of trash," I thought as I recalled last evening's nightmare. How can I help break the chains that seemed to strangle this family's every gasp for air? I continued to look at Sara while sensing my emotions clouding my mission's objective and instead getting angrier with Sara's husband. I wanted to pounce on Benjy and give him a couple of black eyes! I suddenly got into a weakened spiritual state. I could feel a deep ache slice into the middle of my heart. I could see my aura's bleach-white shadow changing into black rays as my hands wrung tighter together to control the involuntary tremors that possessed me.

"Oh God, help me. I feel so weak! What's going on? I feel sick to my stomach and I can barely stand up. Man, I'm not feeling good. What is going on?" I felt a lack of coordination with my feet while feeling nausea surging up my throat making its way toward freedom. Joyful!

"How can I be feeling this way when I'm already dead? Pearl, I need you, what is happening to me? Pearl!" I hoarsely said as I clutched at my stomach, tumbling onto the floor.

"Candace, Candace. Wake up, sweetie," a soft yet strong voice called out. "Candace!"

"Pearl, Pearlie, is that you?" I asked as she slowly lifted my body off the floor.

"Yes, Candace, it is. What in the tarnation are you doing? You are supposed to be helping Mari, not taking a nap!" the voice tinged with humor asked. "Did you miss the *no-sleeping* clause in your contract?"

"Pearlie, you are far from being humorous. Will you please zap me out of this, or are you too busy rehearsing for a Whoopi Goldberg role?" I snickered back at her as I finally felt the blood seeping back into my system.

"Now, now, sweet child, no need for snide remarks. I just love and adore Whoopi Goldberg and her jokes are so much better than mine! Do not go messing with my girl, you feel me?" Pearlie snapped back. "Now, you have simply experienced the repercussions of self-imposed vengeance and hatred. You are not here as a vigilante. Nor were you sent down to earth to give rebirth to feelings you felt when you were alive. You were chosen to bring guidance and hope to an innocent young adult like you that is falling into the hands of abuse. You need to tell her and have her understand she has the possibility of great things to come. You should focus on the emotional needs of Mari, not on your own."

"OK, OK, understood. I would say I'm just being human, but I guess in my situation, that wouldn't be too convincing, would it?" I retorted.

"No, it wouldn't seem as though it would, sweetie," Pearl responded a tad more sweetly.

The front door opened, and I noticed Benjy entering the kitchen with a beautiful large bouquet of red roses. Benjy, with bowed head, meekly stepped up to Sara and gently called her name.

"Sarita, I sooo sorry. I no mean for yu to cry. I need to sleep and yu yelling and yelling at me, yu made me hit yu because I need sleep and I get angry. Yu know how I get when I tired and wanna sleep. Yu know, right? My beautiful Sara! Yu know I no wan to hit yu. Yu are a good and beautiful wife," Benjy said as he gently pulled Sara slowly to him, grabbing her by her butt with his free hand.

"Benjy, yu no need to hit me tat hard. It hurt me. It hurt my heart, Benjy."

"Sarita, my beautiful and wonderful baby, yu are my heart. I no wanna hurt yu. Yu know tha. Yu are my baby, yu know tha, right? I love yu, why I wan to hurt my baby and make her cry?" Benjy asked as he pulled Sara even closer and nuzzled her head into his shoulder. Sara's body slowly lost its stiffness and she gently sniffled as her tears dampened her cheeks.

"Deeze flowers are berry preetie. Tank yu, Benjy. Yu want café now? I make yu eggs and bacon wit bread. OK?"

"Hmmm, tha good, Sara. Berry good." Benjy turned and stepped toward the kitchen table while Sara turned to make Benjy his breakfast. I notice a slight smirk on Benjy's face as he sat on his seat at the head of the table while he waited for Sara to serve his breakfast.

"He knows he's got Sara where he wants her. She's not going to stay angry with him. He's got her hooked back on his side again. You scumbag!" I murmured as I watched the hypocritical drama unfold. Sadly, all I could do was shake my head.

"It's all about choices. Your decision at this time is different from Sara's decision. Maybe a number of years ago, when you were alive knowing what you know now, you might have acted differently. You have a different perspective now. That perspective is what needs to be offered to Mari. It is not up to Mari to decide for her mother and brother. Mari needs to find her own way and then she can help her mother and family," Pearl whispered to me.

The bathroom door opened, and Mari reappeared, looking slightly more awake.

"Ma, are Jenny, Richie, Titi Ana, and Tio Pablo coming over tonight?"

"Yez, yur cousins, aunts, and uncles are coming for dinner. Luisa and Ramon are coming wit their children. Make sure yur room is picked up and clean. OK, *hija?*"

"Ah, great." Mari grimaced at the thought of her other Aunt Luisa and Uncle Ramon also joining them for dinner. She disliked the thought of those two whining brats, Ramon Jr., age six, and his brother, Manuelito, age four, coming over to spoil her fun time with Jenny. She just knew they would get in her face, asking her to play stupid kid games and then gripe when they lost. She sighed, hoping for a miracle of a twenty-four-hour bug that would attack them and force them to stay home in bed. If that happened, it would affect the entire family and they all could stay home since she didn't care for her aunt and uncle. Aunt Luisa was so loud and stupid. She was always making jokes that were either mean or dumb about others. Mari figured everyone just tolerated her because her oldest daughter ran away almost a year ago and had never been heard of again. Sofia was sixteen years old when she left. She was so cool! She would always come over and listen to music with Mari and even showed her the latest moves in the "big teen" dance world. She would bring over her teen magazines and then they would fantasize about being married to all the hottest stars. Sofia always played with Mari's hair and makeup on her. Mari thought she looked like a rock star, and Sofia just looked at Mari and reminded her she did not need makeup to look absolutely beautiful.

Several months before she left, Mari noticed Sofia would give her big hugs and she detected sadness in her eyes. Later when Sofia and her family would come to visit, she noticed Sofia would want to sneak to the fire escape and smoke cigarettes. Sofia also stopped wearing what little makeup she used to wear, hardly ever smiled, and didn't even talk much. She started eating obsessively, she stopped playing with Mari's hair, fantasizing about rock stars, and playing with any makeup altogether.

Boy, she missed her! She was the only one that really got her. Then there was Uncle Ramon, who always gave her the creeps! If Mari was Sofia, who knows, she might have left too.

Mari's uncle always made her really uncomfortable. He was so rude when he spoke, always making sexual jokes that were disgusting. Mari hated it when he made her sit on his lap even when there was a chair available right next to him that she could sit on. He was so weird! He always had a way of bumping his hand "accidentally" on her boob or butt. Ugh, she really disliked him! Mari's thoughts of her evening's upcoming disaster with her family were interrupted when Sara started banging the silverware and plates on the table.

"This is going to be a really shitty day! I can just feel it. Breakfast is not going to be any better. I can just feel that too. Hope I don't get the burnt toast this time," Mari mused as she broke away from her own thoughts to start helping her mother finish the breakfast meal.

CHAPTER 8

"What did I forget? What can I do to make things better with Mari's family?" I thought as I helplessly stood by Mari, feeling her emotions and hearing her thoughts. What's the key to help Mari start some type of support system in which she could speak about her problems at her house? Provide someone to speak to Mari and arrange a place for Benjy to speak about why he has to hit versus talk to Sara. I so wished I had the ability to reach my attorney. I would have this matter fixed in a second, but I no longer had access to my family's resources. It was sad to stand by and see Sara become a punching bag for Benjy. My mind went back to my Spiritual Guide's Course 101. I needed to think of everything I had learned prior to coming down to earth.

"OK, everyone, get yourselves seated. Not much time to get you trained, get you tested, and then let you loose with your Case Supervisors. Come on, get in your assigned seats. You all received your seat numbers when you got your books for this class. If you do not remember what seat number you belong in, just check inside the book flap and you will see your name with your seat number on it," Senior Case Guidance Supervisor Lynn softly yet powerfully said as she guided her new students into their seats so she could start their Spiritual Guide's Course 101 on time. Lynn had ten weeks to get the new guides, twenty-five in all, well prepared, and ready to handle their earth cases. It was going to be a tough go, but Lynn had seen her share of tough classes in the past.

Lynn became known to all of her students and Spiritual Guide friends as Mama Lynn. She had been diagnosed with breast cancer at the young age of forty. She was a vibrant woman full of determination to beat the illness that was knocking at her door. She had fought with all her strength, along with her doctor's help, to bring the cancer down to its knees. She had succeeded for twenty years. The defeat of cancer was a feat few during her era overcame, but it was something Mama Lynn accomplished. She would not let anyone treat her like an invalid and treated others in the same manner. She struggled to maintain her lifestyle as normal as possible, knowing the steps she needed to take in order to maintain the upper hand in the fight against breast cancer. She had set out to beat this health enemy with dignity. She would drive to the store without a wig or pick up baby lizards that were abundant in the South and use them as earrings so she could entertain her grandkids. Mama Lynn and her grandchildren would giggle so loudly that many times it would be difficult to decipher who was laughing the loudest, the children or Mama Lynn. Mama Lynn felt life dealt her these cards and she would not begrudge the lessons she would learn until the end of her days. She spent her life surrounded by loved ones.

During Mama Lynn's wake, nearly the whole town showed up to the modest little church that was situated in the outskirts of her Florida town. The parking lot was closed off so the church staff could place chairs and speakers so all the people that showed who had been affected by Mama Lynn's passing and wanted to pay their respects could hear the service. Hours were spent with family members and friends recalling how Mama Lynn would live on in their lives. Many happy and sad moments were shared with all who had come to celebrate Mama Lynn's next journey. Although many tears had been spilled that afternoon, everyone left the small church with the exuberant feeling that Mama Lynn had been with all of them all day as many slapped their legs and wiped tears of laughter as jokes had been told of her adventures.

Back in the classroom, Mama Lynn was trying to instruct twenty-five new Spiritual Guides into their seats before the buzzer sounded to let them know the day's session was over. She needed to get their attention before these young wannabe guides wasted any more time trying to find their seats. In particular, her thoughts fell on Kyle Jackson, the infamous K-Man.

"OK now, ladies and gentlemen, what part of 'get to your seats quickly' do you not understand? Please let me know if you do not have a seat number inside your book flap," Mama Lynn sternly announced. "I would say each and every one of you is older than five years of age. I think by now you would know how to read and search out your seats. Now get to it!"

"Yo, Moms, be cool. We're getting there. It's all good," a young man said.

"Yo, yo home dog, do I look like the woman you grew up with? Don't call me Moms. My name is Senior Case Guidance Supervisor Lynn. To some of you, I will be known as Mama Lynn. I will let you know when you will have the privilege of calling me Mama Lynn. You dig? Did you understand that, home dog? Now, do I need to write it on the board and maybe draw some pictures so you can understand me better?" Mama Lynn smiled sweetly as she stared directly at the young man whose name was Kyle Jackson per her attendance sheet.

"Yo, it's all good, teach. My seat is right here. Look, I'm sittin' down. See?" Kyle smiled smartly at Mama Lynn as he stared back. Mama Lynn already knew who she needed to spend extra time with during this course. She already knew about Kyle, known as K-Man to all of his spiritual guide friends. She had background information on all of her students. She always received a full file on each of her student's family history, student's fall with death, and why they made it to her class. Each of her students had a special mission with someone on earth. It was Mama Lynn's job to make sure they were aware of not only the subjects chosen but also how the guides would react emotionally to become effective spiritual guides. They had a mission to do. They were chosen because they were the perfect ones to do these missions. No mistake about that. However, they needed to learn so they can reach their potential prior to connecting with their case subjects, while they both embarked on their new journeys together.

K-man was sixteen years of age. He had spiky black hair with lots of gel holding his hair in place. If he had to bludgeon someone to death in self-defense, he would be in good shape. He could easily turn his head toward his aggressor and charge. He had a small silver hoop nose ring pierced in his right nostril. He could mesmerize many with his big hazel eyes, which gave him an upper hand on many arguments. With a thin and muscular 5'11" build and a confident stride, he was able to deter anyone asking why he wore long-sleeve T-shirts even during the hottest days of summer. No one knew of his thirty-plus cut scar marks on his arms, which would reveal all the self-doubt and insecurities this young man carried with him. His life had been hard. He lived through a stomach illness that caused many missed sleepovers at his friend's homes since he never knew when bouts of severe stomach cramps and diarrhea would take up most of his nights. Doctors in his hometown were stumped by such incidents and could never prescribe or provide an adequate treatment plan for him since he did have other factors that would be displayed in stomach illnesses. Additionally, his mature insight to his peers made it difficult for him to truly fit in. K-Man's need to talk about life and the future would bore many of his friends, who preferred to play video games or talk all night long about girls they thought were hot and perhaps and an easy lay over K-Man's philosophical talks. Those times created a dark place for him and found him falling into a deep depression he could not understand. K-Man would take on all the guilt, thinking he was some type of freak since no one would want to be around him because he did not always think the way many of his friends did. He never truly felt like one of the guys. Yet he thought they were a pack of airheads who were just interested in clothes and gossip about other girls who would not sleep with them. These times would cause K-Man to distance himself into music, a channel of escape he knew would never betray him.

His mother had undergone a very hard life with a number of marriages that never worked out and never made sense to K-Man. His mother's life was ended when she was crossing the street one day after work, one block away from home, when an assailant strung out on crack provided a deadly stabbing to her heart for the sake of twenty dollars cash in her purse. K-Man was looking out the window, a habit he had grown accustomed to when it was nearing six o'clock in the evening since that was the time his mom would always seem to cross the street near their home after her long hours at work. K-Man remembered seeing a thin man crossing the street simultaneously as his mom was crossing the opposite block, nearing each other's path. He had noticed the man edging closer to her, and that action had gotten him apprehensive but never thought anything of it until he saw the man break off his mother's purse and push his mother to the ground. Frozen by fear, K-Man watched as the man pulled his mother by her blouse up onto her feet while yelling obscenities into her face for not having more money. K-Man watched his mother's hands try to loosen the maniacal man's grip from her blouse and watched her tears flowing endlessly down her cheeks. Her nonverbal body motions indicated his mother was trying to calm the man down and loosen his grip on her. The man spun his hand quickly to his back trousers pocket, extracting a switchblade easily over six inches long. Knowing K-Man must leave the window and rush to his mother's defense or run to the phone sitting on his living room end table and dial 911 to beg for help, he was glued to the window as though becoming one with the windowsill, feeling captive of the scene he was watching across the street. It was all so surreal and nothing seemed real. It must be a dream because otherwise he would have been downstairs kicking major ass in defense of his mother. Why hadn't he moved? Why was he such a coward? That was his mom, the woman who had always been by his side even after his dad had died from a heart attack one evening while his family was eating dinner at home. K-Man was only ten years old. He had loved his dad with all his heart. His dad had always been his hero, having patience when K-Man had done his best to solve a situation whether it was something simple like going to the park instead of sitting down to do his homework. His dad was more to K-Man; he had been his friend. More than once, K-Man had thought that if he hadn't given his dad such a hard time about getting his homework done, maybe, just maybe, his dad would be with them. K-Man had felt guilty for years about that and had never mentioned it to anyone. He figured he was too much of a freak for his dad to want to stick around. Maybe his dad was better off without him. His dad was in a better place than having to be around him—the freakazoid.

Now K-Man had lost his mother too, and he had done nothing but watch someone else take her away from him. He had done *nothing*. He had sworn to himself the day his mother had been laid to rest that he would never allow himself to be a coward again. He would let others know they could never mess with him or anyone he cared for. If anyone else would want to ever enter his life, there was a very slim chance of that—indeed.

K-Man had been a sole child in his family. His mother worked relentless hours to keep food on the table and maintain a roof over their heads after his dad had died. Several years later, his mom tried dating, but guys would never stick around. Perhaps it had to do with the fact that his mom would tell her dates she had a son and it did not help that K-Man gave them the evil eye along with major attitude whenever the *dates* came around to have dinner, head out to a movie or cheap dinner. He remembered a time when one of his mother's dates, and there were not many at all that even warranted being invited to dinner, had come over with a bouquet of daisies for his mom. The dude seemed OK but not good enough for K-Man to leave him alone in the living with his mom. While K-Man was acting like he was ignoring the dude, he caught him sneaking a look at his mom's butt when she bent over to pick up a napkin that had fallen to the floor. Right at that moment and there, K-Man knew he would not like him. Since dinner was still cooking on the stove, he went into the medicine cabinet and pulled out a box of laxatives that were in the form of a chocolate bar. It was a relatively new package since he noticed only one laxative bar had been used. K-Man pocketed the laxative bar and dissolved most of the bar into the chocolate sauce his mother had steaming in a copper thingy with a candle underneath it keeping the chocolate melted for dessert. After dinner, K-Man announced he would bring the copper pot and serve it to his new guest so his mom could relax and enjoy some time off her feet. Although he noticed his mom had given him a quizzical look, which he ignored, he poured two ladles full of heaping chocolate onto the dessert plate of his mom's date, which had a slice of angel food cake. He then topped off the dessert with fresh strawberries. He placed the ladle back onto the spoon rest since his mom was allergic to strawberries and he knew she never ate dessert on her dates since she never wanted to gorge herself in front of her potential *soul mate*, K-Man sat down smiling and looking quite pleased as his mom's date smiled and stuffed his face with cake, strawberries, and best of all, chocolate laxative.

"Yo, man, you gotta have another helping of dessert. I mean, *my* mom slaved pretty hard on the dessert for ya. I know you're not gonna make her feel bad by not having a second helpin', right?" K-Man said as he stared the suitor right in the eyes, daring him to say no and knowing he didn't have the balls to do so. Plus, K-Man thought, "He thinks he's gonna get some from my mom tonight. I don't think so!"

"Ahh, yeah, man. Go ahead, I'm gonna get another helping. It is really delicious, Lucy. Absolutely the best I have ever eaten. The chocolate has a different taste to it that I can't seem to place. Different but good. Real different!" the date said as he helped himself to another slice of cake, serving of strawberries and slathered the cake and strawberries with the chocolate, finishing with a dab of whipped cream.

"Yo, man, you can't forget the cherry on top. Aside from the chocolate sauce, that's the best part." K-Man snorted as he reached in the cherry bottle and pulled out a cherry and slapped it on top of the suitor's dessert.

"Lucy, are you sure you're not going to join me in a least at little bit of dessert?" The date smiled provocatively at Lucy as he picked up the cherry and ate the cherry off the stem licking his lips seductively at her not caring that her son, K-Man, was sitting next to him.

"Naw, man, she don't want any. She wants to just watch you eat and let her know how good the dessert is. We *both* do," K-Man curtly responded to the date prior to his mom having the opportunity to open her mouth in response to her date.

"Hey, as a matter of fact, let me add some more chocolate to that cake. That's the best part and it didn't look like ya added enough to it," K-Man said as he picked the ladle up and added a heaping serving before the date could object to it.

"Ah, OK. Yeah, man. Thanks. Thanks a lot," the date said in a way as to not offend K-Man but definitely not wanting any more chocolate. He still couldn't place the taste that seemed flavorful with the chocolate sauce but realized he needed to eat his dessert as to not offend Lucy and be out of the playing field with her.

A couple of hours rolled by when K-Man heard his mom's date excuse himself from her in a rather abrupt and hurried manner.

"Lucy, listen I need to head on home now. Thanks a ton for dinner and a real nice time," the suitor mumbled as he quickly got up from the sofa where he and K-Man's mom had spent the last couple of hours sharing stories while K-Man sat in the love seat watching television.

"Hey, man, what's the hurry? The night's still young. You sure you don't want to stick around and maybe get some more dessert? I know my moms and me won't be eating much of it."

"Ah, no, man. That's cool. I ate way too much as it is. Thanks though," the date said as he picked up his car keys from the cocktail table and tried to make a dash to the door.

"Well, ya wanna see some b-ball? There's a Knicks game coming on the tube here in a few. Supposed to be a good game. You sure you wanna miss it?"

"Kyle, thanks for the invite but I really need to head out. I have a really early start at work tomorrow. I appreciate the offer. Maybe next time. Cool, bro?"

"Yeah, whatever," K-Man said without looking at the date.

"Why, Kyle honey, that was really nice of you to invite Jeff to watch the game with you. Jeff, are you sure you won't want to stay a while longer?" Lucy eagerly said as she followed Jeff quickly through the kitchen and down the corridor to keep up with Jeff's pace as he walked out.

"Lucy, the evening was fantastic! Really, it was. I truly appreciate the invitation to see the basketball game but I really have to head out. I'll call you." The date's voice trailed as he opened the door without looking at Lucy and taking the stairs two by three steps at a time as he hurried out of the building.

"Hmmm, that was odd. I don't remember Jeff saying anything about working tomorrow. I didn't think he worked on Saturday mornings," Lucy mused as she was walking back into the living room, not realizing she was speaking out loud.

"Yo, Mom. Don't worry about it. He's probably a dork and forgot to tell you about it. Plus, maybe he had to run somewhere real quick and couldn't hang. You might've been too much of a woman for him," K-Man mentioned. "Mom, I know what it was. He realized he wanted me instead. You weren't his type. He came to realize I was the one he had always dreamed of. He wanted me but realized he couldn't have me so he wanted to go home to get drunk and call the doctors to finally set up the surgery. I showed him his sensitive and feminine side." K-Man continued smirking and put his hands on his hip as he pranced across the living room to his mom's side. As he reached his mom, he placed his arm around her shoulder and leaned into her neck.

"Mom, I am sorry. You were too much woman for him. He came to understand that you were way out of his league. You were just too much of a capital W for him. Just too much!" K-Man said as he turned to his mom with an angelic look on his face.

"What do you mean capital W?"

"Mom, come on. You know, Woman with a capital W. You got your pieces in place and a good head too. Mom, please, you are embarrassing me. You did not know that?!"

"Oh, Kyle, you are too much. The question still is what did you do to him?"

"Mom, please, I ain't done not'ing to him. He just wigging out," K-Man said as he strutted back to his seat and gave his mom a wink as he smiled at her.

Mama Lynn quietly chuckled as she brought her thoughts back to the classroom and her students were finally settling into their seats.

"Welcome, ladies and gentlemen Spiritual Guides, to what I hope will be a spiritually awakening adventure for you and your mission subjects. Keep in mind we will be focused on the futures of our new subjects while keeping mind our subjects' pasts. There will be much to learn, so let's get started."

"Why should we be here if we can't be human again? I mean, we are D-E-A-D. We're over on the other side. Besides, I'm bored. Need to get back to my rocking out. Have a new lick I want to learn on the guitar."

"Serenity, I understand you are quite talented. Wouldn't you want to learn how to teach your subject some of your musical guidance? Perhaps that is the talent you and your case subject have in common to get through whatever is ailing him or her."

"Mama Lynn, see, it goes like this, no one can imitate the great Serenity. I mean no one!" Serenity mentioned as she looked slyly at her fingers as though they were made of gold and she was keeping it a secret from the rest of the class.

"Girl, you must be on something 'cause whatever it is, it is making you hallucinate! I mean H-A-L-U-C-I-N-A-T." Jason, a fourteen-year-old Spiritual Guide, laughed loudly as though he made the funniest joke he had ever heard.

"Yo, genius, hallucinate is spelled, H-A-L-L-U-C-I-N-A-T-E. So much for what you know!" Serenity retorted at Jason.

Mama Lynne had read in Serenity's file she was pretty self-conscious about her talents and tried to use self-grandeur to hide her true feelings about her insecurities regarding her musical skills. Mama Lynne knew the mission Serenity had ahead of her and what a great match she would be with her earth's subject. The challenge Mama Lynne would have was getting Serenity, and many of the other Spiritual Guides, to recognize that some failures are bound to happen before sculpturing a raw stone into a priceless gem. Serenity had had the talent to be among the top musicians of her time, especially at such a young age. Unfortunately, Serenity found herself so depressed one day that her typical cutting episode that relieved her emotional pain hit a vein when Serenity cut too deeply into her thigh. Serenity would now have someone else to live her dreams through if she achieved her mission with her earthling.

Her mother found her outlined in her own pool of blood in the bathroom later that afternoon. Serenity's mom had gone down to ask how she was doing and see if she wanted anything in particular for dinner. Two evenings prior to Serenity's death, her parents became aware of her cutting urges, the need to feel something or feel alive even though it was dangerous. Serenity and her parents had long conversations into the wee hours of the morning, yet Serenity could not let go of the darkness that surrounded her and robbed her of her many musical awards, accolades, and self-awareness of how she would change many lives.

Yet in class, all Serenity would ask Mama Lynne was that she arrived home, wherever that may be, and "Dude, why am I here? I mean, like I don't even believe in this religious stuff. I thought I would come back like a tiger. You know—a beautiful Siberian tiger. Yet I look cooler but I'm not an animal. I figured I would be reincarnated into something different and then go talk to people and get them freaked out. That's the truth, Ms. Senior Case Supervisor Lynne. I just want to tiger punch or claw someone's face if they get mean to someone else," Serenity would say as she air fingered a guitar neck and placed one leg on top of the table.

"Spiritual Guide Serenity, life and the beyond may not always seem as clear as you have imagined it to be. Be ready to trek in my class. It will enlighten and expand your horizons, especially knowing that you hold someone's life in your hands yet all you can do is whisper a word, phrase, or sentence to make sure your case subject will respond to your beckoning. It is not easy but you made the cut, so to speak. You are here because you are special. That is the same reason why the rest of you are here in my class. Coincidence? I do not believe so. I believe in Special. Understand?"

Serenity nodded with a different semblance, one of curiosity. The rest of the class seemed introspective as well. "Maybe now we can get somewhere," Mama Lynne thought as she started calling down the name list. She knew everyone on the list was seated in her classroom, but she still had to call roster. "Doesn't everyone know there are some perks here? Ugh, bureaucracy! Oh well, no matter."

Then we had Eduardo. Mama Lynne looked at him, knowing he would bring a lot of know-it-all attitude to her class, from what she detected of his file. The oldest of the bunch, twenty-eight years of age, was from Argentina, and he died trying to rescue his wife from a suicide attempt. He simply sat back in his chair as his eyes darted from one Guide to another, taking in all they had to say but not really caring at all what was told within the class.

Eduardo had tried numerous times and several methods to help his wife accept their marriage had many challenges that he alone could not fix. He had attempted to make marriage issues go away by being complacent; however, issues started to discombobulate its universe. Any methods and suggestions professionals recommended took too long. His wife wanted a quick fix to many years of turbulence. It was time for his wife to face reality. His wife could not accept her husband had simply fallen out of love with her. One morning, Eduardo stepped in front of a mirror realizing he did not know who the other person was staring back at him. He loved his family, especially his children. He prayed his children would one day understand all the sacrifices he had done to keep his family together at the risk of losing his identity. All he remembered of his marriage were the days he arrived home from work and entered his key into their home's door lock. It seemed to block out his air as he entered his house.

Unfortunately, Eduardo's attempt to help talk his wife off of a cliff resulted in Eduardo's death as his footing plummeted him to his death within the ocean's mountainous edges with no probability of resuscitation. He was dead upon impact.

"Spiritual Guides, this course, I hope, will remind you again of how fragile life can be. You all know this, otherwise, you would not be here. Just remember, there is someone out there that needs help and you will be that person's potential lifeline. You can help if you focus on your task. This is not about you. This journey is about your case subject. Ideally, you will learn a thing or two as you travel on the path with your subject."

CHAPTER 9

Around 7:00 p.m., the steady flow of aunts, uncles, and cousins filled the Santiago residence. Delicious aromas of oregano, garlic, and Spanish condiments scented the kitchen area. Glasses filled with soda were passed to the younger members of the family, while beer and alcoholic drinks were made available to the adults. The men sat congregated around the television set, exchanging heated conversations as to which team would be the New York Mets' next victim as the playoff would near its end.

As Mari crossed the living room to give her father a cold beer, she wondered if he would take her to see a baseball game this year. She recalled the fun she had at the ballpark with her dad several years ago. It was just he and she. That was it. It was so much fun! The stands were packed with people wearing Mets T-shirts and caps. She could almost smell the roasted peanuts, salted pretzels, and hot dogs as she reminisced those great afternoons. Her dad would patiently explain to her why the players were able to run to the base and stay there when other times they had to go back to the dugout. He wouldn't get upset when she would pull on his sleeve so he could tell her why the chubby old man was coming out of the dugout to argue with the umpire. He simply picked her up in his arms and hugged her with a smile that was brighter than the sun.

"He just fightin' for his player, hijita. The man with the bat did not swing all the way and the umpire said he was out and the batter had to sit down. The man that came out is the batter's coach. He makes sure that his players are doing what they are supposed to do so they can win this game."

"Wow, Daddy, he's like their guardian angel, looking out for his team. Except I never saw an angel get so red in the face and angry before. Also, I think he said some bad words, Daddy. I don't think guardian angels are supposed to say bad words." Her dad just picked her up again and laughed. The more he laughed, the more it made Mari laugh. Her dad even caught a foul ball that night when it flew near the seats they were sitting in. They had great seats. They sat a few rows behind the dugout. He handed the ball to her so she could put it in her treasure box. And boy, did she treasure it! She had to treasure it since she didn't remember the last time her father had taken her anywhere again. Her eyes moistened since she couldn't figure out what she had done to upset him so much that would make him forget about her and not want to take her out again on a special afternoon together.

Oh well, it was just a couple of days anyhow. What difference did it make anyway? Besides, I am a lot older now. That was kid stuff.

At least that's what she wanted to believe.

Several of the younger children engaged in a lively game of tag, provoking menacing looks from the mama hens sitting at the kitchen table. As each child acknowledged the glances shot toward their direction, the liveliness of the sweat-inducing game came to an immediate halt. Instead, coloring books and crayons were pulled out of the book bags brought by many of the children.

After an hour had passed by, lids were removed from pots and pans so heaps of food could be served for all to eat. Dinnertime was the usual montage of conversations being carried on at the same time by all. Silence now outweighed the gregarious festivity as the family devoured the food. After the typical desert of flan and strong espresso coffee was served as the evening's treat, the ladies commenced to clear, wash, dry, and put away the dishes as quickly and efficiently as a well-paid assembly line in the finest restaurant. Feeling satisfied every piece of crumb was whisked away, the ladies filed into the living room area to converse with the men.

As soon as Luisa sat down, she turned to Sara.

"So, Sara, did you hear 'bout Hector beating the shit out of Lola? She get hers, huh? She been on Hector's case about moving her out of his parents' house to their own apartment. I mean not'in' was wrong living in thee basement of tha house. Oh no, do yu tink she was satisfied? No, she wanted a bigger place. Maybe she need to start working those long hours her Hector does so she can know what it feel like to work. All she do is sit around the basement and take care of her kids. Tat is it. Well, Sara, you know what a pain she be when she get her hair up her butt 'bout sometin'."

"Luisa, she no have to have her face hit just because she wants her own house. I mean a house she call her own. She have four children and she now have her seventeen-year-old sista, since her parents just died. The roaches leave tha place 'cause they didn't have room to run around," Sara retorted.

"Oh, Sara, yu must have been talking to her and feeling sorry for her, right? It time Hector took off his wife and show her who tha man's in tha house. She have tha coming for a lon time. Hector no get a night out with his friends without Lola complaining about it," Benjy piped in.

"Oh, and she always calls Hector at the pool place to check on him when he go out with tha boys. If he no be home by 1:00 a.m., there come the phone call," Ramon announced as though he had just told them that evening's best kept secret. "Man, I would have pulled my pant down and thrown her on thee bed and show her who thee man of the house is. I mean, the man works hard all week. He pays the bills to feed their faces and she gonna tell him when he need to go home. I don' tink so! All he wan to do is have som fun wit the boys to no hav thee stresssss."

"Oh yeah, bro, I know wha yu mean. I mean that Lola have got a good-looking butt, yu *culo* and her face no look bad. *Hombre*, a man need to control his family. Got to show them who thee man of thee house is and get respect," Ramon added as he slapped his hands on his thighs.

I simply shake my head in disgust as I notice Sara slump back into her seat.

"What an asshole!" I mumble as I feel the heat of my temper rising. I hate hearing Neanderthal men talking like that. Respect my butt! I would take a frying pan and slap it over his head if I were his wife! From the corner of my eye, I spotted Mari slipping out of the living room and heading toward her room. Just as she was about to enter her bedroom, Ramon called out to her.

"Mari, come over here, girl. *Nena*, let your uncle take a good look at you and give you a big hug."

"Crap, crap, crap," Mari whispered under her breath as she pivoted back into the living room. She put on a forced smile and turned to her uncle. "Damn Jonathan, he always gets out of these stupid family visits. I bet he says he has to go to work to just get out of being here with these people. Arghhhhh!" Mari continued to whisper under her breath as she slowly walked toward a very slow death under the hands of her uncle Ramon.

"Tio Ramon, you just saw me when you first got here a couple of hours ago. I still look the same." Mari smirked.

"Mari, don't be rude," Luisa snapped at her. "Yur uncle just wanna be nice to yu and show yu he loves yu."

"Sorry, Tio," she responded, barely audible.

"Ay, girl, no problemo. Come here and sit with yur uncle a few minutes. I wanna hear how you be," Ramon told Mari.

"Tio, I need to go start on my homework since I have—" A high shriek from her bedroom had her bolting toward the sound. As she opened the door to her room, she saw Manuelito pushing Ramon Jr. away from him and running past her to seek comfort from his mother.

"Ramon, what are you doing with my iron?" Mari asked him as she snatched the hot iron away from him.

"I was trying—"

"Ramon Luis, come here righ now," Ramon Sr. yelled out.

"*Papi*, Daddy, it not my fault," Ramon, Jr. started whining as his eyes swelled with tears, imagining what was going to happen to him after he reached his father and left the safety of Mari's room. He could already feel his father's hand on his face before he was able to explain to his dad how he fell victim in this whole mess. His head dropped, and tears started rolling down his face as soon as he reached his father's side.

"Yu know why I call yu to me, Ramon Luis? Wha yu doing to your brother?"

"Manuelito, come here!" Ramon yelled for his younger son.

"Papi, Ramon was trying to iron my pants. He told me to leave my pants on so it will be easier to iron and it will look better since it be on me already. He said if he iron my pants on me, I didn't want to waste time putting them on and then putting them on the ironing board and then take them off again and then we can go play sooner. But he burned my butt! My butt hurts, it feels like it is on fire!" Manuelito said as he continued crying and really hamming it up so his father would beat Ramon Jr. and not him.

"What in thee hell wrong wit yu, Ramon Jr.? Are yu crazy, boy? Why yu ironing yur little brother's pants while he wearing them?" his father yelled as he grabbed Ramon Jr. by his shirt collar and jerked him close to his face.

"I was just trying to help him dry his jeans since he was scared he was going to get in trouble when he dropped his drink on his pants, Papi. That's all. It was an accident. I was just trying to help him!" Ramon, Jr. answered his father through sniffles.

By this time, Luisa had swept her youngest son into her arms and headed to the bathroom to put cool water on his behind.

"Get out my face. Go to yur mother and help her wit yur brother. I no like being embarrassed in front of everyone by yu be stupid!" Ramon shoved his son toward Luisa's direction.

"I'm verry sorry, Benji. I no know wha get into tha boy sometime. I try to punish him to teach him righ from wrong, but he do stupid things. I no understand."

"*Ay, hombre*, no problemo. He jus be a boy. I know yu put the belt to him. Yu wan him to grow up to be a good boy," Benjy said as he tried to make Ramon feel better.

Ramon Sr. slowly nodded his head, accepting his friend's sympathetic words. His eyes diverted to Mari, and he motioned her over to him.

"Ay, Mari, come here. Thee boys good now." Mari sighed as she slowly went to her uncle's waiting lap.

"Sit here and talk to yur Tio Ramon. How is school going?" he asked as he leaned forward to hug Mari while on his lap.

"It's OK." Mari lurched forward, trying to break her uncle's grip. Her uncle merely pulled her back and smiled as his eyes darkened.

"That bastard!" I hiss.

"Take a chill pill, Candace. Not now," Pearl whispers to me as I suddenly realize she was next to me all this time.

"Tio Ramon, I really need to finish my homework. I have a test on Monday and I need to go study." Mari twisted as she tried to get up.

"Oh, OK, Mari. I jus wanna talk to yu. But if yu no wanna to spend some time wit yur tio, tha is OK. I jus wan to know how my niece is doing. I understand," Ramon said while looking innocent and letting go of his grip while he raised his arms and shrugged his shoulders.

Mari pushed away quickly, bursting out of his arms, nearly falling headfirst into the coffee table. She rapidly regained her footing, with embarrassment, turned, and ran to her room, closing the door firmly behind her. Relieved to be back in her room, she quickly discarded the tinge of guilt slowly forming in her stomach from stretching the truth to her uncle. Oh well, I do have to study for Monday. I just don't have a test. She glanced at the clock and saw it was nearly nine-thirty at night. Hopefully, she could stay in her room unnoticed by the others until after they left.

CHAPTER 10

She was roused by a sharp knock on her door.

"Mari, get up. It is time to go to church. I no wan to be late," her father called out loudly.

"OK, Papi. I will get up. Is anyone in the shower?"

"Yez, yur brother. But he coming out righ now. Get up so yu no make us late for mass."

Mari stretched her arms and legs, hoping to release all her kinks from her night's sleep. She lay in bed, listening to the clatter of breakfast dishes being placed on the table and hoping she only heard the voices of her parents and brother.

I sure hope no one slept over, she thought, cringing at the thought she would have to deal with her Tio Ramon, Titi Luisa, and those two brat kids of theirs before she was fully awake. Pretty quiet out there. Yep, I think the coast is clear. Now all I have to do is make it to the bathroom and wake myself up so I can make it to the church pew and then fall asleep again while no one is looking.

"Pretty dumb to have to wake up early on a Sunday morning so some priest can put you back to sleep," Mari mumbled as she tossed her feet over the side of her bed. As Mari fished around her closet for something to wear, her thoughts took her to that morning's church time.

"OK, let's see what the sermon will be about today. Maybe the bald-headed priest will talk about giving money to the church so they can continue having church on Sundays. Or maybe, he will talk about love thy neighbor, as God loved us. Give me a break. The only love anyone has in this neighborhood is love for self-preservation. Maybe he will talk about being happy with what you have and not be jealous that someone else has something more than you do. Yeah, like I really want to have something that someone else in my neighborhood has. Give me a break! They don't have anything, so how can you be jealous of what they don't have? Or, I wonder if he is going to talk about when you are married, how you don't need to think about doing bad stuff with someone else's wife or husband. Yep, we haven't heard that one in a long time. I bet he is gonna talk about that. Oh God, I hope not. That would only get Mami and Papi back fighting again when Ma asks what the priest talked about today at mass. I can definitely go another day without the screaming, cursing, and worse than that, the hitting. I hate when Papi hits Mami. It isn't right!" she thought as she felt her stomach turning into knots. Oh well, nothing she could do now except take a shower and hope for the best.

After Mari finished with her shower, she quickly swallowed her oatmeal in record time so she wouldn't get her father upset by having him wait on her while she finished her breakfast. She noticed her mother had her robe on and was probably not going with them to church as usual. She rarely went to church with them since she called the churchgoers hypocrites, whatever that meant. What was really odd is that her father never strong-armed her mother into going to church with them. He never seemed to like it when she didn't go, but he never slapped her around for it. He would just slam the door on his way out when he left for church. He made sure she felt the vibrations of the door slamming to emphasize his discontent with her decision to stay home. He would always make the point that the entire family should go to church so that God would be happy with them and bless them. Everyone should be at church worshipping instead of cleaning his or her homes or watching television.

Mari saw the enormous reddish brick building come into sight as her father drove their car down the street. The church had been there over seventy years. I noticed it was in dire need of a face-lift. There were several windows that were boarded up, with half the glass missing. There were lewd remarks written in red, blue, and yellow paint scribbled on the sidewalls. Shattered beer bottles adorned the front yard with someone's McDonald's bag spewed alongside it. Lots of cigarette butts and several used needles adorned the curb. A pathway of cracked stone stairs led to large saint statues decorating the entrance of the church's wooden arched doorways, reminding everyone that entered its chamber of the sacrifice felt by Christ's crucifixion. Many portraits hung along every wall of the church.

Mari could hear the loud clamors of the rusty church bells as they echoed within the small church area so loudly it almost felt as though the bells were clamoring within her head. Her father parked their car at a parking spot right in front of the church. They quickly got out of the car in a robotic manner and approached the church doors. "Here we go, one hour of how you are going to the bad place if you do not tell the priest your sins. You should also feel guilty since you lived your week doing bad things and did not feel sorry for them. I mean, you can't be a Catholic if you do not feel guilty about something. Better yet, how you need to care for your family so they will know you love them and realize that heaven can be here on earth as well as in the sky. Boy, is that a good one," Mari thought as she dreaded every step she took that led her closer to the church doors.

"OK, God, we are here. We got up, we came to church, we are praying, we are kneeling down on this thing, the kneeler cushion. Now you tell us how much you love your son. We see pictures and statues of his mama holding him very sweet like. We know you are looking down on them real lovingly and that you care for them a lot since the priest tells us that all the time. And . . . and . . . you tell us and you tell us our daddies should take care of us. Did you ever have to tell your son that? 'Cause you see, our papi doesn't do that no more. At least not that I remember. Do you think that he treats Mami like he does and ignores us a lot 'cause he doesn't see you caring for your son and wife that way? I mean, maybe that's why Papi treats Mami the way that he does. Maybe that's why he treats Jonathan and me the way that he does. He just doesn't see you doing that!" Mari almost shouted out her last sentence before she realized she had been in her own little world and was now hearing everyone around her belting out the words to a hymn from their hymnal book.

"Yes, sweet sister. How can you feel anything different when life has provided you with a different set of rules than the ones that are preached inside this room? Life doesn't have to be cruel and filled with hate or tarnished with a warped sense of love by the administration of the belt," I thought as I could sense Mari's unease when she entered this religious institution. I myself had never fully subjected myself to the teachings of the church. I had come from a long line of Baptist believers. I remembered I could not listen to rock music since it would supposedly bring evil thoughts to my mind and, even worse, conjure devil-worshipping practices. I also recalled I could not wear pants to church or even entertain the notion of befriending someone from the homosexual persuasion that would even admit he or she was homosexual in their society. So sad! There was to be no interacting with people who did not believe the way that her family believed, or you could be swayed to the wrong side of the tracks.

"You know, Pearl, it's too bad that so many people think the only way they can receive peace and happiness is if they are beat hard by the big guy that lives in a faraway place in heaven. I don't get it. I mean, they forget that he is wanting to help us. I know I used to think that I was not good enough for him to do anything for me since I wasn't 'perfect.'"

"I know. I hear that a lot from your buddies."

"Yup, I used to think it was worthless to have to deal with church, religion, and all the 'Is God really up there?'"

"I know, Candace. I have heard so many teenagers like yourself struggling with that very same issue. You don't see God and can't hear him or her, like many of you think that God can be a woman and not necessarily a man. It is normal to feel that way. It feels silly to deal with getting up and going to church. It doesn't make sense when it may not be the truth."

"Pearl, it just seems like everyone who has got a major problem or is lost in his or her own way are the only ones sitting in those pews. I just felt like if I were a 'loser,' then I should go to church. If I weren't a 'loser,' then I don't need to go. So if I went to church, everyone else would see that I am a 'loser.' That make sense to you? I sure lost myself on that one!"

"Yes, Candace. In an odd way, it does make sense to me. Many feel the same way you do. If you are feeling insecure, feeling lost, don't feel any hope left in this world, and do not have any place to go but further down in misery, then those are the ones that need to fill the church pews. I totally get it."

"It's hard to feel like anyone can help you from a divine source if you don't feel or hear him while getting hit with brimstone and fire. Why add to an already existing sense of helplessness and abandonment, when people want to be with God, by whipping them with guilt?" I asked Pearl as we both walked into the church. "Everything seems to come across harsh even though God is about love," I added as I felt Mari so close to me. I understood her emotions. I had those same feelings myself until now.

"It's simpler to look at a person's heart to see the joy or hurt it can provide instead of concentrating on life itself and see what it can provide if people change. Why not refuel your vulnerable spirit with words of love that will linger for another week until it is time again to have your soul embellished with another sermon? I never had that as well. I had it now. It's funny how you can feel a sense of love and purpose after you are dead. Looking at where I am now, I would have given anything to get help and live a real life in a real world. You live most of your life seeking love, security, and a sense of financial well-being and feel chained by that need. If only we can have these emotions prior to leaving to a new world. Now it is about changing the world, one person at a time. That is what I need to do with Mari. Provide her the encouragement she needs to make a difference in her life," I thought as I simply looked at her sad face sitting in the pew.

As I looked at Mari, her brother, and father, I regretted taking my life. I felt angry since I really wanted to become a doctor. I wanted to become a neurosurgeon. Very, very few women would ever fill that occupation, and I wanted to be one of those few women to examine the brain. I wanted to change the world of medicine. That will never happen now. This life was way different, and I am really lucky I am here instead of just lying in some box somewhere. Now my actions will rule what I become in this world. I have a really scary life since my actions will be what dictates Mari's life if she listens to me. But I chose this by taking those pills so I could get away from my own life as my father's sex slave.

Mari's father had already scanned the church for his favorite pews and, to his delight, found they were vacant. They usually were. They were right smack in front of the priest's pulpit. Perhaps it provided him with a stronger sense of forgiveness for his sins, or redemption. Who knows? Benjy strutted up the center aisle toward the pew, stepped aside when he reached it, and motioned for his daughter to go in and then his son. Once his children had taken their seats, he sat, leaned down to pull the kneeler cushion so they could all kneel and say their prayers before the services started.

I felt repulsed as I stared at Benjy push his face deep into both his palms to say his prayers. "Hypocrite!" I muttered to myself. Her eyes shifted to see the children bow their heads as they followed in their father's silent instructions. Once Mari and Jonathan were done with their prayers, they quickly seated themselves back into their pew and read the church bulletin they had received when they arrived at the church doors. Their father still knelt in place for a few minutes before the organ music commenced playing. I noticed Mari stare at the huge wooden crucifix centered high above the altar and close her eyes after a few minutes. Her lips moved slightly as she mouthed unspoken words that only she and I could hear.

"God, I don't understand how you can allow people to be so mean to each other and yet come to you as though they were saints, looking for you to bless them. How can you allow my father to beat the living crap out of my mother and then allow him to sit in your house without punishing him? Why can't you make him nice like I remember him to be years ago when I was younger? Why can't he love my mom and us the way he used to and the way some fathers do in other families? How can you want me to believe you are a God of miracles when you can't make the fighting in our house stop? I am sorry if I have made you angry with me. I mean no disrespect. You know, right now I am pretty pissed off at you. I just don't get it. Please tell me what to do so my father will stop going out at night and then coming home to bash my mom's face in. I promise I won't do it again. I will stop whatever I am doing that you don't like. All I need to know is what I can do to make the fighting stop. Thank you, God! I mean what I said about doing whatever you need me to do to stop the fighting in my house."

I quickly slipped behind Mari and whispered into her ear, "It isn't anything you've done, Mari. It isn't something you have created. You are a wonderful child with a beautiful spirit. I will do my best to protect you. Sometimes, adults do not know how to control their emotions and tempers. They strike out to those they love because they know they can. Some adults just do not know how to control their feelings. Sometimes, they grow up with mixed-up ideas of how they need to act when they become husband and wife or a mom or dad. Just know that your father and mother do love you in their own way. You are such a special young woman with a wonderful future in front of you. Do you hear me? Don't mess that up. I am here for you."

All of a sudden, Mari opened her eyes and looked around her to see who had slipped next to her when she was talking to the "big guy." She did not see anyone and thought she must have just heard someone behind her whispering to someone else. Why are we here? Mari thought. I just don't get it. We come every weekend whether we've had World War III at home the night before or not. We come here whether my dad has come home drunk or whether my mom has gotten in his face for him flirting with someone and he has used her face as a punching bag. Sunday morning, we get up, get dressed, come to church, and listen to the priest tell us how lucky we are to have God in our lives and how we should never forget to be good Catholics. We can't forget to go to confession so we can tell the priest hiding in the closet what lousy people we have been all week. Then he tells us to say ten "Hail Mary" prayers and five "Our Father" prayers, depending how bad we have been. It usually takes about five minutes to go in that confessional, come out, do your weekly penance, and sit in the pew. The longer you're in that closet, the longer you have to be on your knees and pray. Then everyone knows you haven't been the best kid around since you spent most of the mass in that closet and on your knees. In the meantime, people are out there beating on their wives, kids, and everyone else they don't like. But it's OK because you can go into that closet and some guy in a robe will tell you to say some prayers and bingo, your sins are all gone!

"Yup, you are made clean again," Mari said aloud without realizing it.

"What?" Her brother looked at her like she was nuts again.

"Nothing, nutcase. Just thinking about something."

"Thinking about what? How you're gonna be a nun when you grow up?"

"Yeah, right. That is so it. That way I can talk to my buddy priests, and when you get in that confessional, they will tell you to say a ton of prayers and everyone will know what a real big troublemaker and jerk you really are!" Mari sneered back at her brother.

"Uh-huh. Whatever," he retorted. "They'll know it's just you lying. They'll know what a wonder dude I am for putting up with you for so long. They'll just laugh in your face *again* and try to kick you out of their church."

"Be quiet, you two! Sit up and listen to the priest when he is talking. Learn something," their father reprimanded them sternly. Jonathan leaned over to Mari. "Hopefully they will send you to Russia or maybe to the moon so you can be a nun at an alien church or something. You look like one already. Might as well go join them." Mari threw him a quick "bite me" look and turned to her own thoughts again.

"Wonder what it would be like to be a nun?" she thought. "I would so not be a nun. Be in those long robes, I don't think so! Plus having someone telling me what to do, say, and behave. Nope, not for me. It would be like I would be married or something but there would be no husband or kids. Hmmmm, now that might not be too bad. At least I wouldn't get slapped around or nothing. Nah, still not for me." She muffled a laugh at the idea of her being a nun. For even thinking about what her dumb brother said. He is so stupid!

"Wow, I can so relate," I told Pearl. "My church was so freaking weird! Lots of people thinking they were better than you and then thought *they* had a direct line to God, like they had a 'red phone' or something to him."

"So, you think they were weird, huh?" Pearl asked.

"I guess maybe weird is not the right word for them. I think stuck-up or having a chip on their shoulder. You know, they just acted as though they owned the church or were better than anyone else who came through the church doors. I mean, I remember one time our Sunday school teacher for the teenagers would not allow a teenage girl to come into our class since she had HIV. She received it during birth while having a blood transfusion since she had a deficiency in some type of blood cell. There was this big meeting between the members of the church and the pastor as to whether that girl should be allowed to go to the damn class since there was another girl who was the daughter of one of the deacons that had leukemia. The parents and other members were scared it would somehow affect the daughter as if she would get AIDS by just sitting next to her. Plus, I heard one deacon say that having someone in our church with HIV might 'hamper the growth of our church with new members.' We might *scare* them off knowing we have someone with AIDS. Ugh, how stupid!"

"That church congregation is not reflective of *all* churches, Candace. Those people may have learned those ways from how their parents acted with them as they grew up. They could have also been very conceited or simply did not understand how to show the true love God has for his children, *agape*, unselfish love. They are ignorant! You, on the other hand, are very different. You were not allowed to be a child and learn childlike ways. It was taken away by an adult's distorted way of thinking."

"God, if you are really up in heaven, then show me that you can stop this mess. You say it is wrong for husbands to cheat on their wives and hit them like they are a punching bag. Prove it, God! Make this world safer! Truly protect us from those we love. Why should I believe you? I can't see you, I can't hear you, and you have not made my life easy at all. Why should I believe you really exist?" Mari stared blankly ahead, staring right through the priest as he was speaking.

"You should believe because it is true. You have people who love you and surround you if you really listen to their whispers," I softly said to Mari.

Once again, Mari looks around to see who is talking. She sees no one.

CHAPTER 11

The church service finally finished. Mari, who half-listened to the sermon, and Jonathan, who was staring at the teenage girl five pews away, jumped up as soon as they saw everyone bow their heads, curtsey, cross themselves, and start moving toward the door. They were finally done with the Sunday morning ritual. *Hallelujah!* They were now free to finally go home and relax.

Sara left a note she had gone grocery shopping since they were very low on food and they were expecting family for dinner the next evening. Mari remembered her mom mentioning she wanted to make some sautéed chicken, rice, salad, and some cheese flan for dessert. Yum! Mari smacked her lips as she thought of the dinner she would eat later that evening.

Benjy snatched the note from Mari's hand since she saw it first. As soon as he finished reading it, he threw it down on the table with disgust.

"Carajo! Ay, mujer! Damn Satan's woman! She cares only for herself and no for family!" Benjy mumbled under his breath. Mari, hearing every word he mumbled since she was standing right next to him, rushed into her room for fear he would backhand her in the face like he had done in the past when she was near him and he had been angry. Jonathan ran into his room, grabbed his work pants and shirt, and then slipped into the bathroom, hoping no one would see him. He had to go to his part-time job at the department store. He knew if his father saw him getting ready for work, he would give him a lecture about working on Sunday instead of spending time with the family. No time for that! He only had forty-five minutes before he had to report for his shift.

Benjy didn't notice the flash of the silhouette rushing to the bathroom. He just went over to the refrigerator and grabbed himself a beer. He slouched down on the sofa, turned on the television, and searched for some baseball. The play-offs were on and Benjy did not want to miss a game.

"So much for time with the family!" I said sarcastically.

Mari went to the kitchen, grabbed the rice, thawed the chicken in the microwave, and grabbed a couple of cans of beans. She seasoned the chicken, taking special care to add in enough olives for her father since he would get irritated if he did not have enough of them on his plate. She grabbed two other pots and started cooking the rice and beans. She tasted a tad from each pot, and once she felt they were perfect enough so she wouldn't get yelled at by her parents, she left the kitchen. She would leave dessert for her mami to make and hoped her mom would still have time to make some of her delicious cheese flan. Yum! She briefly smiled, feeling certain tonight would render some good grub as she lowered the fire and slowly crossed over to her bedroom. She noticed her father had gone over to their bar area and grabbed the Bacardi rum and poured a lot of it in a glass with some soda and lemon. He typically makes his Cuba libre drink when he is really angry. Mari's stomach started turning into knots.

"Please do not let this be another one of those days!" Mari thought as she went into her bedroom, flopped, on her bed and started to read her book, *Rapunzel.* After forty minutes, she realized she needed to get up so she could hit the shower before dinner. She just wanted to take a nice warm shower to help relax before she faced the rest of the evening with her family. The sweet spicy smells in the kitchen roused her senses as she strolled to the stove to check on their evening meal.

"Papi, you doing OK?" Mari asked her father, hoping he did not hear her so she would not pull his attention toward her.

"Si, hija, yez, daughter, I am good," her father replied as he noticed Mari's developing body in the thin bathrobe she was wearing. Her father had been drinking rum quite steadily since he had gotten home. He tried not to stare but he couldn't help himself. He just loved the woman's body. He also could not believe how quickly his little girl had developed into a young woman. He felt a tinge of guilt as he continued to look at Mari with eyes that were not of a father but instead of a grown man. He felt he had lost control over his family after he read his wife's note. He felt a loss of respect and needed to gain it back. Respect, to him, meant doing what he wanted, and he wanted his whole family go to church with him, not just his children. Instead his wife went shopping! Yes, he had gotten soft! He needed to lay down the law in his house and show her who he really was, the man of the house. She needed to learn a lesson! Then his son sneaks off for his part-time job instead of drinking a beer and watching the ballgame with his old man. Yeah, he needed to take the reins back and show his family Sunday is a family day, or at least a time when they were in his house. He had to show them all who the man was and what family time was about even if he had to beat it into them. At least his girl, Mari, was with him. Oh si, oh yez, she was his girl.

As he looked up, he noticed his glass needed a refill so he walked into the kitchen to grab some ice and add some more soda and rum. As he poured, he heard the shower running.

"Hmmmm, I might need to check on Mari! See how she is doing and make sure she no need nothin'. I can also play a game wit her," Benjy thought as he continued to babble, already half lost in his alcohol. "Maybe, just maybe, I need to show that young girl she needs to respect the man of the house too. She might as well learn how to fully grow up and be a real woman, not like her mother! Ay, I look like a weak man, tha no good!"

Mari had checked the water, stripped down, and jumped into the shower. She soaped herself up and was rinsing her hair, ready to add some shampoo to it, when she heard her shower curtain slide sideways, bringing in a cool breeze to her warm body. As she slapped the water out of her eyes and face, she saw her father's sweaty face. He was standing there with a weird smile twisted into a smirk. She grabbed wildly for the curtain so she could wrap herself in it to protect herself from his preying eyes. She tried desperately to take hold of the shower curtain so she could shield herself from her father's vision but to no avail; he continued staring and laughing like a madman. She couldn't believe her father was in the bathroom as she was taking a shower. She definitely could not understand and found it repulsive that he was actually trying to look at her naked body. She was so stunned she could not even say anything until ice water started to seethe through her veins. What the fuck is wrong with him? She could hear his sick laugh as he deeply bellowed, "Hide and seek! Hide and seek!"

"Papi, what are you doing? Can't you see I am trying to take a shower? What the hell are you doing?" Mari half yelled as she continued to grab for the shower curtain to hide herself from her father's view and grasp.

"Ahh, I wan to play wit yu. Tha all. Yu no wanna play? Yu used to love to play games wit me. Wha yu tink I do? Ahh bañate! Take a shower! You no fun! You are just like your damn mother! Cold like an ice cube, no fun! No fun! Just like your mother!" her father yelled at Mari as he threw the shower curtain in toward her. He then straightened himself up, smoothed his clothes with his palms as though they were a human iron, checked his hair in the mirror, and slowly closed the bathroom door behind him as he left the room.

Mari waited for a few minutes, inhaling deeply as she tried to regain her strength from the fright she had just endured. She exhaled so hard that all the air she had sucked could finally find a way out of her body. She slowly leaned toward the shower curtain opening, trying hard to listen for noise and trying to hear if her father was still looming around. When she was fully convinced he was not in the bathroom or near it, she opened the curtains and leaped out of the shower, leaving water running, and flipped on the security latch to lock the door. She was so angry at herself for not having locked the door before she went into the shower. She just leaned against the door, dripping wet, with water slipping onto the bathroom tile floor from her body. Slowly, Mari slipped back into the shower and changed the lukewarm water to hot. She simply stood there under the scalding water, allowing it to seep over her body, turning her skin to a bright red glow. She was freezing cold, numb from fright. She finally turned off the shower, grabbed a towel, and dried herself. Her heart was running a million miles a minute. She felt as though she could jump right out of her throat.

She finally heard someone opening the front door and heard the sound of bags rustling. To her relief, she heard the sound of her mother's voice.

"Hola, hello. I home. Where everyone?" Sara called out as she walked into their apartment.

"Benjy, Mari, Jonathan, estoy aquí. I'm home," Sara continued to announce her arrival.

"Damn, I'm glad it's Mami. Now I just hope Papi won't get on her case," Mari thought. Mari heard her mother putting away groceries in the kitchen. When Mari's hands finally stopped shaking, she continued drying herself and threw on her clothes. She wiped down the fogged mirror and picked up the brush so she could put her hair up in a ponytail. Mari slowly brought down the brush and just stared at herself in the mirror.

"What just happened? Gosh, what's wrong with him? Why would he do that to me?" Mari's eyes swelled up with tears that streaked down her cheeks like an overflowing stream as she tried finding answers to her questions.

"God, he scared me so badly!" Mari thought as she wiped her tears away, took a deep breath, and gained enough composure to finish dressing. Mari walked out of the bathroom and headed straight to her bedroom. She saw her mom and ran over to her to give her a big bear hug.

"Hi, Mami, I will come out in a minute to help you. I need to finish dressing," Mari tried telling her mom lightheartedly as she looked the other way so Sara wouldn't notice her red face. The last thing Mari wanted was for her mom to start asking her what was wrong. She wouldn't know how to respond to her if she were put on the spot like that.

"Don't worry, hija. By the time yu are finished, I be done an puttin' away these groceries."

"Good!" Mari thought as she flung herself onto her bed. She lay still, trying to listen to ensure her father was still in the living room. The television was on and she could hear him complaining that one of the baseball players had dropped a ball. Mari still felt a mini explosion occurring in her chest and decided she would continue to lie on her bed until it was of utmost importance to leave her room, her sacred place. She picked up her favorite book and started reading it. She tried hard to lose herself in her book. She imagined herself as a princess leaving reality behind. A handsome, young, kind, and gentle prince would notice her and she would be swept off her feet and taken to her own castle that was far, far away from home. Hell, she couldn't concentrate. Her thoughts kept coming back to what happened in the bathroom with her father.

"Mari, it's going to be OK. You should tell your mom. Maybe that can be the key for her standing up for herself and her family. You are not guilty of anything, Mari! Your father really needs some help and some serious counseling. If that doesn't help, he needs a good ass-kicking!" I whispered to Mari in an effort to console her. I knew how Mari felt. I had felt that same way many, many times before. I tried really hard not to let my anger rise. All I wanted to do was get through to Mari. Unstoppable tears streamed down my cheeks as I felt Mari's loneliness and, worst of all, her helplessness. I wanted Mari to know she wasn't alone. I wished so hard that Mari could see me, but I knew that was impossibility. Mari just kept walking toward Sara. I felt Mari's need to be hugged. Someone she could trust and would keep her safe no matter what! Mari knew her mother couldn't do it. She couldn't even keep herself safe from her father, how could she keep her safe? God, she was so screwed. No one to turn to! But wait, she somehow felt this nagging feeling that maybe she should take a chance and tell her mother what happened. Maybe her mom would stand up to her father and take her and her brother far away from him.

After a few minutes had passed by, Mari was pulled back to reality when she heard her father yelling at her mother.

"Ahhh, yu finally decided to come home. Yu no go to church to hear God's message for yu and instead yu go to the store, *la bodega*. How yu tink tha look to my children? Yu go to tha devil, no to God," Benjy screeched in her face.

"Wha yu talk about? I go buy food for tha family. I have to cook food for yur brother and Luisa and the children. Do you no remember tha they come here to eat? Yu invite them. Why yu treat me like that?" Sara screamed back at him. She was so very tired of being accused of being a child of the devil by her husband.

"I say tha 'cause yu be bad mother. Yu no go to church wit me and my children. Yu no listen to the *padre*, tha priest when he give God sermon? Do yu no wan to keep tha church in our family? Why I the one in tha family tha has to do everything?" Benjy's words were slurred and he could barely keep his crazed look on Sara as he moved closer to her. He was trying hard to keep his footing so she could understand he was being serious.

"Why yu tink I no go to church and hear tha sermon? Yu crazy if yu no know tha!" Sara rebelled against Benjy.

"You tink God no see you? Yu tink yu be better than me an yur children? Yu tink God no watch you be bad mother? Mala!"

"I no bad mother," Sara yelled back at Benjy.

"Yu tink yu better than me? Yu are being a bad mother and have to pay for yur sins, yur *pecados*!" Benjy continued yelling as he lurched toward Sara at the same moment Mari peeked through her door crack. When she saw this, she jumped back into her bed and threw her blanket over her head. She cuddled up in a ball and held her hands to her ears. As she lay in her bed, she continued to hear her father screaming at her mother and furniture being thrown around.

"No more, no more, no more!" Mari kept saying to herself until she finally could not stay in bed. She jumped out of bed and ran out of her bedroom, not knowing what was happening in the rest of the house. She suddenly saw her father grab her mother by the neck. As he lifted her up against the wall, Mari saw her father bring his fist back. Mari dove toward her father, grabbing his fist before he punched her mother in the face.

"No, stop! Don't touch Mami," Mari yelled at the top of her lungs as she stood in front of her father. Benjy's jaw dropped, startled at seeing his daughter in the midst of a fight between Sara and himself. Shame filled his soul. Without a word, he pivoted and slapped Mari on her ear, leaving a high-pitched buzzing.

"Shut the hell up! Yu no know not'in'," he said as he glared at Mari. Benjy immediately dropped Sara, grabbed his car keys, and slammed the door as he as he stormed out of their apartment. He was shocked that his baby girl had turned on him. That ungrateful little bitch! She will learn too. She will learn the hard way. She will learn just like her mother will!

"Finally! Good for her!" I blurted out as I ran toward Mari as she was standing in front of Sara, staring at nothing. I could not help myself; I had to hug her, and there was nothing in my notes, class, or policy book that stated I could not do such a thing with my subject. As I started to reach in to hug Mari, I fell right through her and landed right on my face.

"What the—? I just wanted to give Mari a hug for doing the right thing and I fall on my face?" I yelled as I slowly picked myself up.

Nothing changed. Mari was still staring into space, and all she knew was that she had to protect her mother and take a stand against her father's abuse toward her mother. Unfortunately, she got hurt, but maybe this was the start of her standing up for herself. Why is it that when you want to do something right, you always end up getting hurt?

"Not always, Mari," I softly whisper to Mari.

"I get where Mari is coming from. All she has ever seen is hurt and dysfunction. How do you know what to do in that type of situation? You don't want to get in between your parents since you love them both, but wrong is wrong and right is right. I think Mari really got it right even though she ended up with a tremendous earache," I told Pearl, understanding both sides of the situation for the first time ever.

"Many times, change brings discomfort emotionally or physically, sometimes both. In many situations, it brings forth strength and confidence to a person since they know that what they did will bring hope and change for the better. Mari took the first step, but she doesn't understand what has happened yet."

"Mari feels hurt and pain right now. She also feels confused. You know that! You feel her spirit just like I do. We both know she is hurting deeply and doesn't know what else to do right now. She just feels scared! She went against her father in a fight between him and her mother. That is taboo!" I responded to Pearlie.

"We know that Mari is really scared right now. She doesn't know if she made it worse for her mother, her brother, and herself," Pearl continued speaking softly to me. She knew I felt Mari's pain intensely. I was connected to Mari even though Mari could not see me. Pearl knew she had to guide me on how to provide Mari with options available as I had been taught. You know, Pearl had to teach me the ropes. In the meantime, Mari had dropped down to her knees as she wrapped her arms wrapped tightly around her mother, who was sobbing helplessly.

"Ay Mari, mi hija—my daughter. I sorry yu had to see tha an yu get hit. Please no be angry at yur papi. He a good, good man. He be good husband. He be a good father. He work berry hard to make money so we have food and place to live. Please, Mari, no be mad at him!" Sara sobbed uncontrollably.

Mari could not even look at her mother. She just held her tightly. Her heart was beating like crazy. Mari could not believe what she was hearing. She could not believe her mother was actually protecting her father after he choked her mother and slapped her. Then again, her father was good to them. She had to remember that, just like her mother always does. He just had issues. Mari only wished her father would get his issues taken care of so he wouldn't take it out on them. Right now, she just wanted to kick his ass. She hated him! She was glad he left. Maybe he won't come back and it will just be her, her mom, and her brother.

"Mami, why do you let Papi hit you and treat you like that? He beats you," Mari softly asked her mother.

"*Hijita*, my beautiful daughter, yur father no hit me all thee time. He lof me. I know he lof me with all his heart. He no know how to control himself. He get angry and I here so he hit me by accident. I mean, do yu not see thee pretty flowers he bring me? Nobodee bring me flowers except for yur papi. He get angry and den he feel so bad. He no mean to hit me," Sara quietly said as she lifted Mari's face so it would rest in her palm.

"Mami, that does not look like he loves you. Anyone who loves someone does not hit that person. He will be nice and say sweet things to the person he loves. Papi hits you, fine, he brings you flowers only after he hits you hard, Mami. He does not treat you right. Parents are not supposed to do those things." Mari twisted away from her mother's grasp and squared away at Sara.

"Mari, *mi hija*. Yur papi no like tha before. He be good to me. He would look at me and say, 'Sara, yu are the most beautiful woman I know. Yu are the only woman, *mujer*, I vill ever look at. I be happy, Sarita.' Mari, when I meet yur papi, he bee so nice to me. He call me evry night. He open door of car for me. Always so nice, Mari," Sara softly muttered to Mari.

"Yur daddy lose he new job promotion. He is angry and do no always tink of wha he do. I bee only person he talk to and be hisself. He no talk to nobody. Nobody know him and listen to him like me. He no do tat to me 'cause he do not love me. It be an accident. He angry 'cause of his job. He good worker even though he no get promotion. Yu understand, Mari? He no mean to hurt me. He lof me and yu and Jonathan berry, berry much."

"Mami, you are so beautiful, not just on the outside but also on the inside. Do yu know why I read so much, Mami? Do you know why I do not like to leave my room?" Mari asked her mother.

"Yu like yur books, Mari. I know. Yu lof to read," Sara quietly responded.

"I read because that is the only thing I feel safe doing. It takes me away from here. I read in my books about other princesses, princes, and kids growing up without being scared about what lies around the corner. I read about princesses marrying great princes and also about kids who become great people when they are adults. What do you do, Mami? Why not help us live that life, not just for us but for you too?

"I mean you keep me old, Mami, just like you feel. Why let him hit you and you not fight back?" Mari just stared at Sara, hoping she could find the strength to shake some sense and hope into her mom. Somehow, she felt as though she had heard these same words before. Mari paused long enough to catch a glimpse of air whisking a curtain but continued on.

"Mami, I don't want to live within four walls and not experience life. I want to live the ending of the Cinderella book, Mami. I want to meet my handsome and wonderful prince. I want to live a happy life. But I also know that I can do great things because I am smart and do not have to get married to have a happy life. I don't want to hear you cry and Papi hit you all the time. I don't want to read to take me away from the life we live. I want to actually live it and not read about it. I mean, I don't even know how to ride a bike and I'm fifteen years old!"

"Where I go, Mari? How I pay bills? I OK wit yur papi. He treats me like I need, right? I no need more. I get wha I need and deserve. Also, Mari, I no know where I go wit yu and Jonathan. I no have money. Where I go? How I buy a car to go to work? How I feed yu and Jonathan? How I pay for apartment and get food for you and Jonathan? No be mad at your papi, he yur father. Yu must respect him. He good to yu and Jonathan and me." Sara looked at Mari with tear-filled eyes, defeat written all over her tear-streaked face.

"Yeah, Mami. You are right. I won't be angry at him. I know he is a good papi," Mari lied. She knew her mom had no money to leave. Mari was hoping for that magic pumpkin that she had read about, wondered when it would come to her apartment, turn into a carriage, and whisk her mom and brother away with her to a place far away from this crazy place.

"Mari, yu know I love yu and yur brother berry much. I know you must see what happens wit yur father and me. When tings get really bad, I stay here with him because of yu and yur brother. I love you two berry, berry much an do wha I need to do to make sure yu and yur brother be good in this place!"

Mari had a brainstorm as she felt her energy leave her body. She grabbed Sara's hand and ran her to the wall mirror on the living room wall.

"Look at you, Mami, you are beautiful all the way around, just like a perfectly made chocolate chip cookie, inside and out. I don't want you to wither away. You can go to school to learn English really well and even learn a job skill. I mean, Jonathan and I can try really hard to do well in grades and we can go to college. I mean, you do not want to be an overbaked chocolate chip dried-up cookie. Do you? You know chocolate chip cookies are my favorite! I mean, I am an expert at chocolate chip cookies and my chocolate chip cookie radar says that the other cookies need to look out 'cause you are hot, Mami. I mean H-O-T—hot! Mari smiled and poked Sara lovingly in the ribs. Sara giggled while she pulled Mari to her arms to embrace the very reason she lived her life, to take care of her amazing *hijita* Mari and *hijito* Jonathan. Her children were what kept her going. Mari exaggerated clearing her throat and rubbed her tummy.

"Mami, I mean I can check to see if you are still that hot chocolate chip cookie babe if you bake me some cookies to test them out compared to you. I mean, I will do that for you. You know, to make sure you feel good about yourself. I mean, I don't want you to be all down on yourself and stuff."

"Ay, hijita, yu make me laugh when there be not'in' to laugh about. Yu give me hope tha maybe tings vill change. Maybe yur papi vill get his promotion soon and we can all be happy again."

"Mami, everything will work out. Don't lose hope no matter what happens with Papi, be happy with you. You are letting Papi to come and take away the one thing you have always taught us to do, and that is to have hope and faith." Mari grabbed Sara by the hand and pulled her away toward the front door. Mari opened the security bolt and took the door's security pole while she jarred the door open.

"Hija, wha yu do? Where we go? Yu loca! OK, I vill make cookies. Come to the kitchen, I do it now." Mari was not listening. She just kept a death grip on her mom. She ran with her mother until they had finally reached the building's roof.

"Trust me!" Mari told Sara while she pulled their building's roof door open and ran, finding a brick to secure the door open. Mari found Sara's hand and took her to the middle of the roof.

"Look, Mami, look up." Sara looked up toward the sky.

"Can you see it? Do you feel happy, Mami? I do!" Mari continued looking upward, toward the sky, all the time pulling her mother's hand and pleading for her to look at the beautiful blue sky with sunrays piercing brightly through the sea of clouds and shining on both their faces.

"Do you see it? Do you see the beautiful sky with all the fluffy white animals? There, there!" Mari pointed upward, toward a grouping of puffy white and gray clouds.

"There's our castle, Mami, just like in the Cinderella fairy tale. It's tall and wide with lots of windows and animals around it. Do you see how beautiful it is? Do you? It's just like in the books I have read about castles and forts. Look over there!" Mari grabbed her mother's arm and jerked Sara's chin upward to the east.

"There, right over there. That's the castle you, Jonathan, and I will live in! See that woman in the window with the big smile? That's you with a big smile on your face. That's you. Right over there."

I can see another patch to the right side of the cloud cluster Mari chose to be her castle. Sara simply pulled Mari closer to her side and placed her arm on her shoulders.

"Yez, *hija*, I see it. I see *Dios*, I see God but he no see me rit now. He busy, I tink. *Pero, hija*, I feel happy, berry happy I hab yu and yur brother. Just like the best, chocolate chip cookie. I feel lika I jus like the woman of the castle. Yez, thee castle like yu say?" Sara smiled as Mari showed her the thumbs-up sign on both hands.

"Mami, you be the bom-beedy, bomb-bomb, Mami!" Mari smiled and hugged her mother with all that was in her. As Mari did this, she felt a piece of her got stronger. She hoped it got stronger for her mom too. She decided, right there and then, she had to keep her hope alive, if not only for today. She couldn't think about tomorrow; it was too far away.

"Urrrrrr, that is such a crock of bull!" I screeched out as she threw her hand into the air. "She stays with that scumbag because she is too much of a coward to walk out on him. Then Sara pulls the martyr stunt on Mari. That just really gets me!" Just as quickly as I spoke these words, I fell to the floor.

"Candace, Candace. Come on honey, wake up. You know you aren't supposed to get so riled up. That will cloud your judgment. It will cloud your senses and affect the way you help Mari. You know you will get sick every time you get really angry. That is not why you are here. Come on now, get yourself together. That child needs you! Think good things. Think of how Mari will become a stronger person once you are finished with her!"

I knew I had to regain my composure and strength so I can act upon Pearl's suggestions. I knew if I am to help Mari, I could not allow myself to get so angry and bring my own personal past baggage into play. I needed to maintain focus and think of Mari only. I needed to remember my past only for guidance purposes. I need to focus on what I whisper to Mari so my suggestions will help her not fall into the same demise I ran into.

"Pearl, Mari is taking on her parent's role and responsibilities. She is acting as a mother."

"OK, so how are you going to help her? Understanding what she is going through is the first step. Now what?" Pearl softly yet firmly asks me while looking me directly in my eyes.

"I want to tell her to get the hell out of there and go tell the police what is going on. I want her to go to the police or someone they feel safe with so they can find help. I hope a telephone number can be given to them for places to go to or get help until they get to the point that they will leave and put Benjy behind bars!"

"Think about it. Would you have done that when you were going through your abuse?" Pearl asked me. "Did you want police around asking you all kinds of intimate questions while you were by yourself? Perhaps if you had someone with you and supporting you while you spoke with some type of authority, be it the police or someone else that would be able to help you with your situation at home, maybe, just maybe things would have been different for you."

"I know I would not be here without you, right?" I asked Pearl, with ice lacing my question.

"Right. So what will you do to get her to act differently from you? To not end up like you did? What would you do now in Mari's place?"

"I will tell her that her home's mess was not created by her. She is not the one to blame. It is not her fault that her mother is used as a punching bag even if she continues to tell Mari that she is there because of her and her brother. She cannot feel guilty every time her father abuses her mother. Her mother is scared just like she is. She has the strength to make a change in her living situation. I know Mari is just as scared as Sara is. I think Jonathan is scared too. That is why you don't see him around the house that much. He is running away from the problem."

"OK, that is a good start. It's also about choice. Having the choice to have a voice!" Pearl says as she puts her arm around my shoulder.

"That is a very good start."

I rested my head on Pearlie's shoulder as she rested her head on top of mine. We both stood there watching Mari hug her mom on the kitchen floor.

CHAPTER 12

Mari sat back, watching and listening to her aunt, uncle, and three crazy out-of-control cousins while they were gathered at the dinner table, yakking all at the same time. Mari was not very hungry even though the food had a great aroma. There was so much food. Man, it smelled awesome! Her father had returned just a few minutes before the family arrived. Mari could not even look at him.

Her family was quite animated talking about their work, the economy as it related to the lack of money in their pockets, cars, baseball, and other relatives. Her cousins were being scolded for taking more dessert than entrée and vegetables and using improper manners while at the dinner table. She could see her two younger cousins do the "tag, it's you" game while trying hard not to fall under their parent's watchful eye; otherwise, the tag game would result in a slap on the head by their parents.

"Such dorks. Oh well, same crap, just different day," Mari thought as she looked around the table at her cousins and family. Also, how amazing her father was acting so happy, happy as a lark and was even putting his arm around his mom and hugging her like nothing ever happened earlier today. Such hypocrisy!

She heard someone knocking on the door and immediately knew it was her aunt. Finally, someone will be here I really like and is more in tune with the real world. Mari got up quickly before anyone else and ran to the doorbell.

"Hi, Titi Candi, so happy to see you!" Mari said as she ran up to hug her aunt's neck tightly.

"Hola, Mari. Ooooh, it is so good to see you too!" Candi replied as she returned Mari's hug. Candi loved her niece deeply. She loved coming to see her niece, nephew, and older sister. The only one she could do without seeing was that lowlife brother-in-law of hers, she thought as she entered the kitchen where everyone was seated eating. Candi dropped her purse on the kitchen counter before she greeted everyone.

"Hmmm, that must be Sara's youngest sister," I mused. "She looks so beautiful and full of life. Why does she put up shields so no one can truly see who she is? She has so much energy to give to everyone." I contrived from my brief encounter with Candi's spirit.

"*Hola,* Candi! It is about time yu showed up. I tink we have to tie up everybody's hands so yu hab food to eat," Sara laughingly told her as she stood up to give her younger sister a big hug and kiss on the cheek.

There was a flurry of hug and kiss exchanges as Candi made her rounds to everyone. She generally loved coming over, but whenever she arrived or left, she felt extremely uncomfortable the way Benjy hugged her and touched her in his greetings. "It's just my imagination," she would think as she quickly tried to erase that thought for fear that God would punish her for thinking such things. Yet, that odd feeling persisted every time she visited. Candi was a beautiful twenty-eight-year-old woman with slightly wavy shoulder-length light auburn hair. She had large hazel bedroom eyes that were enhanced by her thick lashes. She was different from her sister Sara in that Candi was rather tall, 5'9", compared to the rest of the females in her family. She had a well-proportioned body that captured looks and remarks from many men she walked by. Her physical beauty was enhanced by her inner beauty. She was an extremely kind soul that always tried to help others at all costs. She was also the only person in their family that had gone to college and obtained a bachelor's degree.

After dinner was over, the normal routine occurred, with the men heading to the living room with their beers in hand to watch whatever sports were on television, with the ladies doing the cleanup in the kitchen and later rewarding themselves with some fresh brewed coffee.

"Sara, how did you get that bruise on your neck?" Candi asked her sister.

"Ay, I be so stupid sometimes. I go shopping and I put this necklace that was pretty but too tight on my neck and I no notice how tight it be until I go home and undress. Stupid?" Sara lied hoping Candi would not ask her anything else.

"Stop putting yourself down, Sara. You are not stupid. I was curious since I keep seeing more and more bruises on you lately. I want to make sure you are OK," Candi replied. She had noticed her sister was wearing heavier foundation on her face and clothes that would conceal her body a little more.

"No, Sara, you no stupid," Luisa piped in to get rid of some of the uneasiness that suddenly overcame them all. Luisa too had obtained bruises and it certainly was not by wearing necklaces too tight. Yet, she knew she could never talk about it for fear of more bruises. Thankfully for Luisa, Sara, and all, the conversations went to other family things and all seemed normal again, at least for a while.

It was nearly 10:00 p.m. before Luisa and her clan headed home. Candi had started to put on her jacket when Sara stopped her midstream.

"Candi, stay the night. Leave tomorrow. Yu no go to work early tomorrow, rit? You have the late shift, rit? Quedate, stay so I no worry 'bout yu outside by yurself late in thee nite. OK?" Sara pleaded with her sister.

"Candi, stay the night. We hab thee room. Yu can stay in Mari's room. Why no go out this late unless yu need to meet man for date?" Benjy added to his wife's request with a smirk.

"Yes, Titi Candi! That would be way cool. You can sleep in the cot in my room or I can sleep in the cot and you can sleep in my bed. There is plenty of room and I don't mind your snoring anymore. Plus, we have not had a good girls' sleepover in a while." Mari lovingly pulled on her aunt's hand, guiding her toward her bedroom so she could quickly approve her sleeping accommodations.

"OK, OK. It is hard to argue with you guys!" Candi laughed. "Thanks, it would be smarter to get a good night's sleep and then head out in the morning after everyone has left for work and school. Plus, I do not have anyone meeting me for a date so I am good to stay the night. If I did, I would have mentioned it," Candi said as she turned to Benjy and gave him a "What is wrong with you?" look.

"Good! I get clean linens for yu," Sara said, oblivious to the look exchanged between Candi and Benjy. I felt the immediate unease around Benjy. She also felt so uncomfortable arriving so late for dinner and disrupting the family's routine. She simply had to finish her master's degree thesis. She had not mentioned to anyone she had enrolled in graduate studies. She had hoped it would be a pleasant outcome but did not want to jinx it yet by letting everyone know she was in school.

Mari led Candi into her bedroom while her mom gathered the bed linens and made the cot up for Candi. Mari got her cleanest nightgown and handed it over to her aunt so she could change and relax. They spent a good hour chatting and playing with Mari's hair on ways to make her look cuter than she already did. Mari simply adored her aunt. She was so funny, vivacious, and always listened to what she had to say. She never judged. Mari almost told her about that afternoon's incident about her father bursting into her shower but decided against it. Why burden her aunt with it? Even worse, what if her aunt didn't believe her? That would devastate her. No, better not to bring it up, Mari thought.

Realizing how quickly time had fled by, Mari and Candi both decided it was time to hit the sack. Several hours after they had turned off the lights, both Candi and Mari realized there was a presence in the room. Mari had softly stirred in her sleep and quickly opened her eyes when she felt something was wrong in her room. As she did, she saw a dark silhouette heaving upon her aunt in the cot next to her. She was still very groggy with sleep and was not sure if she was dreaming or if there was truly someone in her room.

As she refocused her eyes, trying to stay quiet for fear that the man would come over to her as well, she started bleeding as a wave of nausea punched her in the pit of her stomach as she recognized who this stranger was in her room. She heard this man's voice cooing to her aunt not to say anything. Telling her to be quiet. Mari could hear this man shushing her aunt into submission. She could also hear her aunt pleading. "Benjy, no. This is wrong. Why yu doing this?"

"Shhhhh, yu know yu want this as much as I do. Hmmmmm, yu wan it has much has I too," Benjy hoarsely whispered to Candi as he continued thrusting himself upon her.

"No, no, Benjy, yu are wrong. Sara is my sister. Yu are crazy."

As Mari realized for certain this was not a bad dream, she realized the figure that was heaving upon her aunt Candi was her father. She could hear her aunt's tearful pleading to have him go back to Sara and leave her alone. Mari's terrified body stiffened, and she prayed her breathing would not give away the fact that she was awake and saw this atrocious act.

Finally, Benjy released his grip on Candi and lifted his sweaty body off from her aunt. He straightened his pajama bottoms, and wove his hands through his hair as he started to leave Mari's room. All of a sudden, Benjy stopped and returned to Candi's side.

"I will see yu again in my dreams, Candi. I know yu wan me and I come back to yu to give yu wha yu wa," Benjy softly spoke as he headed back into his bedroom where Sara was softly snoring, unaware that he had left her side.

Mari could hear her aunt's snuffled sobs as she slowly turned toward the wall away from her aunt. Mari was numb. She wanted to run to her aunt to console her, yet she was unable to move. She was too scared to reveal that she was awake and just witnessed her father rape her aunt.

"I want to die. I want to go away from here. I want a different life. I want to live a different life!"

"Nooooo!" Candace yelled at the top of her lungs. "How can this happen to her? What an animal! I am supposed to help Mari. Guide her and try to protect her from these horrible situations. I am such a failure!" Candace cried out.

"You are not a failure. You are very special and different, Candace. That is why you were chosen to be Mari's very extraordinary Spiritual Guide. You are her Guide. You are not responsible for her actions or anyone else's that comes into her life. Everyone has to choose for themselves what actions they feel will be best for them. You are merely here to show her that life can have a different ending. Life can yield happiness. It does not always have to be about sadness. People can choose their destinies. They have to simply be provided an avenue and a chance to learn there is a different way to live life. Mari does not know this yet. No one has ever shown her that. That is why you are here, Candace. You are here to whisper to her she is special. She can choose a different way of life. She can trust other people. Not everyone is like her father. In the same way you are special, Candace, so is Mari." Candace's eyes swelled with tears as she listened to Pearl's every word.

"Are there any fathers out there that will protect their daughters instead of violating them? My heart goes out to Mari since I understand so well how she feels. I remember how I seethed with anger about my father and the many years of torment and abuse he subjected me to. I found it hard to believe that my own father would come into my room and hurt me in such a disgusting way and treat me as though nothing happened during the day. It took me into this time for me to fully forgive him."

"Candace, it is good you forgave your father. It is up to God to take care of your father afterward. You have a right to see awardees feel. Now it is time for you to share your strength with Mari," Pearl said as she continued to keep me close to her.

I turned to Mari and said, "Mari, you are very special. Never forget that, Mari. You may feel as though you are in a dark closet with no doors allowing entrance to the outside and may want no doors to the outside since there is so much evil and hurt out there. Yet there is hope. There are people who care about injustice and care about putting an end to hurt and pain. Please know what your father did to your aunt has nothing to do with you. Please do not feel guilty that you did not scream or get up to help her. You are a child. Your father should be protecting those he loves and not hurting them. Not every father is like that. You are special and sweet and innocent. You should not be charged with taking on the responsibility to stop your father. You could have but it is not you who should be punished, it is your father. What he did is way wrong. Go tell someone. Tell your mother, tell your teacher, do you trust a police person or your principal?"

I realized Mari's mother was just as lost as she was. Sara was just her mom, except Sara accepted being the punching bag to deal with the reality of what was truly occurring to her family, while my mother used sleeping pills to take her away to a place she would not have to see what was happening to her family. Two families, two choices.

"Candace, we are not just two very hot-looking angels. We are two hot-looking angels that are here to help guide Mari," Pearl soothingly said to Mari.

"I wonder at times how I can help Mari when I feel myself lost as to what to tell her. I took the easy way out, remember? I killed myself instead of facing what was happening to me. I had to kill myself or would end up killing my father."

"You would not have done that, Candace, and you know it. You are not weak." Pearl adamantly said. "You just did not know how to deal with it at that time. Yet now you are whispering all the right things to Mari to help her through her time of anguish. You are wanting to help her to get help. The help you did not get for yourself. You thought your mother would not believe you, so you chose not to tell her. Yet, you did not give her a chance to do the right thing. You did I give her a chance to redeem herself for doing what she should have to protect her daughter. She knew you were being raped. She simply did not know how to deal with such a situation. However, the past is the past. Now we are dealing with the future and this live young woman that needs direction to get out of the horror she does not need to be in."

Candace kept quiet. "Who would Mari tell?" Candace wondered. Mari's mother was so lost herself and did not have the strength to deal with the ordeal she was facing. She felt Mari pulling up walls and closing herself in. "Who can I tell?" Mari thought.

"What do you mean who will she tell?" Pearl softly asked me. "What are you?"

"Pearlie, how did you know what I was thinking?" Pearl simply tilts her head toward mine as if to say, "Hello, who do you think I am?" I went to Mari and sat next to her. She sat there with eyes closed, taking in Mari's energy and returning her energy with a positive and hopeful force.

"Mari, you are not alone. I am here with you. Talk to me. Let me hear your heart. Walk me closer to your soul. I want to help you. You are special. You can have a different life. You can make a difference!" I said as tears flowed down her pink cheeks.

"I hope so. I want to have a different life," Mari muttered, being barely audible while closing her eyes and placing her blanket over her head.

CHAPTER 13

Mari's head was killing her due to lack of sleep. She forced her eyes open after being awakened by a loud DJ on the radio alarm. She quickly looked over to the cot to see if her aunt was sleeping so she could go over and give her a huge good-morning hug. Also, Mari had an alternative motive; she wanted to make sure her Aunt Candi was doing OK. She loved her aunt deeply and was at a loss as to what to say or do. She hoped her aunt would not ask her if Mari saw or heard anything last night. Mari did not have to worry about anything since her aunt was not in her room. The cot was neatly made and her jacket, along with her pocketbook, was gone. Mari had a sick feeling in the pit of her stomach. She feared she would never see her aunt again. She started feeling her forehead and hands get sweaty although her room was rather cold. She just lay in bed watching the clock move its hands forward, knowing she had to get up and being unable to move. She was terrified she would she would see someone. Mari was so scared someone could tell there was something wrong with her. She was scared someone would learn her horrible secret—her father was a monster. He was a rapist!

"I am too sick to go to school but what happens if Papi comes home early? No, I better get up and go to school. I just wish I could stay home locked up in my room with my book." Mari loved to read her fairy tales. They allowed her to go to a happy place where there was always a happy ending even after a tragedy hits and hope was but a mere breeze on a hot summer day. As Mari thought about staying home, reality hit her. She needed to go to school since she had a test in math and had to turn in a project. Dumb school! But no, it was probably better she went, Mari mused. She slowly got dressed. She grabbed a pair of jeans, old sweatshirt, put on some running shoes, and brushed her hair into a ponytail. She cautiously opened her door, peeking slowly through the door crack for fear someone in her family would be up and about even though it was really quiet. With the coast clear, she robotically picked up her jacket and ran into the bathroom where she brushed her teeth and cleaned her face. She didn't bother to eat breakfast since she wasn't hungry. She did not know what she felt. She simply felt numb, no feelings, shallow—an empty carcass without a heartbeat. She ran out of the house.

She walked to school, not seeing those around her. As if in zombie state, she watched streetlights change, she crossed streets when she was supposed to, even though she did not really know how she got to school. Mari saw her brother leaving the gym and remembered he had gym for his first class and left the house early so he could do some early warm-up. He seemed absorbed in thought as well. She wanted so badly to call out to him but could not find her voice. She did not have the drive to speak to him or anyone else, for that matter. Jonathan stooped down to tie a shoelace, and as he got up, he noticed his sister just a few feet away, just staring at him. He waited for her to approach. When she did nothing, he nodded his head in salutation so she would know he acknowledged her presence. He walked toward her and simply signaled to her to head on to her class as he walked with her. Neither Jonathan nor Mari said a word. When Mari got to her classroom door, she whispered, "See you later, bro," as she walked inside her classroom. Jonathan picked up his pace as he returned to his gym class. He did not want his gym teacher getting into his face this morning. All he could think about today was how to take his mom, sister, and himself far from their house and away from their psychotic father.

His father did not see Jonathan behind the pantry door last night when he slipped into Mari's bedroom. Curious as to why his father was going into Mari's room, Jonathan tiptoed across the kitchen so he could get close enough to see what his father was doing. He moved closer to the door to see if he could look through the door crack and what he saw sickened him. Jonathan saw his father on top of his aunt while he muffled his aunt's sobs with his hand. He wished he could stop the rape that was occurring in front of his eyes and right next to his little sister. Jonathan went back into his room, shivering all over even though he had on a sweatshirt and flannel pajama bottoms. He grabbed his iPod, turned it on, and blasted the music into his ear set. He wanted to tune out the sobs he had heard from his aunt. He had wanted to grab his father off his aunt as a hawk tears into an aggressor that preys on her babies for their next meal. Jonathan was very confused. He loved his father and loved knowing that his Latin heritage was being kept alive by the way his father and mother lived. He loved his father's loyalty to his native island of Puerto Rico and his hard-work ethic that ensured he and Mari understood where they came from and their cultural traits. He recognized his father's inference to the male's "Latin blood" when it came to women and how men perceived their role in the marriage. Basically, the man is the king of his house. He does what he wants. Just like the caveman days, the man goes out to hunt for food for his family while his wife stays home to make sure their children are taken care of, the meals are cooked, and if there is desire for more children, then the woman bears the children. Simple! Jonathan thought, as he lay in bed confused at what just happened in his home. Where do the women come into play? Are we as men supposed to take them as we please? The pleas he heard his aunt make did not sound like pleas of a woman that was willing to be "taken." Plus, not all Latin men are like that. I am so very confused!

Jonathan had merely lain in his bed, scared like a total pussy. Yes, he had remembered all of those feelings as he walked to his class. He had wanted to reach out to Mari and ask her if anything had happened to her last night. How could he do that without letting everyone know that he had seen his father go into her room? How could he say anything without disclosing that he had seen someone get hurt that he really cared about and was too much of a coward to do anything about it? No, he had to be quiet. He would make it up to Mari in some way and, most of all, to his aunt when he saw her. He would think of something. Besides, what about his mother? What would happen to her if he would have told her that her husband was caught raping her sister? What then? If it were someone they did not know, it would be OK since he understood his father is a man and a man has needs. At least that was what his father always told him. His mother was always getting the crap beat out of her by his father and she kept blaming Jonathan and Mari for being the reason she stayed with his father. The fact is, Jonathan did not believe a lot of things he would tell him. He hated that his father beat his mother and put her in that crap of a closet. He did not like his father cheating on his mother. But, would his mother leave his father? Where would they go? Would God strike him dead in his tracks for exposing his father? What then? No Jonathan! Man, this sucks!

Jonathan's head hurt just thinking about last night. He did not want to think about it, but the feeling of tremendous failure kept looming over his head. He felt he had betrayed his sister's trust and the protection he should have provided her by not going into her bedroom and ripping his father off of his aunt. Afterward, he would rip his father's face off with his bare hands.

"I think I will take out my bike and help Mari learn how to ride better. That should take her mind off what happened last night if she was awake. Hopefully, she wasn't." She had been hounding him forever to take her out and help her get better at riding. Yep, that is what he'll do. It will make her feel better, and maybe this will show God he wasn't such a bad brother. Nothing he could do now except move on. He could not say anything to the priest at confession since he would be given such a long penance he would spend the whole mass on his knees saying his prayers and everyone would know he did something really bad. No, that was not going to work. Stick to teaching Mari how to ride a bike and forget about the confessional. Besides, what do priests know about marriage, rape, and that type of shit? They never been married, Jonathan tried to rationalize.

The day finally finished, and once again, Jonathan and Mari were back to their normal routine of griping about fixing dinner and doing their homework.

"OK, dinner ready. Mari, come get the plates and forks and put them on table for everyone. Jonathan, go clean yur hands so yu come to table to eat," Sara spoke loudly toward Jonathan's direction as she leaned down to pull his speaker buds off his ears. Sara noticed he had not left his room since she had gotten home from work. He usually would come out after she got home to give her a hug and tease her about how pretty she looks and how he got his looks from her. That was why all the girls couldn't leave him alone. They all wanted him since he was so good-looking. Jonathan barely looked at her as he got up from his bed. He just shrugged his shoulders and brushed past Sara so he could head toward the bathroom to clean his hands.

Everyone, with the exception of Candi, sat at the table for dinner. Candi had left a short note to let Sara know she would not be available for dinner. She would grab a sandwich and get some work around her apartment done. Jonathan ate his dinner without a word. No second helpings this evening. Not even a request for dessert before they finished eating. Very unusual, Sara thought, since she had made his favorite dessert, *arroz dulce,* sweet cold rice with raisins, a family dessert specialty Sara had perfected through the years.

Nina called around 7:45 p.m., but Mari told her mom to tell Nina she was out with her aunt. She did not want to talk to her best friend tonight. Mari wanted to tell Nina what she had seen last night but she couldn't. What would Nina think? Would Nina think Mari's father was a rapist too? Would Nina stop being her best friend if she told her? What if Nina called the police and the police came to her house and took her papi to jail? What would happen to her family? What would happen to her family? What if they wouldn't believe her Aunt Candi? What if they put her Aunt Candi in jail too? What if the police came and put her in jail for not telling them that she had seen her father raping her aunt? What if the police came to her house and took her mother to jail for having given birth to Mari? Ugh, Mari's head started to hurt as she thought of all the things that could go wrong if she spoke up and said something. She loved Nina, and bottom line was that she did not want to lose Nina's friendship. She couldn't take that chance. She had to keep quiet. Mari decided to read her book and hang out in her room for the night. She put her book down and made sure her door was locked with her latch.

CHAPTER 14

The next morning, Candace walked with Mari and Jonathan to school. I stood by the window next to Mari while she was in her English class. I could feel Mari's hurt, confusion, fear, vulnerability, and anger. I had felt all of those emotions years ago when I was alive and wished I was dead so my father's abuse would end. I remembered how I would detach myself when bedtime would bring the night crawler to my bedroom and tear at my soul piece by piece. Right now, I wished I had large beautiful wings like the ones I had seen on angels in the church my parents would take me so I could wrap them around Mari. I wanted to wrap those wings around her and protect her from anything else that might bring her harm. I wished I had had a special guide that would have thought of me during my darkest hours while I was alive.

Mari continued to stare out the window. She ignored her closest friend Nina as she tried to speak with Mari all day long. By the end of the day, Nina simply kept quiet. She sensed something really bad had happened to her buddykins Mari. She wanted to find out what was going on, but as of yet, she couldn't get rid of that barrier Mari had set all around herself. Nina, fourteen years of age, was petite and not as developed as Mari. She would observe how some boys would stare at Mari's figure. She could see in their eyes how they would scope her out. There were times Nina wished they would look at her like that, but if one of them would dare ask her out, she wouldn't know what she would do. So, for now it was best not to open up that can of worms. Besides, boys could be such jerks, and when they grew up, some of them would be even worse jerks. Her dad was nothing like a jerk. He was the best man around. He loved her and her mom. Her dad would take her to baseball, hockey, and even football games. One time, he took her to Shea Stadium, where she caught a ball from one of the New York Mets that had batted a foul ball. That was the bomb! Her father could not be prouder of her, especially since they waited until all the New York Mets' players came out of the stadium. Finally, the player Nina and her father waited for showed up and he autographed the ball. Her dad was so excited and happy she had caught the ball with the glove he had brought for her that they headed to a store and purchased an all-clear glass square box with brass trim. Nina could get the date and player's name embossed on a brass plate that the store assistant placed on the glass box.

When Nina and her dad had arrived home, her mom had placed three chocolate cupcakes she had baked on small plates with a candle in the middle of each cupcake and they sang, "Take Me Out to the Ballgame" except they added to the lyrics, "so Nina can catch another Mets ball." Her mother just sat there smiling. Her father told his wife he was going to take all the knick-knacks off the shelf in the living room so they could showcase Nina's new baseball. Her mom laughed and told her husband next time he was going to make dinner himself if he wanted to eat since he was full of such attitude. Her mom looked over toward Nina and gave her a wink with a smile. After dinner, her dad took Nina to get a glass display box that would show off the ball. She placed her baseball on her drawer so she could see it from all angles of her room. Nina silently prayed her parents would never leave each other. She would not be able to handle it well.

Nina brought herself back and looked at Mari. She wanted to put her arms around her best friend and take away her pain or whatever she was feeling. She knew Mari had a very difficult family life. She would see bruises on Mari's mom's face and body when she would come over to hang out with Mari. She would her Mari's father talk so horribly to Mari's mom, and she could not understand why he would do that. Her own parents rarely raised their voices around her. She usually saw them snuggling with each other like they were BFFs instead of husband and wife. Nina was grateful for her parents.

Nina was an only child and she always searched out Mari for companionship. Mari was such a good friend to her. She was kind and always listened to what she had to say. She would always tell Nina about the latest fairy-tale books she was reading. She would summarize the book as though Mari was the princess instead of Cinderella or some other victorious female character. She was so intense when she spoke about her books. It was as though she lived the character's life. Mari always listened to what Nina had to say and responded to her problems without judgment. Lately, Nina noticed Mari was super depressed. She had to do something to help her friend.

After classes had finished, Nina was walking with Mari when she was surprised to see Jonathan waiting for Mari with his prize bike in front of Mari's apartment building. He would never allow Mari or Nina to even touch the bike unless he told them where they could place their paws on his shiny piece of steel. Nina was happy to see Mari's smile, something she had not seen these past couple of weeks. Mari was still wobbly when she rode a bike and really wanted to gain some confidence. She would always tell Nina she wanted to learn how to ride a bike so she could ride the hell away from her place. She told Nina she could join her if she wanted to, even though she knew Nina was happy at home. Mari knew she would never go to a place far away from where they lived, where the sun shone, the flowers were abundant, and parents walked around with their kids holding their hands and laughing. Yeah, right! Nina looked at Mari as she was gaining more and more steadiness on her bike and remembered how her friend wanted to see and feel what it would be like to go a day without problems. Mari would tell her she was afraid to hope since she did not want to be disappointed if she hoped for a day in her life like that. What did it matter if she hoped?

Nina snapped out of it when Mari threw Nina her books and hopped on Jonathan's bike. Jonathan slowly explained the fundamentals of the ten gears and showed her once again how to stop the bike with the handbrakes or with the pedals. He was being awfully nice to Mari and really careful to make sure she was safe not only with his bike but also with her not falling off. Nina thought it very odd that he had taken today to be so nice when many times he would ignore them, and at times, he would ignore them and treated them rudely. He would call them dweebs and put on his headset then lock himself in his room if they were at Mari's home. If he was at school, he was usually with his friends. He would steal looks to where Mari and Nina were, just to make sure they were all right. Nina knew in her heart that Jonathan loved his sister. He put on that steel look of "I don't give a shit," but she felt inside he really wasn't that way. He just did not want to show it. She thought it was a "macho" thing. Yet, Nina had a huge crush on him. She was insane to feel that way, but a girl feels what she feels. That's why it hurt her when Jonathan ignored them.

Mari seemed to be having a great time now. At first, she got on the bike and she was all over the board while she was riding the bike. Jonathan was getting one hell of a workout! He was trying his best to hold the back of the bike so he could make sure his little sister would not fall off but also because he didn't want his bike scratched up. As Mari gained some confidence, she started riding straighter and gaining speed. Mari started controlling the bike instead of the bike controlling her. She actually seemed to be enjoying herself.

I looked at Mari and Jonathan's interaction and knew Jonathan was trying to find peace and forgiveness by teaching his sister to ride a bike since he knew it was something she wanted to do. He was trying so hard to forgive himself and find peace in his heart. How sad it is to be in such turmoil, I thought to myself. I only wished Jonathan would take his sister and would have a heart-to-heart talk. I hoped Jonathan would open up to his sister. I mean, they're only teenagers. They were lost and needed each other. They both saw and knew the same thing. They knew they were living in a very dysfunctional environment. It would be so cool if they would communicate with each other and come up with a plan.

Mari's ponytail flew high into the air as she got a good wind under it and kept speeding down the block. Her eyes finally opened with excitement and zeal. She allowed herself to feel alive. I slid to her side and whispered, "Doesn't this feel great, Mari? Don't you want to feel this way every day? You can! You don't have to put up with all this abuse. Tell someone. Talk to Jonathan. Let him know what you saw last night. You are stronger than you think, Mari. You are strong and special. You can do it!" Mari simply stopped dead in her tracks. She looked. She looked around as though she was looking for someone or something. She had a distorted look on her face. She rode very unsteadily back to Jonathan and Nina and almost ran into them.

"Did you see someone next to me? Did you hear someone talking to me?" Mari asked them as she looked around.

"Girl, are you nuts? Look around you. Do you see anyone? It was you and my bike," Jonathan told her as if she was having an out-of-body experience.

"I know what it was. The wind. What you heard was probably wind as you sped up and down the street," he continued to tell her.

"No, Mari. No one was around you. Are you OK?" Nina asked her, wondering if she was doing OK.

"I guess maybe it was the wind. Hmmm, it probably was," Mari said as she handed Jonathan the bike back. "I want to head home. Thanks for the lesson, bro. Yak at you later." "I hope you do, Mari. I hope you do speak with Jonathan later. You are loved!" I mused as I saw Mari head home in a faster-than-usual pace.

CHAPTER 15

Weeks had slowly gone by for Mari. Each day felt more dull and unimportant than the last one. Mari stayed in her room reading her books, only coming out for dinner or necessary family meals. She kept to herself quite a bit and rarely spoke much around her mom and brother while doing her chores. Her father also noticed a slight difference in Mari but just thought she was being a typical snotty-nosed teenager and that a couple of slaps in the face would go a long way for attitude adjustment. He would watch Mari from the couch in the living room as he watched his favorite programs on the television. After a couple of beers, her attitude did not come into play as much as her blossoming body. He was so proud she was growing up so quickly and into a beautiful young lady. He'd longingly watched her, smacking his lips and tasting her body, as well as his beer. That's my girl!

"What a disgusting pig!" I told Pearl as I clutched my hands, trying hard not to lose my temper. I had been working hard at not allowing my emotions to take over my good sense. I saw Benjy's wanting eyes as his skin started a glossy semblance as it became dewy with perspiration.

"Candace, he is not your focus. You know that. I know you are trying to do your best and not deviate your thoughts. Believe me, I know you are doing your best. So don't let him get in your way of helping Mari," Pearl lovingly told me.

"You are right, Ms. Pearlmeister. I can't let him get under my skin. I cannot expect from him what he cannot give. How can I or anyone else think he can provide Mari with normal fatherhood when he himself does not know what that is?"

"You got it, sweet stuff. You got it! Expectations are what get everyone in trouble. We think someone will act in a certain way when they themselves do not know how to do so.

"We expect a parent to love their child and protect that child from harm. Yet if that parent may not have known how to protect a child and is dysfunctional as a person, how can he or she do the right thing as a parent? Understand what I mean?" Pearl asked as she pulled me next to her. I was trying to wrap my arms around her and understand how people can be so crazy. Pearl seemed to appreciate me. I had come to her as a very novice dead person. Pearl understood she could not dictate her subject's future or decisions. She learned her subjects had to choose what they felt was right for them. That was what free will was all about, knowing the facts and choosing what you felt was right for you. She never wanted to impose on her subjects. Pearl wanted to love them through the process. She had whispered as hard as she could to her subjects. I had surrounded myself with my own protective device during my abuse. I had created a fortress. That fortress was thick and could not be penetrated by anyone or anything. This fortress told me that nothing could hurt me. It was my barrier. It was my protector. I felt nothing. The fortress became the only thing mentally and emotionally could go to protect myself from my father's intrusive body. Yet, the fortress could not protect my body. I opted to take another road. I chose my own destiny instead of another dead-end road. In hindsight, I wish I had chosen to live and become a loving person; however, I fell into someone else's control—my father's. I had lost the will to battle. I did not know how to fight to keep my life and my dignity. I never told anyone about my ordeal, pain, and my dirt. I had chosen to be silent and lose myself into an isolated demise.

I chose not to listen to the many whispers Pearlie had tried to get across to me during my turbulent years when I was alive. Pearlie had revealed to me she had been my Spiritual Guide when I was alive when I first started this journey. I think she may have said that to be honest with me from the beginning that we can't decide everyone's choices, no matter how difficult it may be. I think that is why I have a special kinship with her.

Pearl felt all along she wanted to wrap her beautiful glittery wings around me, from when I was young until now. She had been with me from the first moments my mom had taken her first real drinking binges until the out-of-body encounters I had with my father. Pearlie had told me everything. We had a "come to Jesus" moment when I had first come under her supervision. She told me how she wanted to scoop me up and protect me from my father and the shell my mother had created for herself. She screamed at me, yet it still came out as whispers to my ears. My tears had become her tears. Yet Pearlie, yes, my Pearlmeister, could not do anything but look at what I had become, a beautiful child with a hollow body. My Pearlie wanted to tell me what to do, but she knew I had to choose my freedom. I had to make my choice to what road I would walk or crawl. I had chosen to forget about the world and simply be swallowed by hurt and pain. My Pearlmeister had to deal with my death and not allow it to affect her future with her other cases and Spiritual Guides. Pearl put her head on top of mine and gave me a good-angel bear hug. "You are not a failure," she whispered to me, bringing me back to the present.

Mari woke up the following morning, dreading the day in front of her. Another day. What she dreaded most about this day was that it was Friday. The weekend was upon her. She had to deal with being home with her family! She had to become social and rejoin her family in their activities. She had to deal with her mother asking her what was wrong with her every five minutes. Oh well, she would deal with it. Then Monday would once again roll around and she would handle that too. It would be simply one more day until that special day she could pick up a bike and ride her way out of her present living situation. She thought of riding across country. She wanted to feel the wind caressing her face while it flowed through her hair. She wanted to live a life that did not exist for her. She had to believe there was something better out there. There had to be a life that wasn't as bad as this one, the one she was living now.

Her day at school was a pretty typical day. Nothing new or exciting occurred, nor did Mari want to care about anything new or exciting. She just wanted the days to go by quickly. The bell rang for her last class, so she gathered her books as she watched Nina near her desk so they could head home together. They both walked in silence, as was the norm lately. They were almost out the school doors when Mari remembered she had left her favorite fairy-tale book in her English classroom that was on the second floor.

"Damn, I forgot my book. Got to go back and get it, Nina. Come with me," Mari asked her friend.

"Nope, no can do today, Mari. My mom is waiting for me to hurry up and get home so she can go to work since Grams is not feeling well and can't stay home. Sorry, girlfriend! Please don't be mad," Nina apologized.

"No problemo, sisssster! I can manage. Have a great weekend. Look and see if you can come over or something, OK? Oh and by the way, let me leave you with something so you can remember me by," Mari responded as she farted really hard and loud and then ran down the corridor, laughing her ass off. She took a corridor she typically did not take when she was heading home, but this route was the closest to her classroom.

"K, Mari. That totally bites!" Nina shouted back as she ran outside the school doors so she wouldn't be late going home, yet smiling since she had not heard Mari invite her over to her home or laugh in a number of days. She missed Mari's laugh and smile and hated the idea she was not available to be there with her friend. Hopefully, this was an indication she was back to her old self.

Mari ran quickly up the stairs to her English classroom. She retrieved her book from inside her desk where she had left it and ran through the hallway to a different stairwell, which would lead her closer to a school exit closer to her home.

"Mari, stop! Don't go down that stairwell! Mari, stop!" I urgently whispered as I ran side by side with Mari. I wanted to grab Mari but could not do so. I knew my limitations when it came to working with my case.

Mari ran through the stairwell door and down the first flight of stairs, taking two steps at a time. As she turned the corner to take the final flight to the outside exit, she found herself staring into the faces of four boys on the left side of the stairwell and three girls on the right side. All of the kids returned her stare. She quickly walked down the middle of the stairs. As she approached the last couple of steps to the floor landing leading her to the outside, she felt two pairs of hands grabbing her butt with a strong grip. She tried to swat at the hands, but as she did, she felt another pair of hands reaching lower and deeper into her butt and her vagina area as they slid their hands inward. Deeper. She finally reached the last step and turned to make sure they would not follow her. As she faced them, they all screeched with laughter. She barely noticed all four of the boys grab their groins, asking her if she wanted some. She quickly turned away and ran out the school exit. She could still hear their laughter as the girls joining in and calling her a "baby pussy" accentuated it! Mari continued running until she had safely reached her apartment. She was trembling so badly she dropped her keys twice before she was finally able to open the door to her home. She hated herself and her life! Mari was breathing so hard she thought she was going to have a heart attack. She had not even realized she was crying until she reached up to brush her hair out of her eyes and felt her face was soaked by tears.

"Ahhh, I so want to help her with this, Pearlie," I softly told Pearl, who had also been watching the whole scene unfold in Mari's school. "I need to help her deal with this in a way that she won't be scared to go to school."

"I know what you mean, sweetie. I know what you mean," Pearl whispered back. "The question is, what do you plan on doing to help her?"

"I am going to suggest she tell Jonathan and since Jonathan is a popular basketball player, he will let the rest of the other players know. I am going to suggest she tell her guidance counselor, and since Mari doesn't know who the kids are, Mari won't be in danger of getting beat up by the kids who touched her for ratting them out. The guidance counselor, Jonathan, and the basketball team can casually go down the same stairwell at exactly the same time Mari went down the stairs today. She will also join them but she will be in front, followed by her brother, the guidance counselor, and all of Jonathan's friends. Unless her guidance counselor can come up with a better plan that will keep Mari safe and anyone who goes down that stairwell, then that will be the plan for the next day. The guidance counselor had already advised the principal of the school about the challenges and dangers of those stairwells where lights nor security cameras were not available to protect the students. The incident had been logged and hopefully, this plan would work without inciting another incident.

"That is a very good start, Candace. A very good start," Pearl mentioned to me.

Mari gathered her composure and headed straight to the bathroom. She locked the door behind her and ripped her clothes off. She could not believe what had just happened to her. She felt so violated. She hated herself for having gone down that stairwell. She hated that she went back for that stupid book.

"I hate life! I hate those kids. I hate my school. I hate life!" Mari yelled out. She started the water on hot and jumped into the shower to scrub away those pawprints on her butt. After a while, she just sat down inside the tub and let the water fall on her, continuing to scald her skin.

"I don't know how much I can handle. I need someone to talk to. I need someone to take me away from here!" Mari thought as she drew herself further into a fetal position.

"I just need someone to help me. If I tell a teacher or guidance counselor, I won't be able to tell them what the kids looked like since I ran out of that stairwell so quickly I do not remember their features. What do I do?" Mari sat down on the floor and stared at her hands.

"This is hopeless!" Mari said out loud. "Just hopeless."

"Nothing is ever hopeless, Mari. You can tell your counselor. She will be able to help you. Give Ms. Johnson a chance to help you. Just go talk to her. Also tell Jonathan what happened. He has lots of friends and everyone can help," I whispered. I sat on the toilet, leaning my head against the bathroom wall. I felt Mari's anguish. I sensed how dirty Mari felt. I knew I needed to talk to Mari more and make her understand there was help out there.

"How do you know?" Mari whispered back, not realizing she was speaking with a Spiritual Guide.

"I know because I went through a traumatic experience similar in nature to yours. Let me help you. Bottom line, what you do is your decision. Just know I can really help. I too will always be here for you," I whispered back.

"OK, this is great. Now I am talking to myself or worse yet, a *ghost*. I want to be normal and live a normal life, yet I am having a two-way conversation with a spirit. I don't know what to do, yet I do know what to do since I am hearing myself say I know what to do. Oh my gosh, somehow what I just said actually made sense. Yep, I have definitely gone nuts. That's all I needed to add to my day. I am nuts!" Mari continued to speak aloud and put her head on her crossed arms on top of her knees while she sat on the floor.

"It's OK, Mari. You are not going crazy. You are doing OK. Try to relax. I know it's hard. You are so very cool. Just know I have your back. You have many who care for you," I whispered to Mari over and over.

CHAPTER 16

Mari finally got out of the shower and got dressed. She wiped the mirror off with her towel only to see her face with a deep, crisp pink tone and her eyes almost swollen shut because of her crying. She stood there for a few minutes staring into the mirror. She stared very intently at every single feature on her face. After a while, she had memorized every pimple's location on her face as well as the exact number of eyelashes she had on each lid.

"God, why are you letting this happen to me? You say you love me. You say I am your child, and being your child, I am protected through your love. I have never done anything bad to anyone. Why the fuck are you letting this shit happen to me? I didn't even know those kids. I never saw them before in my life. I hate you! You are such a fake. You don't love me," Mari mused as she hung her head down, staring down into the sink while feeling her anger rise. "We go to church to hear those priests say that you do, but you really don't love us, at least not me. Why do you keep having them lie? If you loved me, you would never have let this happen. I have never done anything bad to anyone."

"Why, why are you allowing this to happen to me and those that I love?" Mari yelled as she rammed her fist into the mirror, shattering the mirror into hundreds of tiny shards. As Mari stood there with blood oozing down her hand, she tightened her grip on her fist and not only felt the pain from her bloody hand but also her heart.

Mari was so angry. At this point, she did not care what her mom or dad said about what she had done. She saw the bloody mess in the sink and all over the bathroom floor. She knew she had to come up with something to tell her parents to get them off her back and not freak out. She turned on the cold water and put her hand under the stream. It hurt horribly as the water hit directly on her deep wound. She imagined she might need some stitches since she jammed her fist really hard into the mirror. She did not care. She hated seeing her reflection in that stupid thing. She hated seeing her face, and more so, she hated the fact she had not fought back. She now had two occasions that she could have done something important to help herself and someone else, yet she had not done a damn thing. Why? Why did she just let people do whatever they wanted to her and those she loved, even though it was really hurtful or wrong? She just lay there like a lump on a log without any emotion or simply ran like a coward. She was such an idiot and a chicken.

She finally used a towel to dry her hand and reached under the sink to get some gauze, hydrogen peroxide, antibacterial cream, and two large Band-Aids from the first-aid box. The throbbing in her hand was getting unbearable, but she continued to rinse her hand to clean it out really well. Mari checked to make sure no glass was embedded in her skin. She could not believe what she was doing. She had always had such a weak stomach when it came to seeing blood; however, she found strength to do it now. She felt as though she was having an out-of-body experience. She had put her emotions in check and was now simply doing what needed to be done for her hand. She poured some hydrogen peroxide and clenched her teeth because of the pain. She thought she was going to faint but she kept going. She added the antibacterial cream, tightened the skin together and gauzed up the cut while quickly placing the Band-Aids tightly in place. She had seen her mom do that type of cleaning to her papi's arm one time when he had a cut while working in the kitchen sink.

Mari put her clothes back on and went into the hallway closet to get a broom and mop to clean up the mess in the bathroom. She was so going to get grounded, she thought, but she did not care. If she got grounded for breaking the mirror, she could spend more time locked up in her room, reading her books and not having to face life. All she wanted to do right this minute was go to sleep and forget she existed, but at the moment, she had to clean up the bathroom. Afterward, she could run to her bedroom, lock her door, and lose herself in one of her books. That is exactly what Mari did after she cleaned up. She went to her room, locked the door, plopped herself on her bed, and thought about how she would explain the broken mirror to her parents.

"Ahh, what the hell. They are still going to yell at me and let me know how it was my fault no matter what really happened. So who cares what I tell them? They are not going to care. They are too much into their own lives and problems to care about what is happening to me. Plus, I don't want anything that will make them hurt each other or me more than they are already doing," Mari thought. She would deal with that in a while. Right now, she just wanted to forget life and grabbed a book. Within a few minutes, Mari was lost in her book. She did forget about the incident, the broken mirror, her wounded hand, the hurt, and the cleanup. Mari was consumed inside her book.

"Wow, it's going to be hard to pull her from behind those walls she is developing, Pearlie. This is so messing with her head and I don't blame her."

"That's understandable, Candace. She is so overwhelmed right now with emotion. She is feeling such fear, vulnerability, and low self-esteem. She is questioning everyone and blaming everyone because she is confused, troubled, and frustrated," Pearlie answered me.

"Got it, Pearlie, but it is irritating to see all this happening to her and not be able to make it easier for her or lay some smackdown, like some people say now. I hurt for her. I don't want her to feel it is her fault and that she is all alone. She does not deserve this kind of treatment. Just like me, she doesn't have any support. I want to let her know I am here to help her and guide her through her pain and despair, yet I can't. She can't see me. She can't see my face. We can't have a normal conversation. Just not right, Pearlie. Just not right!" I whispered.

CHAPTER 17

"Mari, *que paso?* Wha happen? Wha happen in the bathroom?" Sara asked, shocked to see a broken mirror.

"I see blood. Are yu OK? Is Jonathan here? He OK?" Sara continued to ask, not looking at Mari nor waiting for an answer. She was scared and surprised all at once.

"Mami, I accidentally hit the mirror with my hand when I tried to grab onto the sink. I was falling down and I hit my hand out trying to find something to hold onto but instead of holding onto something, I hit the mirror really hard by accident. I lost my balance, Mami. I am really sorry to have broken the mirror. I really am!" Mari responded to Sara's questions so quickly she was out of breath by the time she was done talking.

"What!" Sara exclaimed. "Are you OK? *Dame!* Give me. Give me your hand! Let me see it! Yu need stitches. Do I need take yu to doctor? *Ay, Señor querido!* Dear God! Wha else going to happen here! Mari, why yu no be careful? Wha yu mean yu fall down? Wha yu mean yu fall down?" Sara asked, again not stopping to hear Mari's answers. Sara was in her own world trying to figure out how to explain all of this to Benjy.

"He going to be soo angry and I hope he no take it out on me," Sara thought.

"Mami, I'm OK! Stop freaking out! I don't need stitches or need to see a doctor. I'm fine," Mari blurted out to her mother. She was getting irritated at her mom for making such a fuss and creating a federal case about her hand. She did not want the attention right now. She just wanted to be left alone. She wanted to isolate herself in her room and not have anyone near her. She wanted to read her book and become one with the story. She wanted the fairy tale to come true. She hated her reality and the hurt that came with it. She wanted to be the princess with the happy king and queen enjoying the festivities of a jubilant and peaceful kingdom. She also wanted to eventually meet the prince that would sweep her off her feet and live happily ever after.

"Mari, no yu talk to me tha way, *hija!*" Sara reprimanded Mari. She would not be spoken to by her children without respect. She had enough of that by her husband. She shook those thoughts immediately since she was too nervous right now with the situation at hand. Benjy was going to be so angry, angry, angry! Worse yet, he was going to hit her since the money to replace the mirror was going to have to come from his "have fun" money fund. He would never dream of taking it from the house expense money. He was too proud not to pay his bills on his own fun time and then be embarrassed by a bill collector that he neglected his family. Sara also did not want Benjy to take it out on Mari. He had not laid a firm hand on Mari except for tapping her hand when she would get into things that would break when she was a toddler and curiosity was larger than life for her.

"I no wan yur papi to see this bathroom this way. Mari, yu feel OK? Yu sure? Then take the broom and sweep tha floor again. I no wan no one cut feet on glass. After, I mop the floor wit bleach and make sure it clean. Do it now before yur papi get here. He stop at the *bodega* to buy milk, meat, and things for us. I no wan he be mad," Sara softly shared with Mari.

"Mami, he is always mad when he is here. I will take the heat. I don't want him hitting you again!" Mari told her mother in a barely audible tone to be heard by Sara.

"Wha yu say? Yur father no hit me for no reason. I get him angry because I do stupid tings and I am stupid. I no know I have feet. I always falling down and hitting myself. Tha way I have these dark spots on me sometime. I go start make dinner now. Tell me when yu finish wit broom so I mop," Sara blurted back to Mari as she nervously left the bathroom and tried to change the topic to a subject that would be better to deal with. She knew Mari was right. Sara was so upset with herself for allowing Benjy's physical and emotional abuse to her become known by Mari, and worse yet, she knew Jonathan had knowledge about that too. She needed to be more quiet and not be so upset with Benjy. She must be a better wife and learn to understand a man has needs. She needed to realize this is life. He is Latino. He is different from other men. He has needs that maybe other men do not have. She would need to start fixing herself up more and start being nicer to her husband. That is why he is looking at other women. She is not as pretty as the other women he is with. No, no! There are other men in her family and people she knows that are Latino, and they do not hit their wives like Benjy does. But she needed to do better for her children. She did not want her children to know that their father hit her. No, no, that would not be good. Finally, Mari called out to Sara to let her know she was done with the sweeping. Sara quickly mopped the bathroom and then resumed her cooking by the time Benjy got home.

"What a crock of bull!" I snarled through my teeth as I turned to face Pearl, with my hands on my hips and a flushed face.

"I know it is, honey. She is in such denial. Sara is trying to take on her husband's infidelity and anything that is not good within him as her fault. She still wants to feel she has control in her life and situation. She believes that by taking on this guilt and coming up with a plan to become a 'better and prettier' wife, she can stop Benjy from going out. She hopes she can make him stop from having affairs if *she* could be prettier and more of the type of woman that Benjy goes after," Pearl softly told me as she put both her hands on my shoulders in hope of calming my temper as not to bring myself to a weakness episode that I had already experienced when I got really angry and felt a degree of hatred or severe dislike for someone.

"I still have much to learn from Pearlie. I mean, I'm not human, but I am still a start-up Spiritual Guide. I still feel real emotions be they bad or good. But . . . I am trying hard. I'm just not sure I am exactly right for this mission, Pearlie. I just want to kick Benjy's butt clear across the universe. I want to shake Sara and Mari until they come to their senses. I want to let them know that I am here and they are not alone. There are also resources out there they can call or go to that will help them," I responded to Pearlie trying to bring down my temper.

"Yes, you're right, there are many resources out there to include her family but it takes longer, some more than others, to understand this. Candace honey, how long did it take you to understand the options? Did you lose memory of the times you struggled by yourself and did not want anything to do with anyone at all? I am not trying to be mean to you, sweetie, but you took a route that is not recommended at all. You decided to end it all. That is not really dealing with the situation."

"I know, Pearlie. I know. I did not make the wisest choice, and it took me a long time to even come to terms with myself, let alone with anyone else. I learned about so much freedom that could have been had from my abuse after I took my life. But, Pearlie, I made the choice at the time I felt was right for me. Knowing what I know now, I would not have done it. I just want Mari to know there are other choices besides hurting herself and letting herself be hurt by anyone else."

"Well, girlfriend, you best get a move on it. You need to get yourself started with a plan before Mari decides on a choice that will hurt herself and also hurt her family at the same time," Pearl told me as she looked at me.

"Oh, hang on a sec, sweetie. I just got pinged by another Guide. I have to go but just send me a text if you need my help. I know you got this. I really do!" Pearlie smiled at me as she put away her cell phone and disappeared on the spot.

CHAPTER 18

The alarm rang louder than usual, or was it that Mari woke up with a throbbing pain in her hand and a headache that throbbed about as hard as her hand hurt?

"This totally bites. My hand hurts, my head hurts, and I have to go to school, to boot. This totally bites the big one. I wonder if I could just stay home. Nah, I better not. I never know if Papi is going to come home without telling anyone, and I don't want to deal with that shit. Nope, I better get my butt to school," Mari thought sadly as she slowly got herself up from bed and to the bathroom before anyone else.

Jonathan was already up and dressed. He was eating breakfast when Mari entered the kitchen on her way to the bathroom.

"Damn, you look ugly. Have you looked at yourself in the mirror? Shit, if I were you, I wouldn't stop to talk to anyone until was cleaned up, took my psycho pill, PMS pill, and any other girl-type pill that will not hurt mankind. Then and only then should you hit the outside world. Maybe then if I were you, I would say something," Jonathan said after he had glanced at Mari while reading his muscle car magazine. He continued eating and, all at once, felt he had helped destroy his sister's confidence a notch. Felt good to exercise some control in his home even if he was only with his kid sister. She actually wasn't too shabby for a little sis, but he couldn't let her know that. Then she would be all in his face wanting to do stuff together. Nah, wasn't going to happen.

"Bite me, you big dork," Mari retorted.

"You baby. You can bite my butt. You wouldn't need sugar for a very long time 'cause I am that sweet!" Jonathan said while he briefly glanced at her and created his body's silhouette with his hands.

"I'm too sweet for words. Nah, words cannot describe my sweetness," Jonathan said as he winked at Mari and fell back to reading his magazine.

"Yeah, whatever," Mari retorted, her hand and head aching too much to bother with her dumb brother.

CHAPTER 19

Demon Camouflaged in Nice Clothes

Demon wearing classy shirts and designer pants,
Strutting down the streets, letting every woman know what he wants.
I will treat you nice and show you a real cool time.
Come to me, can't you see I am so fine.
You will be treated so great and it's all on my dime.
Girl, all you want to do is grind with me at least one more time.
I will bring you up and drop you down even though you are so fine.
Undress, let me see you see you bare,
Trust me, pretty babe, you won't care.
All you will see is the face of a fine-looking demon that won't scare.
A demon camouflaged in nice fine clothes waiting for you to bare.

"Yeah, a demon in nice clothes, that's me," Jonathan thought as he put down his pen and put away his notepad. He didn't care about this night's activities as he stood up and finished dressing. He picked up his cologne to add his *lady's touch*—his cologne. Not every dude he knew could pay for some nice cologne. He, in turn, would not leave on a date without it. He found that was his magic touch with his dates. He would dash some on and nine out of ten times, the girls would be all over him before the night was over. He was becoming a Casanova like his dad. He was very smooth with the ladies. He would look good, smell good, pick up the ladies, drop them, and move on to the next.

"Just like my old man," he sullenly thought.

"Yeah, smell good, Jonathan. You big dick!" Jonathan said out loud as he threw his cologne onto his bed as he strutted out of his bedroom, not really in the dating mood.

"Jonathan, yu smell so nice and look so handsome, *hijo*," Sara told Jonathan as she turned around so she could see him.

"*Si, hijo*, yu look so berry handsome," Sara complimented her son again.

"Ay, Mami, you know me. I always look good. I took after you!" Jonathan smiled as he gave her a peck on the cheek. I could see how much Jonathan loved his mother and hated how his father treated her sometimes. I also knew Jonathan was moving forward in a dangerous path, trying to be like his father.

"Maybe I can get to Jonathan with Mari. He is going down a path I know is not what he wants." I knew he was going to fall hard if he did not make the right choices and I wouldn't be able to help him. There were times I disliked the limitations of my abilities. I wished I could snap my fingers and do what I wanted with people. Well . . . maybe later as I earn more sparkles on my wing outfit. I heard a door bang and realized Jonathan had left for his date.

"Poor girl!" I thought as I headed to find Mari and spend time with her.

"4590, 4592, 4594, OK, there it is, 4596," Jonathan whispered as he came to a complete stop in front of a conservatively adorned two-story home. He had known Jacquelyn for about a month when she transferred over to the store he worked at uptown. She was pretty cool and had a supertight body. But more important, Jacquelyn got him. She seemed to read his mind. She was magic, yet something was off. He was hoping that feeling would go away, Jonathan thought, as he walked up the front steps to ring Jacquelyn's doorbell. A tall balding man with a stern look opened the front wooden door with an iron gate.

"Hello, are you, Mr. Russell? Sir, my name is Jonathan Santiago, and I am here to pick up Jacquelyn for dinner."

"Oh, you are the famous Jonathan," the stern man answered as his thin lips tightened into a slight smile.

"I heard a lot about you tonight as Jacquelyn convinced me it was OK to let you take her out. So, Jonathan, why should I trust my little girl with you? Why should I let you take her to dinner? I mean, we got food here, you know. I am a pretty good chef. Everyone *loves* my food!" Mr. Russell asked Jonathan, with his eyebrows furrowing and eyes looking suspiciously at Jonathan.

"Oh hey, Jonathan! I thought I heard the doorbell. Dad, why didn't you call me to let me know Jonathan was here? Oh no . . . Dad, please don't tell me. Were you giving Jonathan a hard time? Did you tell him we have lots of food? Jonathan, did he tell you he was a great chef?" Jacquelyn said as she put her hands on her hips and stared her dad down and then gave Jonathan a sad look.

"Well, Jonathan, did I give you the speech?" Mr. Russell turned to him with a surprised expression while daring Jonathan to say anything but no to Jacquelyn's question if he expected to take his daughter out to dinner or, for that matter, anyplace else—ever!

"Hmmm, uh, no. No, Jacquelyn, I barely got here. Your dad and I were just talking about the World Series and wondering who was gonna take the championship. You know, man stuff," Jonathan said as he slowly took his gaze away from Mr. Russell and gave Jacquelyn a meek smile.

"Anyway, it was a pleasure speaking with you, Mr. Russell. I will take good care of your daughter," Jonathan said as he looked at Mr. Russell and raised his hand to shake his and hoped Mr. Russell had approved of his answer.

"OK, Jonathan. Bring her back by 10:00 p.m." Mr. Russell responded to Jonathan with a half smile approving of the way he handled himself. His daughter would not give him grief this time. Ugh, she is growing up way too quickly, he mused.

"Oh, Daddy, we will be fine. Stop worrying so much. Jonathan is not a serial killer or rapist or anything like that. At least not that I know of, I mean, I know he has a dark side, but he told me he is on medication that handles his impulses to throw things around. Did you take your pills earlier, Jonathan?" Jacquelyn said as she quickly gave her dad a kiss on his cheek and ran down her front steps, dragging Jonathan behind her.

"Jacquelyn, he didn't answer your question?" Mr. Russell said as he turned around and locked the door behind him, chuckling at his daughter's wittiness.

"Nice BS there, Jonathan, but it so didn't fly! I knew you were being interrogated by my dad," Jacquelyn said as she waited for Jonathan to lean in and open the passenger door to his car. Plus, it would give a nice impression to his dad who by now was staring at them through the window and would most likely stare after them until he could no longer see the lights of Jonathan's car.

"Hey, please. Do you honestly think your dad wouldn't like me and turn to untrusting tactics? Please, girl, dads L-O-V-E *me*!" Jonathan feigned hurt as he turned toward Jacquelyn with his sad puppy-dog eyes.

"Oh, don't even try that, Jonathan. I know my dad. If he could scare you away, he would so love it. He thinks I am convent material. He said he could 'rent' grandchildren if he wants some. I will always be his little angel." Jacquelyn laughed as she turned toward Jonathan, feeling increasingly comfortable with him.

"No, no. I am not ready to hit the convent circuit just yet. I still have plenty of years left before going out to chase nuns down. Besides, you got a killer body that would be totally lost in a nun's habit. No, don't think it would work for you or me, girl!" Jonathan cracked a loud chuckle as he made some turns and headed toward the restaurant he knew would have great food and not hurt his wallet too badly.

After a couple of hours, Jonathan and Jacquelyn were completely stuffed. Jacquelyn had a primavera dish and a Salisbury steak with potatoes for Jonathan. They could not pass up the tempting chocolate mousse cake with cherry ice cream that they both split. Add a couple of soft drinks and they both could barely get out of their seats.

"That was a really cool place. Thanks a lot for inviting me out to dinner. You aren't such a jerk after all," Jacquelyn sweetly told Jonathan as they walked toward his car.

"Oh OK, I see how this goes. I get some food in your tummy, and all of a sudden, out comes the truth you have been hiding from me. I am so very hurt. It really is a long walk back home for you too," Jonathan responded as he exaggerated feeling hurt.

"Jacquelyn, are you up for a drive? It's only eight-thirty and we have until ten tonight before I hand you over to your dad. Sound good?"

Jacquelyn was starting to get mesmerized by Jonathan's charm and felt that maybe, just maybe he wouldn't be a jerk and hurt her like some of the other guys she had gone out with. At least she didn't have to pay her own dinner or both, for that matter. Not a bad start, Jacquelyn thought.

"Sure, why not. I don't have anything better to do tonight." Jacquelyn giggled as she flirted back.

After a few minutes of driving, Jonathan turned off to a one-way road that led them to a deserted parking lot where a structure was being built, and it had a terrific view of the city.

"Wow, this is a nice spot. I didn't think we had this type of spot in our neck of the woods!"

"Yeah, I found it out a while back when I was driving around. It's a great place to be alone with your thoughts. No one is usually around when I drive out here."

Jacquelyn snuggled back into her seat and stared at the bright stars etching animal designs in the sky. She could see a dragon shooting fire as it ran after a bunny. *Poor bunny, dumb bunny to be around a dragon*, she thought as she stared at the day.

"So what do you think Jack is gonna do when Jenny quits next week? Do you think he's gonna flip?" Jacquelyn asked Jonathan, to break up the silence in the car.

"Naw, he'll just overwork the rest of us peons until he finds another sucker to take her place."

"Do you really think so? I just don't see him doing something like that?"

"Oh yeah, he will. He'll make it miserable for Jenny until the day she quits. You know the type."

"Ahh, so you talking from experience? Have you made it difficult for girls who don't follow your every desire?"

"Me? Naw, woman. Not me. I'm just a sweet teenager who wants to do his job at work, be nice to customers and even nicer and sweeter to his coworkers. You know the type." Jonathan smiled innocently.

"Yeah, she should be nice and ready to tango to a home run next time we meet. At least go to second base, or hopefully third base, when we out again. Yeah, freaky time," Jonathan mused.

"Yeah, she should be nice and ready. Jonathan will hit that. I mean, I will be over her. Damn, I could be just like my old man." Jonathan visualized and the thought was not as appealing as he first thought.

"Pearl, I am not sure he is moving in the wrong direction. I mean, he hesitated. He was thinking about following his father's footsteps and yet he seemed off," I mentioned to Pearl, who was looking through some file folders, while we sat in the backseat, and texting someone.

"Candace, you know his destiny. He will go the direction he wants to go. Neither you nor I can interfere. Besides, we are primarily here for Mari. If what happens to her affects Jonathan by her doing, then it is a different story."

"Pearl, am I just supposed to sit here and watch him turn into the abusive pig his father is? I mean, he seems to be wavering, but I have no idea in what direction. I might be able to help him *waver* in the right direction if I have the opportunity. He is just going to use Jacquelyn and not care. I mean, he's just seventeen years old. He doesn't have to end up like his father. Yet, there is something bugging me about him, I can't seem to put my finger on it," I pleaded to Pearl.

"You know, little angel, you are right. He has so many options to change his destiny but those choices come from him. We can't interfere with him and you know it. The only person who can hear you is Mari. She is your subject, your case, and the person you can influence by your words. Mari and those around Jonathan can help him change his course in life. You can help him via Mari, except Mari is not paying attention to him. She is focused only on her mother. You know this," Pearl softly reminded me although I did not want to hear her.

"I know, Ms. Pearl. I just need to move faster with Mari and make sure she gets it like I never did. I need to make sure Mari is not a statistic like I was. I was nothing else but a number."

CHAPTER 20

"Hey, how was your date last night?" Mari asked a very sleepy-eyed Jonathan while he was in the kitchen preparing a glass of juice before he headed back to his room. Jonathan nodded.

"It was cool. Pretty much like any other date I have any of my female species."

"What do you mean by that? That sounds tacky!" Mari smirked at her brother.

"What? She is a girl I work with. I liked her body, and she wasn't a total airhead to talk to. Simple. I probably won't see her again after a couple of times. I don't want to be tied down. Simple. Besides, what do you care?" Jonathan snapped.

"Whatever, jerk! You are sounding and acting more and more like Papi every day. How pathetic is that!"

"If you don't want to hear how my life is going, then don't ask!" Jonathan screeched. "Besides, Papi is cool. He knows how to treat his women. No more, no less. I love Mami but she can be a nag sometimes. She is always getting in Papi's face and then he is forced to deal with her. I hate him having to slap her around but a man's got to do what a man's got to do."

"So you think Papi is right to slap and hurt Mami?" Mari got real slow in order to get it together before getting near Jonathan. She was scared of what she might do to him if she was right next to Jonathan right now at this very second. He outweighed her by at least fifty pounds. She might not be a genius but she wasn't a fool.

"Pearl, Pearl, get over here quick, Pearl, please!" I pleaded for Pearl as she quietly listened to the drama between Mari and Jonathan unfolding.

"Now, Candace, you know I am going to have to rein you in, so why are you doing this to me?" Pearl softly told me since she knew the path I was headed.

"What? Can't you see what is happening here? Jonathan is actually trying to defend his stance regarding his father."

"Candace, Jonathan is simply acting out what he sees and is being taught. He sees how his father treats his mother and he sees those actions as gospel to how a man treats a woman. He doesn't understand that a man should treat his wife respectfully and should talk instead of hit. They should simply talk things through, but where you have raw emotions, it is not easy unless you walk away for a few minutes to calm down. I mean, Jonathan does not know that women treat men very poorly and can be very abusive to them too. Unfortunately, violence does not make any distinctions between men and women, even though men statistically are the abusers," Pearl sympathetically told a very solemn-faced me.

"You could say violence has many faces," Candace softly added.

"You know, short stack, you just can't handle having real men around." Jonathan smirked back at Mari.

"Nope, I don't think that at all. I just haven't seen any lately," Mari spat right back at Jonathan.

"Besides, I know that you act all cool and crap but that is only because you are chugging down all that liquor from Papi and Mami's cabinet," Mari continued.

"I am not!" Jonathan embarrassedly replied. He realized he had just gotten busted and he was trying to figure out how his kid sister had found out. He had to quiet her down now and find a way to keep her from telling his parents about their missing alcohol. *Crap. I am in deep shit now with Mari knowing what I have been doing,* Jonathan mused.

"You so lie! That is not true. You are the one hitting the liquor. Besides, how would you know if anything is missing? Are you drinking?" Jonathan quickly rebuked.

"No, I don't drink! I know better than trying to be cool just because I am drunk off my butt all the time. It's not cool. Who wants a stinky-mouth idiot sticking their tongue in their mouth when they smell like that?"

"Whatever. You don't know what you're talking about. Who is gonna listen to you anyway? Mom and Dad always listen to me. I am the other man of the house. Besides, I'm seventeen years old. I am old enough to drink if I want to. It's none of your business. Papi and me are tight. There's nothing wrong wanting to be more like him. I like the ass and tits and the girls. They like me back. They get stupid, I teach them not to be. Simple!"

"What? Have you gone really *loco*? You must be crazy! You think girls are just around for you. You think you're all that? Well, bro, you aren't! You're gonna end up just like Papi. He's an old fart going after other women, acting like he's all that 'cause that's all he's got. He treats Mami like shit, and you ain't got the balls to stop it! You just drink, act stupid, and think you're cool. But you ain't. What do you got? Huh, what do you got? Your grades suck, you're a closet drunk. You got skanks after you 'cause that's all that'll have you and you think that's cool. It's pretty sad when your little sister has to show you up by being the grown-up around here! Plus, it isn't legal to drink alcohol until you are twenty-one years old, you moron."

With that, Jonathan pivoted around so quickly and stared at Mari in the face that half of his drink spilled over his shirt. He was beyond himself. His face was bright red. Jonathan decided to back off of his little sister before he lost himself on her face. He couldn't do that to her. Not when she was right. He was trying hard to act cool while knowing he hated what was happening in his home due to his parents fighting. He knew Mari was right about their father. Jonathan knew his father was a pig. He dreamed many a night of slamming him down when he had seen him slap his mother around like a rag doll. Jonathan knew it wasn't right, but he couldn't get up the nerve to do anything about it. He simply accepted it as a normal thing for men to do when women would bitch and complain. Even if the woman was right and didn't deserve to be treated badly by their man. Jonathan felt so torn. He didn't know what to think, especially when deep down inside, he didn't even like girls.

Jonathan had found himself staring at guys more than girls lately. He found them sensual, especially when they took off their shirts and were sweaty from gym class. He felt himself feeling his body react in a manner that he knew was taboo. What was wrong with him? Was he a homosexual? Naw, he couldn't be. That's not the way to be. His father would kick his ass out of the house and then where would he go? He has never known anyone else that was homosexual in his family. No, it would be disastrous!

Besides, the only times he actually did something remotely different was when he was checking out male porn at his job when he was locking up one night. He did it just for kicks. Besides, his friend Lorenzo was cool and he was gay. Lorenzo never made fun of Jonathan when he would ask him questions. He was just curious. Lorenzo was really cool about it. He told Jonathan all the secrets of the homosexual world, like how to tell if another guy was gay so you wouldn't get your ass kicked by a guy who wasn't. He also told Jonathan how to get into a girl even though it does nothing for you, but you don't want to let on you're not feeling manly. Plus, how to get along in the real world where they lived and no one knows you're homosexual. It had been working 'cause no one had said anything to him at all about him even remotely resembling a homosexual guy. Nah, he was cool. All the girls loved him. They thought of him as a cuddly bear. His nickname was Huggy Bear Jon. Girls just cooed after him. He was the man! Wasn't he? What a freakin' joke. Jonathan remembered his sister and her big mouth and got back into the moment with her.

"Whatever. I'm done trying to be nice to you. Just shut up and do whatever your stupid self does in the afternoons. Don't care, don't want to care," Jonathan responded as he loudly shut his door behind him as he simultaneously put his headset on his head to listen to his music as he carefully balanced his orange juice in his hands.

Mari got up quickly, losing her appetite for any afternoon snack. She quickly thought how quickly Jonathan was turning into her father or at least trying to act like him.

"Don't want to have two Papis running around in this house. I think I would shoot myself," Mari thought as she overdramatized her brother's actions in her head. She went into her room, locked the door behind her, and thought increasingly to herself how many responsibilities she was taking on. She went to her bed, pulled up her mattress, and retrieved her diary that was hidden midway under her mattress and box spring.

"Ahhh, how are you doing, my trusted friend?" Mari thought as she found her last entry and started to write.

Well, I finally got the nerve to tell Jonathan what I thought of him and how he was acting more and more like Papi. Of course, he is just a boy! He acted just like a boy—dumbbutt!!! Mari wrote, referring to her confrontation with her brother a few minutes earlier. She continued:

Yeah, he acted real dumb and macho like some type of Rambo. How dumb! I don't get why a cute girl like Jacquelyn would even go out with him. She actually seemed smart! Mari chuckled to herself as she finished her sentence. She continued writing.

The part I really don't get is that Papi doesn't even do much with Jonathan anymore, yet Jonathan just thinks Papi is cool. Well, Papi isn't so cool. I am getting to really hate his guts the way he treats Mami and the way he just came into the bathroom, sneaking looks inside my shower curtain while I was taking a shower. That really creeped me out. I felt so scared! Mari wrote as she felt her hair on her neck rise while she recalled the shower incident with her father. She continued:

I love Jon, but I am really, really scared he is going to hurt someone by punching him or even her really hard or getting a girl pregnant or having a father or boyfriend beat the crap out of Jonathan that might even kill him. Then again Jonathan is Mami and Papi's perfect little angel. He does no evil and that is bull. Mari took a deep breath before continuing writing again. That is what her Aunt Carla used to tell her when she got all frustrated and stuff.

"Honey, just take a deep, deep breath. Take deep breaths so all that yucky stuff that does not belong in your body goes out into the far, far galaxy. You are too precious to have all that yucky stuff in you. Besides, you are just too cute, just like me! If you have yucky stuff in you, then you get wrinkles on your face and that means that your Aunt Carla has wrinkles on her face too. And we both know that is just *not* true, don't we?" Mari's Aunt Carla would always tell Mari when Mari was younger and would get upset.

Anyway, once again, Mari refocused her thoughts to Jonathan. Mari felt scared for him. She had gotten up from bed many times when she heard him in the kitchen. Mari sneaked a peek to see who was in the kitchen. She caught her brother pouring Bacardi rum in his mug and then taking a can of beer with him into his bedroom.

Mari continued to write:

I am scared for my brother. Even though he can be a royal pain in my butt, I still love him. It scares me that he is driving and, worse yet, he talks about girls that he dates in such a crappy way. That really sucks to be them!

"Ugh, I wish she could see me and we can just talk."

"You know you can, baby girl!" Pearl said to me. She knew how frustrated I felt right now. She had to deal with other Spiritual Guides that were in training like me that had much zeal and a zest to conquer the human race and make it so much better. I am a special trainee. I want to achieve Pearl's stature before long, but first I need to get me some wings. Pearl understood how I felt. I really respected Pearl and she understood how I felt through the agonizing abuse in the hands of my father while my mother ignored a lot of it. She knew I felt as though my parents really failed me. Having gone through all of the unspoken abuse led me to be a meticulous and vivacious Spiritual Guide at the hands of Mama Lynn, Spiritual Guide teacher extraordinaire! Mama Lynn had patiently taken my enthusiastic impatience and molded it to be a virtue of determination. Mama Lynn had taught me to seek and finish the tasks at hand, no matter how difficult. I had more than fulfilled those expectations.

"I can try to will her to feel my essence, you know," I defiantly told Pearl.

"Yes, you can. You can do so much more to your subjects so they can feel your presence, but you know in your heart and soul, it would not be the right thing to do right now," Pearl reminded me.

"I know. I know." I retreated humbly before Pearl.

"I just want them, Mari, Jonathan, and Sara, to have a chance at normal family life. Not like I had. Mine just dealt with a father who forgot what it was like to be a father to a child. My father, father of the year candidate," I sourly told Pearl.

"I know, baby girl. Just remember that true forgiveness allows you to think clearly and become a truly free soul. Nothing is in the way to making good decisions. In the same manner, it is up to them to make their own decisions with nothing interfering except clear thoughts and the whispers of a beautiful Spiritual Guide."

"I know, Pearlie. You are right and thank you for the awesome compliment," I whispered to her.

CHAPTER 21

Mari walked into her homeroom class feeling completely drained. Mari had spent most of her evening wondering if Jonathan would ever speak to her again after confronting him about his drinking. She knew her brother was really proud, and it probably got him uptight that his little sister put him down.

"Why do boys have to be so dumb?" Mari said under her breath.

"What?" her friend Sylvia whispered to Mari. Sylvia was just a few months younger than Mari but had become Mari's protector in school. No one messed with Mari when Sylvia was around. She was 5'10" and she was only fifteen years old. She wouldn't put up with anyone being mean to other kids and, most of all, her friends. She lived with her psycho mom since her parents split a couple of years ago. Sylvia always told me she thought her father left since he couldn't deal with her mom's crap any longer. She was just bonkers! Sylvia would tell me stories about her parents and her homelife. Sylvia mentioned that her mom had a good job and would make sure she presented a "better than you" façade to everyone. Sylvia would always tell Mari how her mother would make sure that Sylvia called her every evening from her dad's house when she was staying with him. She would make Sylvia tell her everything they did and ask who else was around. She also made Sylvia wear beat-up clothes and raggedy sneakers when she went to her dad's house so she could ask her father for more money. Then her parents would fight again and many phone hang-ups later, her father would give in and send her money, more money that she usually used the majority of it on herself and the remainder on Sylvia.

"You see, Mari, my dad's remarried now and she can't stand it. She hates the fact that there is no man at home she can go psycho on besides herself. I mean, she would make life miserable if my dad would even talk to any of their previous friends. She just wanted Dad to be by her side twenty-four hours a day and seven days a week. She would tell everyone she knew how miserable I would be when I would go visit Dad but I really did like going to see him. I just couldn't say anything about it."

"Why couldn't you say anything?" Mari would ask.

"Well, because she would totally freak out on me! She would start yelling at me and tell me that I didn't love her anymore. That I loved my dad more and the slut he was living with. She would then make me stay up and do homework all night long without any breaks. Kinda a punishment because I would like it more over at Dad's house. One time the police came over and talked to her and me. The police guy told me that if I would ever get scared of her and she would start pounding on me for no reason, I could call 911. They would send someone over really fast. Depending on how bad it was, I mean, if she really beat me hard and even broke an arm of mine or something, they could take me away from her and I might be able to live with my dad. I don't know about any of that. Pretty pathetic, huh, but I don't want my mom away from me because I really do love her. I just wish she would go to the doctor and get something that will calm her down. Some other kids have had this same type of problem and some of the parents would go to a doctor and get some pills and it would help them calm down. It's all that prescription stuff. We will see what will happen!" Sylvia would always end her stories with that same sentence.

Sylvia always had hope life would change in her home. I also felt hope for her. I just wished I could feel the same, Mari mused.

"Oh, and the one that put her over the edge was when I mentioned to her I wanted to stay with my dad for Christmas break when he was headed out to see Grams and Grandpa. My mom really hated that I really wanted to go over to San Francisco in California and hang with my grandparents. You see Dad's wife would also be there and I would be spending a lot of time with her too."

"Wow, San Francisco? That's tight! I've never been anywhere except for New York and Puerto Rico to visit family."

"Yeah, well, I would go bag groceries if it got me out of house and I wouldn't have to hear my mom tell me that she loved me more than anyone else in this world and that included dad's *shit of a wife* since I was her blood. You see if you weren't blood related, you couldn't love anyone else the way your family loved you. That is so weird! She would always be dogging Dad's wife and calling her names, gossiping to her friends how my dad's wife would go spending a lot of money so that my dad never had enough to feed me when I went over to his house. Just complete lies."

"Man, that is low!" Mari blew a long whistle after she heard her comment. She had met Sylvia's father and his new wife and she thought they were really cool. They also allowed Sylvia to bring her friends over and never judged them. I never even heard them say anything bad about Sylvia's mom except that she could sometimes go psycho city, but they would only say that when they thought Sylvia was out of earshot.

"Yeah, dude, she's trippin'." Sylvia shook her head as she remembered her mother acting stupid. It would really make Sylvia feel really low since she just wanted to be a normal kid. She didn't want to choose sides between her mom and her dad. She really loved them both. She had two homes. Mari really felt for her friend. It really stunk being caught in the middle.

"Yeah, check this one out." Sylvia just kept venting to Mari. Sylvia wouldn't stop talking about her homelife for a while yet. Mari really enjoyed Sylvia although it was hard to tell her anything about her own family. She was scared that Sylvia would tell their teacher or something, then Mami and Papi would get really angry with her because she said something to a stranger, even though Sylvia was one of her best friends. Sara would get angry because then Mari's teacher would know and it would be someone else getting into their lives. Her mom would punish her by slapping her or not letting her see television after school. Or what about if her father would punch her like her mom? Or even worse, what if he would keep her in her bedroom closet because once her mother mentioned to her Aunt Nilda that her father was having an affair with another woman from down the block and he found out about it and he stuck her in the closet for the full weekend. He then made her clean up the closet inside with ammonia, cleaning tools, and her bare hands. Her mami had red marks for weeks on her hands.

Mari remembered her father slapping her mother so hard that she got a really bad nosebleed. Then her papi grabbed her mom by the hair and threw her into their bedroom closet. He then locked the door. Benjy only opened the door when he smelled poop from the closet. He would open the door, pull her mother out again by the hair, and make her clean the inside of the closet. He would push her into the kitchen so she would make a drink for him but then threw her back inside. He also took the cords to the telephones so none of them would call anyone if they noticed she was in the closet. Totally nuts and scary!

"Tha wha happin when yu do sometin tha no right. Yu know? Tha happin because yu shay sometin to *anyone* an yu wil go there too. Yu hear me?" Mari remembered her papi getting angrier when he would look at Jonathan and Mari staring at him while they cowered in the couch and went back to staring at the television.

"Yes, Papi. We hear you," Jonathan told their father without looking at him.

"Yu look at me when yu tok to mee, *hijo*. Yu need to control yur woman when she do sometin stupid. *Estupida!*" He howled as he repeated stupid in Spanish and stared directly at Jonathan.

"I know, Papi, I know," Jonathan slowly said as he stared his father down.

"Yu Mari. Yu need no do to me wha yur mami do to mee. She no good!" Benjy yelled as he ran over and kicked the closet door where he held their mother hostage. He kicked the wooden door so hard he made a dent in it.

"Yu no say not'in' to no people wha happin in this house. *Mi casa!* My house! Yu hear me!" He strutted over to Jonathan and Mari and leaned over barely a half inch from their faces.

"*Mi casa.* My house," Benjy whispered as he fell over onto the couch where Mari and Jonathan sat. He was fast asleep, knocked out by the quart or two of rum.

As soon as Mari could see her father was not getting up anytime soon she would go into her room, latch her door, and dig out her diary, and started her pen to flow freely on her pages. Her diary was the only thing that allowed her to feel free to speak her mind without judgment. She could write all the happenings that would occur to her, her family, or friends. Her diary would not talk, but she knew her diary was the only thing that kept her sane from the craziness in her home or school. She wrote:

Papi did not want to think anything was wrong with them or anyone else. Privacy was very important to him. I guess Papi wanted to teach Mami a lesson for telling my aunt stuff about him and the other woman from down the block. I remember Jonathan had asked Mami her nose since it looked really big but she said that she had bumped into her bedroom door since she had not realized it was open when she walked into their bedroom. I didn't think it was true since I saw Papi slap her directly on her face really hard. I thought he had slapped her nose off her face but she still had her nose, it was just bleeding. My papi kept Mami in the closet for two full days back then. She didn't go to work those two days. Jonathan and I had spent a sleepover at our cousin's house, which was weird since our aunt went to pick us up at school. That never happened before. Especially since Mami and Papi were on vacation from work. After we got home from my aunt's house, I noticed Mami had been crying and cleaning the bedroom closet all afternoon. I heard Mami sniffling while she was on the phone with my aunt when Papi was out with the "guys" and Mami said she had been kept in a closet for two days. Well, I better go for now. Will write more later, Ms. Diary. With those last words, Mari closed her diary and put it back in her secret hiding place. Sylvia was coming over in about five minutes, so she needed to hurry up. No one could ever find out she had a diary. TMI—too much information and too many secrets.

She could never tell Sylvia or anyone, for that matter, anything of the crazy stuff that happened at home. That would be bad.

"I mean, maybe Papi would put me inside my own bedroom closet for a couple of days. Or worse yet, what if he forgot I was in it? Then I would die in a closet." No, she could never tell anyone anything. Papi would kill her if he ever found out or maybe even kill her mami. That would be worse and it would be her fault. Nope, she would never say a word. That secret would always be hers. Mari needed to remember to write all this down in her diary. If she was ever thrown into her closet and she was forgotten in there, at least someone might get her story if they found her diary in her secret hiding place. No, she would die. No one would ever find her diary in her secret hiding place. Mari spent months trying to figure out a place no one in the world ever find her diary. Mari slipped out of the house and got to the schoolyard without anyone noticing she was gone.

"Yo, earth to Mari. You alive?" Mari felt Sylvia's hand pushing her shoulder back.

"Oh yeah, girl. Sorry. I forgot you wanted me to keep awake." Mari feigned a smile, acting like she was just teasing Sylvia. Good. Sylvia had bought it, she just kept on talking like Mari had been listening intently to her story.

"I really like spending time at my dad's house. I also like spending time with my two sisters over there. They're pretty cool and actually, you know normal. I mean they aren't crazy valley girls with their boobs hanging out and wearing these tight pants so that guys will notice them. They're pretty cool and are actually, you know, normal. They're pretty down to earth, plus, they would really like to play football and wrestling. Pretty cool, huh? Also, my psycho mom, I mean, Mari, check this out, she actually made me call a lawyer to let him know I didn't want to go to my dad's home because they wouldn't feed me. Geez, unreal. I had to go looking all sad and stuff. I wanted to tell the lawyer the truth, but then my mom would find out and she would make my life a living hell. Yup, kept quiet and played the game. I just don't get it. Why don't parents just get along?" Sylvia asked Mari as if Mari would enlighten her knowledge to the ailments of parental silence.

"Yo, dude, I am just as lost as you are. Parents are just weird. Period. No sense worrying about it. I think, though, you should tell your mom's lawyer that your mom's crazy. I have a mom and dad that are crazy. Just be glad you only got one psycho mom and not a psycho dad to go along with her like I do," Mari told Sylvia as she put her arm around her shoulders. Mari so wanted to really talk to Sylvia about everything that was happening at her house. She just couldn't bring herself to break the secret she held at her home. Just too dangerous. Her diary would just have to do. She'd write away her fear and hope tomorrow would be a better day for her.

"OK, Mari. We just got to work a little closer and harder together. I got used to see it's OK to talk. You can trust others, the same way you want them to trust you. They're not going to think you're weird. You may have to take a chance that someone will help protect you and keep you from your father's monstrous grip," I whispered to Mari as low as I was allowed by the spiritual guides' code of ethics guidelines. I needed to be careful to follow directions; otherwise, I would have to go back to Spiritual Guide's Course 101. Although I enjoyed Mama Lynn teaching this course and I've learned much, I did not want to move backward, I wanted to move forward. More than anything, I wanted Mari to open her eyes and her voice so her words to others who would be willing to hear them would be listened to. I knew many people would help Mari with her problems at home. Mari just had to let go of her fear.

I realized the reality of Mari's fear. It was real. Mari's father Benjy would make Eskimos buy igloos from him. Benjy was that much of a silver-tongued devil. Yet, I had to try to convince Mari to speak with someone she could trust. That was the problem: finding someone that Mari could truly trust. She really liked a lot of people, but she was terrified at bringing them into her dark world. Sylvia would be the ideal person, I thought; however, getting Mari to let go of her perception that her father would punish her was going to be tougher than I realized.

"Well, dudette, I'm at my next class. See ya, wouldn't want to be ya!" Sylvia laughed out loud as though she had just made the most hysterical joke of the decade.

"Yeah, you know you'd want to walk in my shoes, be me, feel my presence all day long!"

"Girlfriend, I was with you all morning and I sure didn't see you smoke any weed or take any drugs. Somehow, you must have had some early-morning long-lasting drug to think I'd want to be you!" Sylvia responded to Mari.

"Whatever, girl!" Mari said as both girls high and low slapped each other's hand. "I better jet to my next class before Mrs. Anderson gets all weird on me. She's like ninety years old, when they want her to have a heart attack 'cause of me."

"Yeah, well, when she sees your face, your face will give her the heart attack! Ooooohhh, yes, I did say it!" Mari laughed as she got up to leave up and go to her next class.

Mari decided to take the janitor's stairwell to her classroom since it was a shortcut to her next class. She knew it was off limits, but she would often take that direction when she was cutting it too close for comfort to get to her next class. She only needed to go down two staircases, make a quick last left and walk a few feet to the right, and there would be her class. Mrs. Anderson would yet have another day of life without a heart attack due to all of her students being in class on time.

Mari slid down the first staircase, taking two to three stairs at a time, but when she turned into the second staircase, she was confronted with several teenage girls and boys on both sides of the staircase. She'd seen these kids before. They were known for being major troublemakers in her school. Panic and terror hit Mari at exactly the same time. *Crap*, Mari thought. *I really need to act like I'm going down the stairs without an issue, otherwise, they'll give me an issue to worry about*, Mari continued thinking. Mari looked straight ahead and tried to fly down the stairs quickly, yet by the time she was going to hit the fifth stair, she felt a strange hand cop a feel of her butt, from her vagina all the way to the top of her waist. Mari started to feel sweat soak her for head and neck. Her hair stood up at the nape of her neck.

"What the hell! Leave me alone!" Mari yelled back at the pimply-faced fat kid who was throwing Mari kisses when she turned back to find out who had groped her butt.

Mari continued down the next two stairs when she felt another hand reach out to her and grope her butt again. When she turned around, all she could see were all the kids laughing and catcalling out to her.

"Yo, baby. You want some more where that came from!" a voice from the far top of the stairwell yelled out to her.

"No, don't go, I have something especially for you." A male skinny kid with his dingy white trunks showing out of his jeans that were five times too large for his build.

"Naw, she won't know what to do!" Mari heard a female voice say as she was reaching for the doorknob that would lead her to some form of safety. Hopefully, no one would jump her and rape her right then and there. She needed to hurry up and open up that door. What would she do if she couldn't open it before someone grabbed her? She didn't have a cell phone. She didn't even think she had a voice in her. She felt completely mute. No, she had to reach the door and run out of that stairwell. Ugh, she hated school! She just hated people. She just wanted to die right now, right there. How would those assholes feel about that?!

Mari leaped to the door, and luckily, it opened easily. She ran out and kept running. She ran past all the classrooms where students were seated in their seats and teachers were just arriving to start their daily routine of teaching their math, social studies, history, political science, etc. She even ran past Mrs. Anderson, who had just started to write something on the board with her special light green chalk that she always used to signify the topic of the day in her classes. Mari didn't care. She just kept running and running until she reached this school's front glass doors. Mari didn't stop running until she reached her apartment door and had to stop her running in order to grab her key from her backpack so she could open the door to her safe haven, a place that would provide her asylum, even though she hated to be there most of the time. She was really happy to see it appear in front of her now, after all she had endured.

Mari quickly put her key into the door lock and opened the door. She closed the door and just slid down to the floor as she felt the door hide her from the outside world. Mari sat there holding on to her backpack as though her backpack was shielding her from any precarious situation the world was going to present to her. After ten minutes or what seemed an eternity to Mari, she took a deep breath, stood up, and walked over to her room, where she robotically changed from school clothes to sweats, T-shirt, and running shoes. She put up her hair into a ponytail and went into the kitchen to start dinner per Sara's instruction to Mari and Jonathan.

Mari tried and tried again to become motivated to start dinner for the family, but she kept recounting in her mind her horrid incident at school. Having been unsuccessful at cooking, Mari stopped and ran into her bedroom, where she quickly pulled out her diary from its hidden spot and started to write. She wrote:

Dear Ms. Diary,

*How have you been? My day truly sucked big time! I was actually having a good day goofing with Sylvia and I almost, almost for a split second was going to confide in her and tell her what has been happening at home with my folks, but again I chickened out. I really feel I need to talk to someone and tell them about the hell I am going through at home, in school, but I am really, really scared to do it. Then this afternoon, I was booking all the way to class so my old teach doesn't freak out because I am not there yet, and these kids—*Mari just stopped; her hands were shaking like a leaf. Mari just stared at her diary, wide-eyed, as tears flowed down her cheeks. Her body started to shake and she joined her hands together, trying to make the trembling stop as she struggled to finish her thoughts to the one source, the one thing she knew would not betray her trust, her diary. She continued to write:

These kids just take their nasty hands and start feeling me up. I felt so scared. I felt as though these kids were going to take my clothes off and just rape me. Like gang rape, you know?! It was horrible. I started to run away and I heard them all laughing like I was some type of coward and idiot. I felt so violated and used. I just wish I had never gone through that stairwell again. I have used the janitor's stairwell before without a problem. Today all these kids were there. I just wish I had been someone else, like maybe Sylvia. Sylvia would've kicked all of their asses. I know she would have! She doesn't put up with anyone messing with her. I had this happen before, why now again?

I don't want to go to school anymore. I just want to stay in my room by myself with no one bothering me or needing me. Not even Mami. I love Mami but she needs to deal with Papi herself. I wish I could tell Mami and Papi about what happened, but then those kids will get me and kill me. It would be worse! Wait, if I am dead, I wouldn't have to deal with this stuff. I wouldn't have to be scared all the time. Naw, I think I am going to talk to Sylvia. She'll know what to do. I know she will.

OK, Ms. Diary, I better get back to cooking or my parents of government kill me anyway and I won't need to worry about any hassles. I always LOVE talking to you, Ms. Diary. Bye, I will try to talk to you tomorrow, OK? With that, Mari closed her diary and placed it back into its secret hiding place. She felt as though her whole life had changed in a flicker of a second. Once again, she felt reenergized and went into the kitchen with the thought of cooking dinner, wondering where Jonathan was, since he was supposed to help her. He was probably out there hitting on some girl again, acting like he was all cool and crap.

"Mari, I am so proud of you. At least you want to talk to Sylvia about what happened to you this afternoon. Listen, girl, I've been there. It isn't right for you to go through this by yourself. You deserve more than that. You were violated, although those kids didn't take your clothes off, they still messed with you sexually. You really need to talk to someone!" I yelled the last sentence to Mari. I so wanted Mari to listen, talk, to find help. I wished I was human so I could help Mari help herself. I felt so helpless. All of a sudden, I felt as though I was the biggest loser among all the Spiritual Guides. I couldn't believe I could be so lousy as to let down my subject. Mari needed me. I also had to prove it to myself that I would be able to help someone with situations like that. I have been through so much myself, and the thought of Mari having to feel so distressed and anguished was breaking my heart.

"Pearl, does this sound messed up?" I asked Pearl who looked up from writing Spiritual Guides' evaluations.

"What is it, Candace? What revelations have you come upon today?"

"Well, Pearlie, O Wise One," I said as I peeked over Pearl's shoulder to see whose evaluation she was writing, "I know this sounds really, really screwed up, but it felt good to just have someone come in to hold me. Damn, Pearl, it was my psycho demented sick father! How weird and mental is that? It makes me sick to even think that. I mean, it was important to me to have my crazy perverted father come in and do the nasty with me, even though it was a sick thing to do. I took myself to another place when he was getting his rocks off, yet it felt good to have him at least think of me. Fucked up, isn't it? Ooooops, sorry. I guess I'm a Spiritual Guide and shouldn't talk like that. Why couldn't he just want to be with me in a right way as normal fathers do with their kids? God, I just wish I was dead after he left! Then again, now I am. It doesn't feel any better. I am just more determined to help others be free."

"Candace, you have never truly experienced a true parental love from either of your parents. Your mother hid herself behind the bottle and was oblivious to your needs or, for that matter, anyone else's. You were not provided a fair shake in life, and you reacted in the only way you knew to get away from your horrific life. Unfortunately, you did not have anyone for you to talk to or trust," Pearl softly tells me.

"Yes, Pearlie, you are so right. I definitely didn't have anyone to talk to. I just had my books and my very special getaway spot by the meadow I would run to so I could get away from them and get away from life. That helped for a while, but then the nightmares would start all over again and again."

"It seems then, Candace, that you have plenty of work left to do with Mari if she is to get a better chance in life. Go talk to her. I feel pretty certain she'll respond when she is ready."

"Pearl, when will I know if she's ready?" I asked Pearl.

"Oh my girl, you will know. Mari will tell you in her own way. She'll let you know. There will be times when you think you are talking to a brick wall. Don't give up! Many victims of domestic violence will try to ignore the fact that their loved one, their soul mate made in heaven, is really a devil incarnate. That husband or father or boyfriend or even fling would not hurt them. Why, that loved one treasures the ground they walk on, when in reality, the person who hits his or her loved one just to keep them in line is just that—a hitter. It takes time to change a person's mind as well as their heart. Think about it, how did you feel when you were going through your own abuse?" Pearl hated to remind me of my past, due to the deep bruises it had left on my heart, but she needed to make a point that would help me empathize and grow as a Spiritual Guide. Pearl hoped to open the gates that she knew held me back, my shackles that bound me to my past and did not allow me to move to a level that would not only help my subjects but me as well.

"Pearl . . ." I hoarsely spoke, just an octave above a whisper. "It was different back then. It was my father. My mother ignored the fact that he would come into my bedroom almost every night for numerous years. She ignored me! She allowed him to hurt me. She never came in and hurled him off me. She never had the courage to confront his sickness and perverseness. It's different with Mari. Sara will help Mari if Mari just opened her mouth and spoke out and broke Sara's silence." My voice was barely audible. Pearl heard me without a problem. When someone becomes a Spiritual Guide, all physical senses are heightened and the body becomes an incredible unbreakable temple.

"Candace, you can do this. Follow your heart and it will lead you to the hole that Mari has left open for someone to throw in a life preserver. She is waiting on you. She needs your direction. Mari just needs to push to speak out and know that she is not the only one going through that prison she is in. Go out there and speak to Mari as you wished someone had spoken to you when you needed your own special angel. I believe you can do it. It isn't just about getting your wings. It's about helping a very beautiful girl who is living in a very messed-up home, seeing darkness even though light lives within her. She has what it takes to make a difference in her life and the life of her family. She just doesn't realize it is not her fault that she is not able to tell right from wrong. No one has been around to help her when she has needed someone to believe her or protect her from others. She has always had to hold on to secrets and protect others so she could consider herself useful."

"OK, Pearlie. I will try to reach out so Mari will understand not only her life but the lives of her mom and brother depend on their future actions. Also, the life of her sicko dad depends on her as well. If Mari continues to be quiet, she will allow Benjy to continue to hurt her mom and she will allow Benjy to teach her brother some very lousy lessons. I feel something horrible happening. A storm is brewing and Mari will be swept up in it if she does not rise above it.

"Candace, it is up to you to see to it that Mari is not swept away by the storm. Own the moment. Know you can reach Mari. She deserves another way of life. If you cannot believe in yourself, then how do you expect Mari to believe she can escape the chains that will envelop her soul? You can do this. I know it. If I did not feel it in my own heart and being, you would not be here. Candace, it is up to you. Reach out and release your soul so that Mari's spirit will not be lost. Remember your spirit? The spirit within you, it does live!"

CHAPTER 22

Mari woke up with a huge headache this morning. She tried to figure out what she did the night before that would land her with killer pounding inside her temples. Take aspirin—check! Take a shower—check! Change into sweats and a T-shirt—check! Mari had seen this movie where the lead actress used the "check" method to make things happen for her. Mari thought it might get her more organized and make things happen for her just like it did for the actress. So here we go, talk to Jonathan about his date—check! Nope, scratch that, not sure of this topic. Major question mark. Shoot, what was she supposed to do? Write down the task and then put a question mark? Don't write the question down, but then she might forget about the task, or did she just write the task down and then put a blackened circle next to it? Ugh, way too complicated. Just write the damn tasks down and check the list to make sure she wrote down all the stuff.

"Anyway, too early to deal with my stupid brother," Mari thought. She had been thinking about talking to her brother for several months by now and getting more in tune with him. She thought it might be the mature thing to do. "I mean, I am sixteen years of age. I am getting to be a complete adult now, almost, kinda sorta," Mari thought. Plus, Jonathan had been acting like an ass, and he seemed to be acting more and more like her father. Mari already had to deal with the craziness of her dad; she couldn't deal with Jonathan becoming Papi II, especially since he was just seventeen years of age. "I mean, one horndog is enough around my dumb crazy house. Let's not add another one," Mari mused. She was getting really concerned about her mom. She noticed her mom sported another couple of deep purple bruises on her arms and she noticed that she had some deep red marks around her neck. That really scared Mari. Mari tried to broach the subject with her mom, but Sara always said she was OK. Sara had either tripped or fell down or, get this one, Sara mentioned to Mari she had pulled her scarf too tight around her neck and she forgot she had her necklace on and that is what caused that crazy red mark around her neck. Weird! Mari had a gut feeling that her mami was hiding stuff from her ever since she started to help her friend Rebecca, who lived in the building next to theirs, with her orchestra music.

Mari was first violinist and Rebecca was second chair. Sometimes, both Rebecca and Mari messed up on their violins, and they kept swapping their orchestra seating more times than they raised their violin bows. It got pretty competitive with Mari and Rebecca. Yet, Mari and Rebecca were the best of friends. It seemed the violin was the other thing that kept their minds off their lives.

Rebecca had had a pretty rough time of late. Her mom had just gotten remarried and Rebecca now lived with two new sisters. They were pretty cool and all, even though they were slightly younger than she was. But her new sisters were constantly calling their mom and letting her know about everything that was going on in Rebecca's house, even though nothing was going on. Her two sisters, Brandi and Matti, were really cool when they stayed over. Rebecca's stepmom had some mental issues and was constantly trying to create problems with Rebecca's mom and homelife. Oh well, some people cannot handle people moving on in their lives, even though life was miserable with them. This crap of her sisters' mom butting into their lives was making it really challenging, especially since it was really great when her sisters were there. They would play board games, chat about the latest music, and the latest crushes they had on movie stars and musicians. Hopefully, the grown-ups would get it together and leave things alone. Why can't people like it when others are happy? I guess it was just jealousy. Her sisters' mom was just jealous and didn't like it that Rebecca's mom and her new stepdad were happy.

Rebecca went on to tell Mari that she heard her mom and stepdad how much this stupidity of dealing with lawyers all the time was draining them of money that they could spend on the kids and how it was making her sisters change when they first got to her home. They would be really mean to her mom and really snotty with her stepdad, but after a couple of days, they would start to get better and life would get back to normal. She remembered her sisters telling her how much they wanted their mom to remarry and be as happy as their dad was now with Rebecca's mom.

I guess a lot of the kids have issues too; Mari was not the only one.

Rebecca just wished parents would realize how their actions hurt their kids. It was more about parental egos than it had anything to do with the kids really being unhappy. She kept saying that all the time they saw each other, which was all the time! After that, they would both get into their classical music. After their rehearsal, Rebecca would tell Mari how she was going to be a famous violinist, she and others would have to pay to see her play in all of the famous stadiums. She was going to get a degree and move out of their crazy neighborhood. They both knew that their classical music didn't seem to do anything to the kids who were forced to go and see the orchestra. Maybe there would be one kid who did not have deaf ears and he or she would hear it and would feel how they did. That would really be cool.

CHAPTER 23

"Yo, Mari!" Jonathan banged on Mari's door as he shouted her name out, making sure she was awake so they could walk to school. This was Jonathan's senior year and there were only four months before he would graduate. He could not wait. He thought about going to college but wasn't sure if he could handle dealing with professors and more schoolwork. Yet, watching college girls and guys flaunting their stuff around was enough to get his interest going. He had applied to several colleges but had yet to hear from them. He hoped he would be accepted deep down inside but knew it might be a major stretch. He just wanted to leave his home and not deal with his parents fighting all the time even though he hated the thought of leaving Mari behind to deal with everything. Whoa, that was news, Jonathan thinking of Mari and her potential living arrangement at home. Naw, she'd be OK. Papi knew better than to mess with Mari, Jonathan thought.

His papi wouldn't hit Mari like Jonathan knew he hit their mom. Mari had always been his daddy's little girl. Jonathan always got smacked in the face or with the belt while Mari always got away with something she did that made Jonathan look bad. No way his dad would hurt Mari. Jonathan had also noticed his dad was getting more vicious and more frequent on his verbal and physical attacks on his mom. He needed to stop it, but there were times Jonathan felt confused as to what to do or say, and there were times he felt his dad should smack his mom for mouthing off on his dad. A woman should not be accusing a man of being unfaithful or needing to do anything, right? Jonathan loved his mom, but she shouldn't be allowed to do anything that would not be cool with his dad being a man, period, or should she? Ugh, he was so confused.

Mari was different. Jonathan felt that she would get her ass kicked over and over again before she got what it meant to give a man his place. Mari always got all weird and screwed up when it came to women's rights and what a man or woman should be. Mari always felt a woman had the right to be her own self, the way a man always had the right to be what he is, a man.

"Why can't a woman determine her destiny?" Mari would challenge Jonathan, with fire in her eyes. He just said what he always said and felt at the time, "A woman is a bitch. She should take her place in the kitchen and have babies." Jonathan knew that would piss her off and he would always taunt Mari. He didn't feel that way all the time, although sometimes he would feel that women would be better off if they just hung out at home and let men do what they were supposed to do—work, pay the bills, and go out to have fun on the weekends. Responsibilities were taken care of, right? Bills were paid, food was provided on the dinner table with the man's hard-earned money, so it was time for the man to go out at the end of the week. He did not understand when Mari would just stare at him like he was some kind of alien. "What?" Jonathan would ask, not knowing why the hell Mari would look at him that way. He just figured Mari was just on the rag and acting crazy. That was the all-encompassing period! That time in the month when girls would get all weird, emotional, and just downright strange. It really wasn't what guys did wrong, it was just girls and women acting all crazy and making guys do things they wouldn't normally do. It was all their fault because they were girls and had to have the rag. That was the time when guys had to leave them so they can become sane because if they stayed with their girl partners, the guys would go nuts. It was called "period time-out." That should be made a national monthly holiday. That way, guys wouldn't get blamed for every damn thing girls do that is really bizarre because they were on their periods. They shouldn't be blamed for being insensitive, callous, and piggish. It was a time where guys could safely all hang out and leave their girlfriends or wives to their thing and the guys could do their thing. What's wrong with that?

"Yo, you ready? Got to hit it. Can't be late again. The principal's got a hard-on for seniors again this year. You are late, we get detention, but there is a possibility of summer school before we can graduate. It's crazy. Don't need the bald-ass principal getting to know my name."

"Yeah, got it. Am almost done. Just need a sec and I will be ready to fly the coop," Mari responded automatically, not thinking about her brother's potential plight with summer school if he was caught being late. She was too preoccupied with her own issues. How could she approach her stupid horndog brother about his date and how he feels about her or just girls in general? Mari had to get Jon's thoughts on what was happening at home. What the heck, just ask and knock it out.

"By the way, have you seen Mom lately?" Mari asked Jonathan as she waited on him to secure the four sets of locks on their front door. Don't want to give burglars a chance to get into their place with easy access, right?

"What about Mami?" Jonathan answered, just slightly acknowledging her question.

"Haven't you seen her arms lately and her neck? She's got some major marks again. Just wondered if you had heard her fall or trip on anything," Mari asked Jonathan nonchalantly as they ran down the stairs in their apartment building, heading out to school.

"Naw, you know Mami. She can be kind of clumsy sometimes. I mean, I have never seen her fall down or trip or anything but if that's what she said, then that's what happened. What's the big deal?" Jonathan asked, knowing where the conversation was going. He just wanted to get the conversation over and done with by the time he got close to school. He didn't want his friends seeing him talking to his kid sister. It might give them the wrong impression about him. Jonathan didn't want his friends thinking he was going soft, even though all of his friends knew, hands off when it came to Mari. No one messed with her. It was an unspoken rule among all of his friends. All of the sisters or brothers were off her as a harassment target. No one messed with each others' families, period.

"I was just worried about Mami. Don't you care about her?" Mari jumped on Jonathan when she noticed he was being so flippant about their mother.

"Look, I am not Mami's keeper, you got it? I am not around home much and did not see anything happen to her. Got it? If Mami fell, she fell. Big deal. We all fall sometimes."

"Look, moron, get your head out of your ass. Mami hasn't been doing real good. She barely talks to me anymore."

"Then that's your issue. Not mine. Talk to her about it."

"Look, I think Papi is messing with Mom, OK?"

"Finally!" I squealed as I jumped up toward Pearl. "Pearlie, did you hear that? Mari finally admitted to Jonathan that something abnormal is happening to their mom. That is huge!"

"Yes, Candace. It is wonderful. But your job is far from done. The first step is to have your case subject acknowledge something is wrong. The next step is to let your subject understand that she must move forward with some type of positive action to help the situation. Recognizing a bad situation at home is occurring doesn't fix the problem. That would be like a patient admitting there is a health problem. The sickness will still hang around unless the patient is brought to the doctor's office or hospital for the sickness to be taken care of, the illness will still linger unless the root of the problem is seen and the right type of medication or modification of life is made. The same will occur to Mari if she doesn't take a proactive step to the next level. Whisper to Mari the potential of a life without fear, a life where young girl can go to sleep without screams or thumps in the night, and sweet dreams instead of nightmares will happen," Pearl gently suggests to me.

"Jonathan, did you not hear what I said?"

"Mami's a big girl. She can take care of herself."

"What?! You think it's OK for Papi be to smacking Mom around like she is some type of rag doll? You think it's OK for Mami to be walking around with black eyes and bruises not only on her face but on her body? What's wrong with you?"

"Look, dork, that's between Papi and Mami. What do you want from me? I stick my nose in their business and then they get all back into one another and I'm the one they take things out on because I got into their stuff. You know that they fight and they make up and it gets back to normal at the Santiagos'. Mami ain't going nowhere. She will let Papi do whatever to her. She'll take it 'cause that's what she does. Not getting into their business."

"So that's it? Figured you wouldn't do nothing. I'll take care of stuff. Next time Papi starts in on Mami, I am good and getting into his face. I don't care what he does."

"Yeah, well, whatever. You'll be the one to have the black eyes and bruises instead of Mami."

"At least I'll be doing something instead of letting Mami get beat. I guess I gotta be the one to wear the real pants in this house." Mari stared at Jonathan as she hiked her pants up on her hips to stress her point. After a few seconds, Jonathan runs his comb through his hair. He starts heading to school. Another day in school, another day for checking out the girls and figuring out who is going to be the lucky chick that he gets to go out with him on a ride they will never forget. The games one has to play to be a man.

CHAPTER 24

"Yo, dude. Did you see Scott checking you out? He is so eyeing you," Rebecca whispered as she leaned over to Mari while hiding behind her science book so she would not be spotted by Mr. Evans, or Bob as he preferred his class to call him. Not that Bob would do much. He was Mari's and Rebecca's hippie science teacher. He came into class with tie-dyed T-shirts 95 percent of the time. He even tie-dyed his lab coat so it would match his T-shirts. Yeah, he was weird, but he was pretty smart when it came to science. When it was time for his class observation by other teachers or the principal, he would wear a tie over his T-shirt and have his class call him Mr. Evans. Oh, and he would still wear his crazy as lab coat.

"Rebecca, you are crazy, girl. He is not interested in someone like me?"

"What are you talking about? Why wouldn't he be interested in you? You are hot! He is hot! Hmmm, hmmm, hmmm, it is just too hot in here. I think I need to get up, go out, and forget about this class today." Rebecca winked at Mari and she pretended to put her books inside her backpack so she could leave class. Mari just closed her eyes as she giggled. When she opened her eyes again, she slowly twisted in her chair so she could shoot a glance toward Scott's desk. To Mari's surprise, he was staring right at her and he smiled. Mari smiled back and quickly turned forward in her chair.

Mari and Rebecca were both startled as Bob noisily jumped on his desk when his beaker started to spill a concoction of blue and green foam over his lab table. He started to wail he was going to die, while pulling his pants up dramatically. As he jumped up and down, his green and blue polka-dot goggles wiggled on his face. The crazy scene Bob was making made Mari forget about her embarrassing Scott moment. He saw her looking at him. Hopefully, the Bob jumping dance would make him forget about the embarrassing moment as well.

"Mari, turn around in your chair and look away from the lab table," Bob called over to Mari as he stopped his table dance. "I tell you what, so I know you do not peek up here, turn your chair toward . . . let's see, oh I know, Scott. Turn your chair toward Scott." Bob had noticed Scott looking at Mari for a while now in his classes. Bob had dealt with students who had pretty lousy home lives and he dressed up every day in his crazy outfits to give his students a reprieve from crap at home. Get their minds away from home for at least forty-five minutes and focus on school and the opportunities in the world that can help at least some students walk away from their home saga into a new and happier future life.

"Mari, are you with me? Earth to Mari, earth to Mari, come hither, Mari." Bob chuckled as Mari simply stared at him as though she had been called the owner of a fart that had ripped throughout the classroom.

"What? Why do you want me to turn my chair toward Scott?" Mari struggled with her words as her eyes opened wider as she spoke to Bob.

"Well, Mari, you are the lucky student who has just entered Bob's science emporium. Your mission, should you choose to accept it, which, by the way, you will do so, otherwise you will have to clean the mess up here after class, is to tell me all the ingredients used to make this crazy volcano. What you miss, Mari, Scott will have to name off until everything of this amazing volcano has been tallied off the volcano-making list."

Crap, Mari thought, what am I going to do now? That will teach me to pay attention to Rebecca with her crazy ideas. Oh well, I just need to remember what I used when I created a foaming lava trail on Jonathan's underwear that he left on his bed one day when he went to take a shower. She had taken his other four pairs of underwear and run mustard down the crack so it would look like he had messed himself. That would teach him! Hmph! He had been a royal pain and had gotten her in trouble with Mami and Papi. She had to stay in her room during the entire weekend without any television or phone privileges. Mari searched her memory as she faked a cough to gain her some time. OK, I got this. Crap, now Scott is really going to hate me. Oh well, who cares what Scott thinks. I don't like him, well, maybe not a lot.

"Bob, since you have green lava coming out of the volcano, I think you used some kind of green soda and some green Mentos candy." Mari immediately looked at her hands as she could imagine seeing the tiny drops of sweat covering her palms.

"Scott, what else is used to make our monster volcano?"

"Wait, um, I don't think I missed anything. Did I?" Mari immediately tried to come to Scott's rescue. As she looked over at him, he just sat there relaxed, with the cutest smirk on his face that she had ever seen, on anyone. How could he be relaxed while she was going to be dripping sweat onto her jeans from her palms? Dude, you really are cute! Mari allowed her mind to wander for just a millisecond.

"Bob, Mari was right on with her answer," Scott confidently answered as he looked over at Mari while answering their science teacher.

"Normally, I would say you are both correct, but you both missed the most, and again I must say *most*, important ingredient of the volcano-making masterpiece." Bob used his intonation of words to give a very scientific flair as he answered Scott. Bob hesitated for a couple of seconds before he spun and leaped onto his desk, taking his goggles off midair and stretching his arms outward.

"Me! You missed the most important part of the experiment. The scientist—me! So, since neither of you remembered me, your beloved teacher, renowned inventor in the scientific realm and future Pulitzer Prize winner. Of which, I hope I can recover from feeling so hurt." Bob feigned immense physical distress. "You will both have to stay after class to clean up this mess." The bell rang, marking the end of Bob's fictitious science emporium. Students immediately picked up their schoolbooks, jackets, backpacks, and ran out of the classroom before Bob could finish his homework reminder.

"OK, you two. Have fun and don't say that I've never done anything special for you. Also, talk and have fun as you clean up all these volcano pieces. You'll find it will make the cleanup a lot quicker and nicer." Bob smiled as he picked up his brown tattered briefcase covered with Save the Ozone and *Weird Science* movie stickers. There were at least four or five different colored neon peace-symbol stickers to give his attaché case a very '70s look.

"Are you OK getting to lunch a few minutes late?" Scott softly asked Mari, breaking the thick air of tension created before Bob left the classroom.

"Yeah, I'm cool. I don't need a lot of time to eat my sandwich. How about you? I can do this myself if you have friends waiting for you." Mari could barely get the words out of her mouth. It almost felt like an out-of-body experience hearing her voice yet not realizing she was talking. It felt as though someone else was talking for her.

"Nah, I don't have a lot of friends except for maybe you? Maybe, kinda, sort of?" Scott asked as he put on a puppy-dog look. As Mari looked at him, Scott crossed his eyes toward his nose, which made him look like a crossed-eye puppy and Mari burst out laughing.

"You are a dork," Mari told him as she started to pick up hardened imitation volcano pieces and threw them into the trash can. "You should get your butt over here and start doing some real work," Mari said in a stern voice, trying to take command of the cleaning assignment. It wasn't working. She started to experience once again the out-of-body experience as she heard herself speak but could only think about his hazel eyes and great smile.

"Ahhhh, Pearlie, I think we have some sugar happening here!" I squealed as I hugged Pearl's arm.

"Scott has a kind soul. He seems to like her all right. Seems like he has had his eye on Mari for a while, she hasn't noticed since her thoughts have been more on her homelife. You never know who is sitting right next to you until you stop to look."

Pearl winked at me as we looked back at Mari and Scott doing classroom cleanup.

CHAPTER 25

"Who was that you were all girlie and dumb with at lunch?" Jonathan asked as he and Mari walked home together after school. He tried to look all cool like he did not care, but Mari knew he did. Deep down inside, she knew he would not let anyone hurt her like her father hurt her.

"Why do you care?" Mari answered Jonathan, giving him the same type of attitude he gave her.

"I don't care, dwarf. Just thinking how bad Mami and Papi are going to beat you if they ever find out you are hanging around a guy in school behind their backs."

"I just sat next to him at lunch this one time. I sit next to girls and boys at a lunch table. Guess what? There are two chairs to a desk and class, and oh my gosh, I sit next to boys there too," Mari exclaimed as she made fun of Jonathan, although she knew he was right on how their parents would react if they ever found out she sat next to Scott voluntarily at lunch. Mari and Scott had pretty much ignored their friends at the lunch table as they joked about Bob and his antics in class. They also talked about some of their other classes they shared.

"Well, I won't say nothing as long as you don't mess with me. Otherwise, I will let them know you were kissing and sucking each other's tongues out. That should get you at least a week in the closet." Jonathan stopped smiling as soon as he mentioned the closet. He regretted the words as soon as they left his mouth. Mari froze in her steps. Neither Jonathan nor she had ever joked about the closet.

"Sorry, Mari. You know I would never let that happen to you," Jonathan softly and slowly said to Mari so he could be sure she would understand what he meant and that he was not playing around.

"Yeah, I know." Mari looked at her brother and they fell back in step until they reached their apartment.

As the days went by, Mari and Scott spent more time together at lunch chatting about their classes, music, television, upcoming movies, and friends. Scott found a way of changing seats with his or Mari's friends so that they could sit together in class. Bob noticed the change in their seating arrangements in his science class but did not say a word. He was happy his classroom cleaning punishment reaped a happy outcome. Bob did not have Scott or Mari stay after class for any more classroom cleanup again.

"So whazzzup with Scottie-Boy, Mari?" Rebecca and Nina both teased Mari and went to Mari's right side, and Sylvia caught Mari on her left side as they caught her by surprise while she was walking out of her history class.

"What are you talking about? Scott is just in some of my classes and he is pretty cool. Plus, his name is not *Scottie-Boy*." Mari teased back as she took off her glasses and blinked numerous times at the girls. She blinked so hard that the girls were did not see the pole they almost bumped into until they felt an arm go across them.

"Hey, you almost made a triple play with this pole if I wasn't here to save you. I would say you girls owe me for saving your lives," Scott said as he smiled at all four girls but focused his attention toward Mari.

"Oh, I don't think so, *Scottie-Boy*," Sylvia tough talked back to Scott.

"Oh, I think you do, Ms. Sylvia." Scott looked straight at Sylvia and then continued to slyly look at her as he put his hands in his front jean pockets.

"I happen to know about someone who has been in my face, hounding me forever for your phone number, especially now that I know a really good, good friend of yours. I could just make ya day, ya know. I'm cool that way. Always thinking of others . . ." Scott joked as he looked up toward the ceiling and nodded his head to some students that walked by.

"I don't know *anyone* who I *want* to go out with in this school. No one is that special," Sylvia piped back at Scott a little less convincingly with her tough-girl act.

"Anyway, gots to go. My stop is here. Call you later, M. See you around, *Scottie-Boy*." Sylvia smiled at Scott as she put her hand by her ear as though telling Mari to call her.

"So who is interested in Sylvia?" Mari leaned into Scott to find out who in the school would be interested in Sylvia. Sylvia was really cute but she was very standoffish and was considered a snob by most guys around the school. It really intrigued Mari that a guy would actually be interested in her friend. She didn't think there was a guy that could be tough enough to handle her.

"I will tell you if you come over to my house and have lunch and watch a movie or play some video games. My mom thought it would be nice to meet you. I told her there was a girl in school who would not leave me alone."

"Naw-ah. You said what to your mom?" Mari almost choked on her words, and she was dumbstruck and horrified Scott would say such a thing to his mom about her or even mention her to his mom. Mari knew Scott and she had become good friends but she wasn't sure if she was ready to go to his house or anything like that.

"Yeah, Mom wanted to see the person that would put up with me voluntarily. I mean she said she does 'cause she's my mom and stuff, but why would you want to hang around me?" Scott laughed as he acted all surprised and hurt by what his mom had supposedly said to him.

"Oh, you can tell your mom that I just used it as an exercise so I can deal with my brother. If I put up with you, it is easier to deal with my bro when I get home," Mari joked back at Scott.

"Pearlie, Mari and Scott really seem to be getting along well. That is really cool. So does this mean all is good with Mari now and I can go to another case subject?" I asked Pearl.

"Candace, Mari will be dealing with some very hard times ahead. I would suggest you get your whispering pipes cleaned up really well because she is really going to need not only Scott but someone else that will give her strength and courage to move forward," Pearl said very seriously as she continued to see Mari and Scott laughing and kidding as they entered their next classroom.

CHAPTER 26

Mari almost had her complete wardrobe out on her bed. She kept trying jeans, blouses, sweaters, skirts, definitely no on the skirts for her lunch at Scott's house later that afternoon. She wanted to look really casual but not too casual that she would look like a slob to Scott's mom and to Scott.

She could not believe her ears when her mami and papi had decided to let her visit her friend today. She did leave out a very important part: her friend was a guy friend. "I mean, why would that matter? Right?" Mari tried to rationalize the lack of information to her parents.

"Mari, I think the jeans with the red sweater would look really nice with your dark hair," I leaned over and whispered to Mari.

"The red will also bring out your beautiful dark eyes. Scott will definitely think you are a total babe, although he already thinks that," I continued to whisper in Mari's ear. It was not an easy feat since I had tried to dodge jeans, blouses, sweaters, and sweatshirts being launched at me when I was a teenager trying to dress up for a friend, but Mari was aiming her clothes toward her bed, not all clothes making it to their destination.

"What?" Mari asked as though there was someone else in her bedroom, yet she knew that could not be since it was 7:00 a.m. and everyone was still in bed asleep. It was Saturday morning and their family usually started getting up around 8:00 a.m. or so, except for Jonathan who usually slept until noon on the weekends when he did not have to go into work early. She must be hearing things again. Lately, it seemed as though she could hear someone saying things, and when she looked, there was no one there. Mari thought she was starting to lose it since she might be stressing due to a lot of tests in school, but she had been doing pretty good with her grades and had thought the tests were pretty easy. Weird!

By the time breakfast had been set on the table and everyone was inching toward the food, except for Jonathan, whom she could still hear snoring from his bedroom, Mari had picked up all her clothes and placed them back inside her closet. She pulled out her favorite pair of jeans that did not have any holes in them but were definitely not new, a sweater, and her tennis shoes. She also decided she would wear her hair loose since it would look best that way with her red sweater.

"So wha time yu go to see yur friend? Do yur friend live close? Do we need to take yu there?" Sara asked Mari as she sat down at the kitchen table.

"No, Mami. I am good. I can walk over to my friend's house. My friend's mom will drive me back since it will be getting dark by then. I will be home in time for dinner around 5:30 p.m." Mari tried to sound casual as she stared at her food and avoided any type of eye contact with her parents. Her father was busy reading the newspaper, but her mom was staring her down. Mari could sense her mom's piercing eyes and heard the nervousness in her voice. This was the first time Mari would be gone for so long to someone's house that was neither Rebecca's or Sylvia's or Nina's or any of her cousins' houses.

"OK. Yu jus make sure yu here at 5:30 p.m. No longer up. OK? Entiendes? Yu understand, Mari," Sara firmly told Mari.

"Si, Mami. Yes, I understand. I will be here at five-thirty today and no later," Mari responded quickly.

"Mari, not sure you are doing the right thing, girlfriend," I whispered into Mari's ear.

"If I say the truth—" Mari said quickly without realizing she was vocalizing her thoughts as she turned around to see who was talking to her.

"Que? Wha, Mari?" Benjy asked as he looked down in time to see his daughter turning around so quickly in her chair that she almost fell on the floor.

"Wha sa matter wit yu? Yu loca? Yu crazy? Hija, yu see too much television. Yu now talking to yursel?" Benjy said as he returned to his newspaper.

"No, Papi, I was just trying to remember something so I wouldn't forget it. If I say it out loud, I won't forget."

"Forget what, dwarf?" Jonathan asked as he barely opened his eyes to sit down at the table to eat some breakfast.

"She must've been uuuuugggglllly if you are up before noon and you were on a date last night," Mari retorted.

"Yeah, she kinda reminded me of you!" Jonathan smirked at Mari as Sara provided him with pancakes, eggs, and sausage as he grabbed his plate.

"Oh no, yu go to the bathroom and brush yur teeth, wash yur face and hands before yu sit at this table wit food. Go!" Sara quietly rushed Jonathan out of the kitchen so he could get cleaned up before he sat down to eat breakfast.

"Good, don't want any of your nasty cooties at this table. It's bad enough you live here!" Mari thought as she gulped down the rest of her breakfast and excused herself to her bedroom until was time to leave to see Scott.

"Well, you must be Mari. Scott told me all about you except he left out how pretty you are." Scott's mother Marilyn told Mari that she welcomed her into their apartment.

"Hmmmm, hello. Nice to meet you, Mrs. Allen," Mari stammered as she felt her ears turn boiling hot.

"Mom, you're embarrassing Mari. Let her come inside then you can embarrass her," Scott joked with his mom.

"You are so right, Scott. Where are my manners? Come in, Mari, and make yourself at home. I am glad you could come out to meet me!" Scott's mom said as she winked at Mari and led her inside the living room.

The living room had a tan corduroy couch with matching love seat and chair. The windows were covered with age-sheer curtains and a deep burgundy drape she designed with swirls of tan, age, and olive green colors. A wood coffee table with books and magazines neatly piled on the corners and a large Bible lying in middle, with the living room also having tables holding tall black and brown steel lamps with round beige lamps, gave a great cosmopolitan look to their place. The walls that were not covered with pictures or drawings were covered with bookshelves holding a multitude of books of all types of genre. Tall pots of green plants lined the living room by the window and several corners of the room. As Mari looked around, she noticed an oval wood dining room table with brass candleholders and burgundy candlesticks. A large hutch with canary yellow dishes outlined with green and royal blue swirls lined the hutch shelves. Round plates on the second and third shelves showcased different places within the world and stood on plate holders provided by the owners. Plates showing photos of the Eiffel Tower, Rhine River in Germany, Dutch shoes from Holland, close-knit buildings in Belgium, waterfalls from Kauai, Hawaii, and stunning brown and white Paso Fino horses in Spain finished the plate collection within the hutch shelves.

Scott's house felt like a home. Mari tried to pay attention to Marilyn as she talked about Scott and his escapades as a child, while he begged his mother to stop bringing up painfully embarrassing scenes from his toddler years. But, Mari barely paid attention to the conversation due to the warm feeling she felt within her soul.

"Wow, now this seems like a home. No screaming, no tension, just laughter, and what looked like genuine love in a real family even if the family was just made up of a son and a mother. Maybe that was the key, no father or was it just my family— we are just screwed up! I wonder if they hide things as well as my family does when people come over," Mari mused.

"Yes, you are right. This area is usually overlooked by many people since we are right at the edge of a major highway and the apartment buildings. Lots of trees cover our homes so you really do not notice the houses from the streets. Where do you live, Mari?" Marilyn asked.

"Oh, we live just a couple of blocks away from our school, in the apartments. Pretty close to school," Mari answered, not really knowing what else to say and feeling a major sense of relief when she saw Scott return to the living room with some refreshments and snacks.

"OK, Mom, you can stop interrogating Mari now. She's cool. She's one of the almost normal ones at school," Scott joked.

"Almost normal? I think I resent that!" Mari piped in as Scott handed her a soda and motioned toward some sandwiches and cookies for her to munch on.

"Yeah, I am the only sane person in that school," Scott told his mother while avoiding Mari's stare while she took a modest bite from a chocolate chip cookie.

"You sound and act just like your father." Marilyn laughed as she playfully tugged her son down so he plopped on the sofa right next to her.

"Where is your father? Is he working?" Mari asked, curious to know if she was going to be handed over to some more interrogation before she could actually sit down and play some video games and eat some lunch, although she enjoyed watching Scott and his mom joke with each other.

"No, Mari. Scott's dad died in a car crash nine years ago. He was killed by a drunk driver when he was heading home from work. It's just been Scott and me making it together this last number of years. Been tough but we've been making it," Marilyn answered softly as she glanced over at Scott, who had been giving her a sideward glance.

"How long were you married?"

"Almost twenty-five years. He was the best thing that happened to me aside from this monster sitting next to me waiting for me to hurry up and do a disappearing act so he can get to his video games."

"Wow, that sounds really nice, must be real nice to have someone like him in your life. Looks like you really miss him," Mari responded as she looked at a family portrait where Marilyn was sitting down in a beautiful dress, with her husband sitting by her side while Scott sat between them, grinning at the camera showing his two missing front teeth.

"Yes, I really do. I miss him every day that passes by. He was an amazing husband and father," Marilyn softly said as she stared at the same family portrait Mari was staring at when she asked the question.

"You do not find people like Scott's father every day. He was very hard to come by and it was not always easy, but he had a way of helping me talk things out. He was a very gentle and happy soul. The only other man with that combination of traits is Santa Claus." Marilyn stood up quickly as she realized her eyes were starting to tear.

"You kids have fun. Mari, there is plenty of food so please do not be bashful. Don't let Scott hog all the cookies," Marilyn said as she smiled over at her son, who was staring at their last family photo together.

"Wow, your mom seems so nice. Sounds like she really misses your dad. I am sorry about what happened. Must have been tough losing your dad. He sounds like he was a good husband and dad," Mari stated as she glanced over at Scott, who had not stopped staring at his family photo since his mom had started to talk about his dad.

"Yeah, from what I remember, he was really great. I remember him always twirling me upside down and scaring the crap out of my mom. He would always come in the house and give my mom or me a hug and kiss before he even took off his jacket or got himself all comfortable. He would always say that you never know what could happen so you don't want to take people for granted. Not even for a second. So who cares if he had to wait a few seconds to take off his jacket or put his lunch box or thermos away. It was a few seconds earlier that he got to tell us he loved us and was happy to see us. Everything else could wait," Scott said softly.

"How about your family, are they tight? Are your parents cool with you?" Scott asked Mari.

"Hmm, not really much to say about them. They are your typical normal crazy parents. Very unlike your mom and your dad. Your parents really seemed happy. Mine are just nuts," Mari mentioned before she realized what she was saying and how easy it was to actually talk to someone about her family.

Realizing he must have hit a nerve by the way Mari had clenched her jaw when she spoke about her parents and hoping to make it comfortable again, Scott straightened up quickly and asked Mari if she wanted a sandwich.

"You got to try these samiches. They are crazy good. My mom is a great cook. She is loony sometimes, keeps forgetting stuff, but that woman can cook!"

"What's a samich?" Mari asked Scott.

"Oh, sorry about that. I meant a sandwich. My dad would always call a sandwich a samich since I could never pronounce sandwich when I was growing up. I guess it just stuck. It became kind of a family word," Scott answered as he got up and put on the television and video game console.

"So, what do you want to play? Or should I ask what game do you want to be least embarrassed about losing in? I am the champ of champs when it comes to video games," Scott kidded as he raised his left eyebrow while daring Mari to challenge him.

"Well, we have the old game system, so you may have one over on me, but I am pretty good. Unless you think that just because I'm a girl, you will beat me." Mari stared right back at Scott, mimicking his look.

"Ahhh, so let the games begin!" Scott said as he slid a video game into the console and jumped over the coffee table while plopping onto the sofa next to Mari.

"All right then, no hard feelings when I kick your butt in this game," Mari joked as she picked up her game controller. She immersed herself into the games that she barely noticed four hours had flown by when she heard her watch beep to let her know she had fifteen minutes to walk back home.

"What's that?" Scott asked Mari when he heard the beep.

"Oh, I have fifteen minutes to walk back home so I've got to go now. Thanks a lot. It was pretty cool hanging out and beating your butt. I better say good-bye to your mom," Mari said as she quickly placed the game controller down and hurried around picking up her napkin, plate, and glass so she could take them all into the kitchen. She didn't want to leave a mess behind. She really didn't want Mrs. Allen and Scott to think she was a slob or anything like that.

"Hey, it's cool. You can leave that there. I'll get it. Besides, my mom said she would drive you back to your place. It's starting to get dark out there anyway and we wouldn't want you to walk to your home," Scott said as he took everything from Mari and headed into the kitchen to let his mom know they needed to give Mari a ride home.

"Man, Pearlie, she really needed this kind of a break before going home," I mentioned to Pearl as she lovingly watched the teenagers playing video games, laughing, eating, and having a good time.

"Yes, you are right about that. Hopefully, Mari will continue to open up to Scott. He is a really nice young man who learned the exact opposite of what was taught to Mari growing up. His family really did and still does have a special bond. Very loving family. Actually, Scott's father is a professor at the Spirits' College. He is a senior advisor there."

"You are so kidding, Pearlie! Have I seen him?" I asked Pearl, wondering if I had met him during my classes at the Spirits' College. I was really curious to know if Scott looked like his dad, and I was trying really hard to search my memory bank.

"Look at me. Was I with you while you went to college? Just because I am brilliant and know a lot of things, does not necessarily mean I know everything that you did before you were handed over to my team. I know that you think I am amazing, but believe it or not, I do have other Spirit Guides to train. You are not the only one." Pearlie looked at me as though she was out of her mind. With fifty-five Spiritual Guides in training, Pearl had her hands full, but she kept up. It was her job to train her team well and up to her Master's standards and plan.

"Pearlie, I know you have a ton of others to train but you must admit I am your most favorite, right?" I nudged Pearl by the hip, trying to get a fun rise out of her. I needed to lighten up the atmosphere.

"We need to head over to Mari's house now. A storm seems to be brewing. Not too sure it's headed toward Mari's place." Pearl looked at me as I headed over to Mari's place. Pearl moved into work mode. It looked like the storm was going to come in fierce and fast, from Pearl's troubled eyes.

CHAPTER 27

Scott quickly leaped out of the car so Mari could get out of his mom's car. They still had at least five minutes to spare, so Mari would not have any complaints from her parents for getting home late, Scott thought. He could not believe what a great time he had, many great memories already being formed due to a couple of hours hanging out with Mari playing video games. Who would have thought, Scott thought, as he reached in to grab Mari by the hand to help her out of the front seat of the car where she sat with his mom.

Mari thanked Marilyn for the samiches, snacks, and soft drinks. She also apologized just a little bit for squashing Scott's ingenious gaming skills. She realized Scott would be a sulking kid for a couple of days so hopefully he would not take it out on Marilyn, Mari teased as she was getting out of the car.

"Thank you again, Mrs. Allen. It was great fun. Thank you also for the right. My parents will be happy I got home on time. Have to run upstairs now."

"Mari, anytime you would like to come by, you just tell Scott and he can let me know. I will be happy to pick you up and maybe even meet your parents too as they know who we are," Marilyn responded, very happy to have met Mari and finally met the girl whom Scott spoke about so much. He always seemed to fit Mari into some topic he and she would be speaking about.

"Thank you, Mrs. Allen. I really need to go now," Mari said very quickly, hoping that Marilyn would forget about meeting her parents. Somehow, Mari did not think her parents would approve of her hanging out with Scott. Nothing happened, but her father especially would not believe her.

"Scott, go walk Mari upstairs so she doesn't have to go upstairs alone."

"Oh no, Mrs. Allen, I'm OK. Thank you though. Got to go," Mari quickly said as she ran toward her apartment building's entrance.

"Yo, Scott, thanks again. Great kicking your butt on the video games," Mari teased Scott as she looked back and reached outward to push open the building's glass shatterproof entrance door.

"Yeah, whatever, Mari. I'll get you next time you come over." Scott laughed as he teased Mari back while getting into their car.

Just as she turned to push open the door, she ran right into her father, who had been standing inside the building entrance door watching and hearing the conversation with Scott and his mother.

"Papi, what are you doing here? I mean, I got home early so would not worry you or Mami," Mari stammered her words as she felt every ounce of color leave her face while her knees almost buckled from under her.

"I go out. Yu no need to know where. Yu go upstair and no go anywhere else. I deal wit yu when I get home. Go now!" Benjy said very loudly and sternly through his teeth as to not make a very big scene since he noticed Scott had turned around to look toward the door when he heard Mari talking to a man. The medium-built man had similar facial features to Mari, except for the intense penetrating eyes that projected evil.

"My, Mari, you OK?" Scott called out as he rolled down his car window.

"Yez, she OK. Yu no worry about her," Benjy answered as he stared very seriously at Scott.

"Yes, sir. Thank you. Just wanted to make sure Mari was OK. Are you Mari's father?" Scott asked as he noticed Benjy walking out the door as Mari ran inside the building.

"Yez," Benjy answered very abruptly as he gave Scott a knifelike piercing look and continued walking, not stopping to shake Scott's outstretched hand as Scott got out of the car when he realized there might be some trouble with Mari and this man who had given her a killing look, and who Mari was apparently very terrified of. It shocked Scott to learn it was Mari's father. He would have never guessed a child could ever look at his or her father in such a way. Then again, he was really young when his father was around, so he never got to see a mean side from his dad. As Marilyn pulled out into traffic to head back home, she asked Scott who he was talking to.

"Oh, that was Mari's dad, I think," Scott answered.

"Sweetie, what do you mean you think the man was Mari's dad? The man either was or he wasn't," Marilyn responded, quite confused with her son's answer.

"Mom, I saw Mari talking to this man who looked really mean, and when I asked Mari if she was OK, the man answered for her, saying she was. But she looked real scared. Gave me the creeps! Hope she's OK. I don't have her phone number or her apartment number, so I can't call or go to her place to make sure she's not in trouble," Scott told his mom. He couldn't shake the feeling something was going to go down but didn't know what it was. Scott just felt it would not be something good. Damn, he wished he had asked Mari for her phone number. Actually, he wished he had asked for her phone number a long time ago. Oh well. He'd make sure she was OK when he saw her in school on Monday. He'd make sure of it.

"Pearlie, Benjy looked pretty angry. I'm not sure if I should whisper anything to Mari since I am not sure of what is going to happen. Do you know?" I asked

Pearl as she stared at Mari standing outside her apartment door with her key in her hand. She was just standing outside her apartment door, staring at her key.

"Candace, I don't know what is going to happen. I suspect it will not be a good thing. I think you might want to get her thinking of some safe places she can go to if her father gets ignorant about what happened today," Pearl answered, feeling apprehensive about Mari's situation. Pearl did not think it was a good idea for Mari to omit information on which friend she was going to be spending the afternoon with, although she understood why Mari did not give all the information to her parents. Pearl understood the nightmare that Mari lived in and the challenges she would be going through as early as tonight, yet Pearl did not know the exact details. All Pearl knew was that it was important for Candace to stay very close to Mari. Pearl knew God had a plan for this family. There would be much to endure tonight. Too much! Mari was going to need Candace more than she would ever need anyone in her life. Pearl only wondered if whispers would be enough to get her through what would occur.

CHAPTER 28

"Mari, is that yu?" Sara called out from her bedroom toward the corridor when she heard their apartment door open and close. She had seen Mari get out of the car with a handsome young man and wondered if that was the classmate she had gone to see. Hmm, she did not see a girl classmate come out of the car. Maybe she was in the backseat of the vehicle. Sara had not seen the intense hatred Benjy had on his face when he glared at Scott. Sara immediately left the window to find out what had gone wrong and if she needed to take the kids and go over to her sister's house. No, that wouldn't be a good idea. The last time she did that, Benjy dislocated her shoulder when he shook hard. No, not a good idea at all.

"Mari?" Sara asked again as she headed toward the corridor.

"Si, Mami. Yeah, it's me." Mari barely answered above an audible tone.

"Wha?"

"Mami, yes, it is me. I am home. I wanted to get here on time so you would not worry," Mari said a little louder this time.

"Oh, good. I no sure it was yu or yur papi. He left rite now. Did yu see him?" Sara asked, trying to get information from Mari to find out how serious tonight would be for her.

"Yeah, I saw him. I did not talk to him much," Mari responded on her way to her bedroom, where she quickly latched close her door once she entered.

"Oh, OK. It good yu got here on time. I no have to worry about yu now. Yu here home, yu safe," Sara responded with a slight sigh of relief.

"Not sure I am safe here or not." Mari quivered as she remembered the look on her papi's face when he saw her a few minutes ago. She would surely go into the closet. The question was for how long this time? Damn, she shouldn't have gone to Scott's house today.

"Mari, it is not your fault that you went to visit a friend. Perhaps being honest with your father when he arrives will help him understand why you omitted some information as to who you were going to visit. It was simply a classmate from school. His mom was home and there was an adult in the house. There was adult supervision. You were never alone with Scott. Not once," I whispered to Mari.

Mari stopped pacing in her room and stared toward her bedroom wall close to Candace's position in her room. Mari just shook her head. She felt sick to her

149

Nilsa L. Cleland

stomach. She slumped onto her bed and hung her head between her legs to get some blood flow toward her brain. She hoped that would help get her strength back. Somehow she did not think that was going to happen. She was simply terrified of what her father would do. She wondered when Jonathan would be home from work and hoped he did not have a date tonight. Maybe, just maybe, he might be able to keep her father from sticking her in the closet or whatever else he had in his wicked mind. She also really prayed her stupidity would not get her mother in trouble.

"Oh God, please don't let my father take his anger out on Mami. It was not her fault. It is all my fault. I am the one that is stupid here, no one else. It is my entire fault. I deserve to get punished for not letting them know who I was going to spend some time with. I am the one who deserves to get beat and stuck in the closet. No one else. I can't let Papi hit Mami because of me."

"Mari, you don't know that's going to happen. Why don't you call the police if he tries anything? Get a phone and keep it near you." I whispered advice to Mari. "None of this is deserving of anyone being beat and dragged into a closet for any length of time. Believe me, I know." I tried to console Mari.

Mari continued to hang her head down until she realized her head was starting to touch her floor rug. As she raised her head and lay back on her bed, she could not shrug off a feeling of someone talking to her. She must really be nuts. First, she really screwed up and lied to her parents, kinda lied . . . no, she lied by not telling the complete truth so they would not go ballistic and ground her from visiting Scott. Second, she ran right into her papi as Scott and his mom dropped her off so that her father saw that she was with Scott and not a girl from school, and third, now she would get beat up or put in the closet or, worse yet, get her mami hurt because of her stupidity.

"Damn it, how could I be so dumb, dumb, dumb!" Mari jumped up from her bed as she shrieked her self-anger.

Mari got down on her knees, put her head in her hands while she closed her eyes, and started to pray.

"God, I know you are really busy and all, but I really, really need your help right now. I really messed up. I am sure you already know what happened but if you weren't around and don't know why I am calling out to you right now, I will give you a real short version since I am just too scared to think of everything at this moment," Mari said into her hands as she clenched her eyes shut.

"I did the most stupid thing ever. I did not tell my parents that I was going to hang out with a guy friend from school. Honest, that is all he is, I think. I mean, I like him but it is not like we are going out or anything. All I did was have lunch, meet his mom, and play video games in the living room. His mom was in the house throughout the whole time. She even drove me home. But Papi saw Scott drop me off, so he knows that I wasn't hanging with one of my girlfriends from school. I am really scared that he is going to hurt me or throw me in that closet for a couple of days. But even worse yet, I am so scared he might hit Mami because of me. God, I don't know if you know, I mean, I thought you know everything but if you knew everything, then you would know how bad Papi hits and hurts Mami. It is really scary!" Mari heard herself say. She was trying so hard to pray so that God would really hear her.

"Mari, it's OK. I learned that God does hear you. Keep talking to him. Reveal your innermost thoughts to him. He won't judge you. He really does love you. I know that now," I encouraged Mari as I knelt down next to her.

"Let me get beat instead of Mami, please do not let him hurt her. She is not at fault. He beats her too many times." Mari sobbed softly as she prayed.

"Mari, hija. Adondes estas? Mari, are yu in yur room?" Sara called out, thinking she had heard Mari's bedroom door close.

"Si, Mami, I am here. Yes, I am in my bedroom." Mari coughed a couple of times so that her mother would not think she had been crying or anything else had been wrong. The last thing she needed was her mom breathing down her throat about what was wrong. Yet, maybe she should tell her about her papi seeing Scott dropping her off, so that way, her mom could be ready for her dad. Maybe it would be better if he would not take her by surprise. God, she hated this! Why should she at sixteen years of age have to worry about what her father would do to her mother because of a small mistake, well, maybe a big mistake, Mari thought.

Sara, sensing something was more than wrong, asked Mari to come out and talk to her.

"Mari, Mari? Hija, wha tha matter? Yu look like yu see a ghost," Sara asked as she saw Mari opening her door and coming out into the kitchen light.

"Nothing, Mami. I'm OK, but I think you need to know something before Papi comes home," Mari told Sara.

"OK, wha happen?" Sara asked.

"Mami, I went to have lunch and play video games at my friend's house from school," Mari started very slowly.

"His mother was there the whole time."

"Mari, what yu mean *his* mother there all thee time?" Sara asked very slowly, this time searching Mari's face for additional information.

"Mami, I went over to Scott's house for lunch today. He is a kid from school. His mother made lunch and we played video games," Mari quickly piped in as she saw her mother stiffen when she took two steps away from Mari as though Mari was infected with some contagious disease. Little did Mari know that Sara was trying to figure out how to handle this new happening with her family. She quickly thought of calling her sister, but that might not work since she did not want to get her sister involved. Benjy had said some crazy things about her, and Sara could not risk putting herself in danger. Sara knew Benjy too well.

"Mari, put some clothes in a bag. I call yur aunt and uncle to pick yu up. I tell yur dad that yu went for a visit and they want yu to stay over the house. OK? Go, do it now. Hurry," Sara quickly instructed Mari as she picked up the phone to call her sister and ask if Mari could go over to stay.

Afterward, Sara finished helping Mari pack a couple of things and both were watching television a couple of hours later, waiting for Sara's sister and husband to pick up Mari as Benjy ripped through the door. Benjy, flushed and smelling of beer, bellowed to Sara.

"Do yu know wha yur slut daughter, yur hija, did to me?"

"Benjy, yu must be tired. Go to bed so yu get some rest and we talk in morning. Get some rest, Benjy." Sara got up to walk toward her husband. Just as she reached him, he pulled back and slapped Sara across her face with such force that she hit the wall and fell unconscious to the floor.

"Mami!" Mari yelled as she ran over to help her mother.

"Oh no, yu no go to yur mami now. Yu come wit me." Benjy grabbed Mari upward by her arm as she fell toward Sara lying lifeless on the floor.

"No, let me go. Mami needs help!" Mari screamed and wiggled, trying to get away from her father's death grip on her arm.

"Oh no, yu no go nowhere. Yu come wit me," Benjy yelled as he pulled Mari up by the arm and pulled her so close to him she could barely see his face and only smell his alcoholic breath on her nose.

"Let me go. Mami needs help! Let me go!" Mari yelled as her father continued to hold her against his body.

"No, yu come wit me. Yu want to be wit a boy. I show yu how to be wit a man instead of a boy," Benjy yelled back at her as he dragged her into her parents' bedroom and pushed her onto the bed. Mari was so terrified that she simply lay on their parents' bed without movement. Her body lay limp without any feeling.

"Noooooo, Mari. Move, girl. You need to get up *now*! Get up!" I loudly said to Mari. I could have been yelling my lungs out, but all Mari could hear was a whisper softly tickling her ears. Just a voice telling her to move, yet Mari could not obey. Her muscles would not allow her to.

"Mari, you can do this. I did not fight for my life when I was in your situation, but you are still alive. You can do this. There really is hope and people who truly love you the way that is meant to love. Get up now!" I pleaded with Mari.

"Yu tink yu disgrace this family wit yu going out wit boys and lying to us?" Benjy yelled at Mari as he ripped off his shirt and yanked off his T-shirt, then he started to pull off his belt buckle.

"What are you talking about? I did not go out with boys. I just went to a friend's house to visit him and his mother, have lunch, and play video games." Mari calmly tried to reason with her father as she anticipated what he was going to do next. She could not believe what she was seeing, not from her papi!

"Mari, that is good. Now try to slowly move over to the edge of the bed so you can get up from the bed. Come on now. You can do this. You are worth more than this. You have so many people that love you in ways that truly is love. This, what your papi is trying to do, is not love or punish. You do not deserve this. Come on now, get off the bed, Mari." I tried to coax Mari to move swiftly yet carefully away from her infuriated father. I shuddered at watching Benjy and seeing his hungry and furious distorted face. He no longer looked like a man but an animal ready to pounce on its prey. It sickened me. I remembered seeing, smelling, and being touched by such a creature. Like Mari, I could not believe my father could have done all that he did to me. Yet, I now knew through my classes at Spirits' College and learning about God's love that this was not right. This is not what a loving father does to his daughter. This is not what anyone should do to any person, be it a daughter or loved one. Mari is sixteen years old, a loving soul who loved and cared about her family.

"Papi, I was scared that you would not trust me. That is why I did not say anything about Scott."

"Who Scott? Was that Scott? I will kill him if he touch yu! But yu must learn lesson first." As he responded to Mari, he turned around and walked over to where Sara was lying lifeless. He grabbed Sara by her hair and dragged her to the closet. He simply threw her inside and slammed the door. This time, Benjy did not grab a bowl with water for Sara. He threw her inside like a piece of discarded clothing not to be used for a while. His eyes, wild with rage, refocused on the bedroom where Mari was starting to edge toward the side of the bed.

"Papi, what are you doing? Papi, you cannot do this. Mami loves you and I am your daughter, the daughter who you love and loved as a baby. Remember when you would play with me and my toys, and you would throw me up in the air but not too high so I would not get scared?" Mari tried to get her father redirected into a different frame of mind. She knew he was not thinking straight, and she was too scared to imagine what he was going to do next. She had never seen her father so angry and crazy.

"It's all my fault this is even happening," Mari thought as she started to silently sob trying not to think of what could possibly happen next.

"Yu disgrace our family. Me. Yu make me look bad. Wha will people tink of me, yur father, letting yu go to a boy's house? Ahhh?" Benjy looked around and then he zoned on Mari's face. He looked at her as she lay on the bed with her red sweater and jeans. She looked so mature. Where had the years gone? Benjy thought. As he looked at her, he started to get aroused again. What is he thinking? That is sick even for him, Benjy thought. Just as he was going to teach Mari a lesson, he jumped on Mari and took her face in his hands, cradling her face like a baby. Where did the years go? What went wrong? What did he do that she go and be a whore? Why she do that to him? He did not understand. All he knew was that he had to teach her manners and not to go wit boys again. No, not go wit boys. As he let go of his right hand off Mari's face and moved it backward, forming a fist with his hand, there was a loud knock on their apartment door. This just made Benjy angrier. He grabbed Mari by her hair and pulled her to his bedroom and opened the closet's door and threw her inside with her mother, who was starting to stir and wake slowly.

"Benjy, wha yu do? Benjy," Sara said as she tried to sit up, but having Mari thrown on top of her made her woozy once again as her head hit the closet sidewall. The close quarters of the closet were not designed for two adult people. The closet was designed for clothes. No room to move around comfortably.

"Mari, I am with you. You are not alone. Please, Mari, when you hear the apartment door open, start kicking the closet and yelling at the top of your lungs. Someone has to hear your cries. Do not give up. I know you are scared but I am with you," I whispered to Mari.

"Sara, I am with you. Help Mari by kicking at the door and yelling. Scream like you have never screamed. Loud, very loud! You do not have to live this way," Pearl whispered to Sara as she stroked Sara's hair back due to the blood. Pearl was able to do more than Mari due to the Spirit status she held. Pearl and I both knew nothing could be done if Mari and Sara did not want to yell or bang on the closet doors. Pearl and I knew it was about free will, the choice of wanting a change or wanting to do something. It was not a matter of being forced to do something but a choice to take chances on helping oneself. I brought out of my pocket a poem I have been carrying forever. I read:

"When we are provided choices in life,
We have the ability to bring realism into being.
Do you choose the ability to see yet are blind to life's atrocities?
Will you instead choose hearing and be deaf to the cries of injustice?
We all have a choice.
Why not choose to have a voice?"

CHAPTER 29

"Benjy, wha happin?" Sara's sister Ana asked as she smelled Benjy's alcoholic breath and perspiration-soaked bare chest after he finally opened the apartment door. His pants had the belt hanging open and his hair was in utter disarray. Benjy's hair was never in a mess. Never! Something is very wrong, both Sara's sister and her husband thought as they looked at each other.

"Wha yu want? Sara not here," Benjy stated as he was about to close the apartment door.

"Whoa, Benjy, wha happen wit yu? We come in and wait for Sara. No problema. We wait!" Ana said as she tried to push the door open and walk inside, except Benjy blocked her way inside the apartment.

"Look, Ana, I need to take a shower and get clean clothes. I have Sara call yu," Benjy said as he was closing the door.

"Benjy, we wait inside. Yu no like us anymore? Wha happen to Sara? Why yu no want us to wait inside? She OK?" Ana asked as her voice started to climb in pitch due to her apprehension.

"Ana, not'in' happen to Sara? She OK. No problema, she no here. Tha all. She no here."

"Where Mari? We talk to Mari until Sara get home. OK?" Ana told Benjy so she and her husband Pablo could go inside to make sure Sara was not in danger. Ana had heard horror stories from Sara and had seen some of Benjy's violence plastered all over Sara's face and body. Yet this time was different. Benjy had never blocked Ana and Pablo from entering their apartment before.

"Ana, Jocelyn is calling me. I be back in a second," Pablo stated as he moved slightly away from the apartment door as he answered his phone. Ana could not believe Pablo was leaving her alone to deal with Benjy, but she could not stop with Benjy right now. She had to know what had happened to her sister and niece. She knew it could not be good. She would handle this herself and let Pablo deal with the phone call he needed to take. As Ana continued to talk to Benjy, Pablo dialed 911 on his cell phone. He wanted to make a play that would take him some distance from Benjy but not far enough away that he could not keep a good eye on his wife.

He had never liked Benjy. He just put up with him because his wife's brother-in-law made him family. Pablo had always felt Benjy was a piece of scum who made all decent men gain a bad rap due to his male ego, womanizing, and wife-belittling behavior. Pablo loved his wife, and it would make his skin crawl when he would defend Sara when Benjy would put her down in front of others. He stopped defending Sara when he saw her left eye half shut and swollen due to a beating she had taken from Benjy, after he had told Benjy to stop belittling her in front of a group of friends. Apparently, Benjy had asked Sara if she was having an affair with Pablo. She denied everything of course, but Benjy did not believe her. A black eye and a dislocated shoulder later, Sara called his wife and asked her to please tell Pablo not to say anything about her to Benjy. Pablo did just that. Sara still showed up with bruises on her face, legs, or arms, unless Benjy had gotten really angry and broken her ribs, arms, or hands. Yet, Sara would never complain to anyone and Benjy continued to abuse her.

"911, what is your emergency?" Pablo heard the 911 dispatcher say. He only prayed he could keep the sound low by covering the telephone mouthpiece with his hand.

"Please, come to 123 General Street, apartment 3. Come fast, something wrong here. Yu come now. Please." Pablo spoke low but slowly so he could be understood and heard by the 911 operator. He had always heard that the address should always be given first when calling the 911 dispatcher for an emergency phone call. He learned this during one of his son's school programs. Pablo and Ana had tried very hard to go to all of their children's school programs where parents were invited. His son's school program was focused on the police department and all the services they offered children and the families in their community. They did not know much English, but they were trying to learn as much as they could as quickly as they could so Pablo could get a better job. He was tired of breaking his back in a restaurant washing dishes. He was a hard worker and liked by his bosses and coworkers. He started an English-as-a-second-language class at their children's school twice a week after work. He was determined to make a better life for his family.

"Sir, are you hurt? What is your emergency?" the 911 dispatcher asked.

"I tink my sister-in-law is hurt. Her husban not led me and my wife go inside to see her. We worried she is hurt. Yu come now please. My niece not come to door too. She may be hurt."

"Sir, what makes you think they may be hurt?" the 911 dispatcher asked and she checked Sara and Benjy's address. The dispatcher noticed several domestic violence calls had been dispatched to this address.

"Sir, who is in the apartment right now?" the 911 operator asked.

"My wife is talking to Benjy, my sister-in-law's husband rite now. He smell of mucho alcohol. He look drunk."

"Sir, do you feel your wife is safe right now speaking to Mr. Santiago?" the 911 operator asked as she searched her monitors to find out which officers were close to the Santiago address.

"No, not rit. Mane now. Benjy no look rite."

"Sir, one moment, please, let me see who is near that address that—"

"Ayudame, help me!" A loud shriek by Sara followed by a hard bang to the closet door by Mari and Sara startled Benjy and Pablo.

"Sara! Mari!" Ana yelled as she pushed Benjy out of the way, knocking him down as she ran down his apartment's corridor.

"Ana, yu stop now. Get out my house!" Benjy yelled as he struggled to get up off the floor.

"What is happening right now? Who is yelling? Is anyone hurt?" the 911 operator asked as she clicked on her controls to radio her officers and let them know the escalation level had risen at this call.

"Hurry now. Sara and Mari are in apartment and they scream." He had also learned this during his son's school police program. The 911 dispatcher will continue to monitor the phone call while the phone is still connected to them. He kept his cell phone hidden so Benjy could not see it and try taking it. Pablo told the 911 dispatcher as he ran to the apartment and pushed Benjy down onto the floor. When he saw Benjy was getting up, he would not let Benjy hurt his wife, sister-in-law, and niece. Pablo did not shut off the call to the 911 dispatcher so she could hear and record all about was going on in the apartment. He did not want to make things worse than they already were for Sara and Mari.

As he and Ana reached the living room, she could see Sara sliding out of the closet through the broken closet wall slats and reaching outside the closet with her hand. Having called out for Sara, she could see Mari being barely pulled out of the closet by her mother due to the weakened state she was in.

"Sara, Sara! Mari!" Ana yelled. "Pablo, call the ambulancia! Call policia! Sara and Mari need help. Call!" Ana yelled to Pablo. Little did Ana know that Pablo had already contacted 911 and help was on the way.

"Mari, help is on the way. You and your mom will be OK. Hang in there," I whispered to Mari as she stared at the walls in front of her, not knowing what to do. She just sat and stared. Maybe the day will pass by and night will fall. Maybe, just maybe, the morning will erase all that had happened and life will be back as it was in the morn. Yet somehow she sensed that would not happen.

"Wait, yu go now. Sara and Mari OK. I take care of them. Yu go now, all good," Benjy said as he had gotten himself up and run down the corridor into the bedroom when he heard Sara, Mari, and Ana speaking. Benjy almost shit in his pants when he heard Ana talking to his wife and daughter. He still thought he might be able to talk his way out of this mess. Why the hell did his wife's stupid sister and her dumb husband have to come by? Now I have to try to get them to go away and not make a big thing out of this. Sara and Mari get what is coming to them. They not know when to shut up and act like proper women. Stupid and now it is their fault, they got me in this mess. Look wha I have to clean up because of my stupid wife and daughter. I no know wha I do wit them now. So stupid.

So stupid! Just as Benjy was going over to get Sara away from Ana's death grip on her, he heard police sirens. Benjy knew the police were coming to get him even though in his mind, he had not done anything wrong. It was Ana's and Pablo's fault that the police were there. They be the ones who make the mess he in now. Then again it was Sara's fault. She be always the one who made a mess of everything. Now he had to clean up after her. Carajo! Mari was part of the problem. If she no got in the way, he would not have to put her in closet with her mami. Why Sara and Mari no act right? He try to make a home and give them everything they need. Why no they appreciate wha he do? Ahh, women! Wha they know? Who care? He no care. He tell police Sara and Mari crazy and they know not'in'. Sara know better than go against him. She have not'in' without him. She know her place. Just as Benjy was finishing his thoughts in his head, he heard her loud bang on his apartment door.

"Hello?" Benjy called out to the door as though the police could hear him from the bedroom. Another loud bang and, this time, the police made sure they announced who they were.

"Mr. and Mrs. Santiago? This is the New York Police Department. If you are inside the apartment or anyone is inside this apartment, please open the door slowly," Officer Williams, a dedicated and no-nonsense New York police officer said as he placed his right hand on his revolver and moved to the right side of the door. His partner, rookie Sally Hays, stood on the other side of the door. After eighteen years on the force, he knew domestic violence calls were unpredictable. Sally was his responsibility, as were the people inside the apartment. He was the senior ranking officer on the scene. It was up to him to ensure everyone would stay safe while they were there investigating the call. No one would get hurt on his watch if he could help it. No one!

CHAPTER 30

"Ugh, this sucks!" Mari thought as she tried to get to her feet. She felt so dizzy and out of it. She had never been locked in a closet that long. The small area she had been crammed into had taken a toll on her whole body and she twisted her torso around to give her mom some type of breathing room. Plus, the smell of cleaning detergents her mom used to try to take away the smell of her bathroom needs in the closet was very intoxicating. Mari's throat was on fire! Remembering her mother in the closet and thinking of how many times her father might have put her inside that trapped box made her angry, hurt, and sad at the same time. How could he do that to someone he loved? How could he stick his own daughter in the closet too? Mari tried to think desperately of what she had ever done to her papi that would make him do that to her. What did she do?

I stood by Mari's side as she tortured herself with guilt for perhaps being the cause of this whole mess.

"Mari, it's understandable why you are feeling all this stuff. It hurts like hell. It isn't fair you have to go through it, as well as your mom, but you will be safe now. Speak with the police, and it's OK to talk with them. They can also help you by having you speak with an advocate that could help you with the homelife. You are not betraying your father by talking to them. If not, a close friend, someone you think can help you to deal with what is happening in your life." I tried to reassure Mari.

"I don't get it. Why? What did we do? What did I do?" Mari whispered in response to my previous conversation with her. Mari in her zombie state did not realize she had spoken back to someone whom she could not see.

"Mari, you are OK now. The police are here and you can tell them what has been going on here. You do not have to live like this, and you can have the police help you out. It may feel like you are not helping your family, but you really are. The police will get you in contact with people who specialize in situations like this if you do not feel comfortable speaking to them. They can help answer questions you, your mom, and your brother may have."

"I don't understand. I don't understand. What did Mami do? What did I do? Why does he get so angry? Mari mumbled to herself as she walked to her room, feeling as though she had the whole world on her shoulders.

"Mari, it'll be faster, you can do it, girl. You're stronger than you think, and right now, what is important is to get to a safe place, and your dad can finally get the help he needs. This is not the way to raise a family!" I said as I leaned into Mari while she sat on her bed.

Another knock was heard from the front door. Sara instantly pushed herself from Ana's arms. Before Ana knew it, Sara was halfway through the kitchen and headed down the corridor. Then she adjusted by the door watching Sara walking toward him. He made no attempt to move toward her. Sara did not look at him. The police officer immediately intercepted Sara as he opened the door wider, pinning Benjy to the wall behind it. The police officer positioned himself between Benjy and Sara, ensuring no one would be able to touch one another.

"Mrs. Santiago?" Officer Williams asked.

"Yez," Sara whispered since she was not able to speak well with her swollen lip. She had hit the back wall of the closet with the side of her face and lip really hard when Benjy threw her in the closet. She had also dislocated her shoulder and was holding her left elbow and arm with her right hand, trying hard not to make a big deal out of it.

"Let's go to the living room so we can talk for just a little. My partner is calling an ambulance so we can make sure you are OK."

"Oh no, please. I OK. I no need doctor. I stay here. No doctor," Sara mumbled out, holding on to a muffled sob. She needed to be strong for Mari. There were just too many strangers in her house and she felt overwhelmed. But she had to be strong for Mari. As she thought of Mari, panic overtook her as she realized she had not seen Mari since she had been pulled out of the closet. With so many bodies surrounding her and voices asking questions, she got lost in the chaos. She had to find Mari!

"*Mari, Mari, Mari. Adonde estas, hija?* Where are you? Mari, Mari—" Sara frantically slipped away from the officer and started to run toward the closet, screaming at the top of her lungs for her daughter, the one person whom she knew she had to be with, the one person whom she had to do her best to protect. But how?

"Mrs. Santiago, your daughter is right in her bedroom and officer Daly. She is OK, as well as can be expected. You can go see her, but it may be a good idea if I can have you answer some questions about the situation beforehand, even though it may be painful. You can go see your daughter, but I would appreciate it if we can get right back to discuss seen what happened earlier while it is fresh on your mind," Officer Williams said as he gently tried to get in front of Sara and seeing Mari for the moment.

Sara ran away from Officer Williams with a look of bewilderment and ran into Mari's room. She pulled Mari up to give her the hardest hug she had ever given her. At this point, Sara simply sobbed into Mari's hair and begged for her forgiveness. "Mari, I sorry. I so sorry. I sorry—"

"Mami, it's not your fault. I can't believe this is happening. We will be OK, Mami. It was my fault. I should not have made Papi angry."

"No, Mari, it no your faul. It my faul I mak sure I mak it better. I fix all," Sara tried to reassure her daughter so she would not be scared. Sara had no idea what she was going to do. What will happen to Benjy? What will happen to her and the children? Who was going to take care of the children and her? How will bills be paid? *Ay, Dios mio!* Oh my dear God, what have I done? Why did I make Benjy angry?" Sara agonized.

"Mrs. Santiago, please let us go back into the living room while my partner talks with your daughter and I may speak with you," Officer Williams told Sara as he gently moved around her, guiding her toward the room.

"Wha about Benjy? Wha will hapen to im? I sorry, I no wan no trouble," Sara pleaded to Officer Williams. She could barely understand what she was saying since her lip had grown twice its size since the officers had arrived at her apartment.

"Mr. Santiago is being questioned by our partners. They will take his statement and we the officers will discuss the situation and find out what would be the best idea or process for you and your family to make sure everyone will be safe," Officer Williams told Sara. He really disliked domestic violence calls. These calls are always dangerous, sometimes deadly. You never know whether those you are visiting are calm or there is a hostage situation that can occur or if the victim will be cooperative with them, many factors and sometimes too short a period to manage the domestic violence calls. You never knew if you would get the complete story from the victim because the person is too scared to tell all the facts. Parts of the story are forgotten due to what might come next. Seeing someone that you loved being hauled away in handcuffs can be overwhelming. The sense of guilt that the victim feels for her loved one being hauled away can immediately change that person's mind. That person's life has just changed and the emotional pain may overrun the physical pain. He understood the domestic violence cycle and the need to break it for victims but the victims have to decide for themselves. They could help as much as they could with information or contacting the local prevention for domestic violence agency for an advocate to come see the victim and the family, but it was still a mess! His heart felt heavy for the children. They always seemed to get the bad rap on this crap.

"Mrs. Santiago, I want you to know that we work with an agency that has people that can come talk to you about these type of situations. They can talk to you about ways you can protect yourself and how to avoid it happening to you and your family again. Right now, they can talk to you about what to expect these next couple of days if you decide to press charges. I went ahead and contacted one of the advocates in the agency to meet us here in case you wanted to speak with her. They will be here in a few minutes if you would like to talk to them or you can just listen to what they have to say. The lady who is coming over speaks Spanish, so it will be easier for you to talk to her. Is that OK?"

"Yez, OK," Sara said robotically.

"So Mrs. Santiago, I am going to ask you some questions about what happened earlier. Do you understand me? We can't wait until the Spanish advocate arrives to ensure you understand everything."

"No, I talk now," Sara said.

Officer Williams took out his notepad and looked at Sara with understanding eyes and a relaxed professional posture. He wanted to make sure Sara would not freeze up on him if she saw Mr. Santiago. He directed her toward a seat that was not in the line of view of the hallway where Mr. Santiago was being held and questioned. Just as Sara was going to speak, a police officer came by and nodded to Officer Williams.

"Mrs. Santiago, I am sorry, but I need to speak to my partner for a very quick second."

"What's up? You headed to the station?"

"Yeah, Jack and I are going to take Mr. Santiago now. His story just does not jive with what happened here. Jana just got here from the prevention of domestic violence agency and is still speaking with the Santiago daughter and her aunt. She can help you out once she's done. Also, Harry from CSU radioed and he has Gail from PDVA also with him. They will be here in less than five. She and he have cameras to take photos of Mrs. Santiago, her daughter, Mr. Santiago's closet, and the home. Depending on how the interview with Mr. Santiago goes, we'll see whether we will keep him overnight or not. We also need to know if Mrs. Santiago is pressing charges. Keep me posted with what's happening. I'll be in the hallway."

"Cool, sounds like a plan. Damn I hate these fucking cases. So much destruction when there does not need to be," Officer Williams mumbled to his colleague.

"Tell me about it. This is my second one of the night and can't wait for my shift to be over already. Let me know if you need anything. Yak at you later."

The policewoman went to check on Benjy and ensure he would continue to maintain his calm while Sara discussed the evening's situation with Officer Williams when he arrived in the living room. He wanted a verbal account of what happened and then he would have her write down a written statement before he left. It would be a long night. He wondered if there was a full moon.

"OK, Mrs. Santiago. Why don't we start with the moments before you found yourself in the closet? What happened?" Officer Williams gently asked Sara.

"Ahhhh, I wash television wit Mari, my daughter, and Benjy, my hosban get very, very angry becoz my daughter went to hav lunch at her friend house."

"Mrs. Santiago, your husband got this angry because your daughter had lunch with a friend? Does he always get this way when your daughter has lunch with her friends? Was this a friend your husband did not like?"

"Her friend is boy. My hosban no lik her hav boyfriends. She too yung. I no tink she do not'in' bad, but Benjy vas drinking and he go crazy. He no bad hosban.

He good to me and children. He work hard and sometime he drink beer. Tat all," Sara said softly, hoping the people in her house would instantly disappear and things would be back to normal.

"I understand, Mrs. Santiago. Please go on and tell me what happened next when your husband got angry. Take your time. I know it is hard but you are doing great."

"Ahh, not'in' really happin. Benjy get angry. He take me by hair and put me in closet. Then I hear him yell at Mari and put her in closet wit me. He just angry. He no mean wat he do. He drink and lose his head. I no wan troble wit *policia.*"

"Mami, you know that Papi did not just put us in the closet. He threw us in the closet. Are you OK?" Mari told Sara as she barged into the living room and hugged her mom. She also wanted the police to know the truth and not a softened-up version of it. She loved her papi but he needed help. Maybe he could get fixed up and they could all be happy again Mari silently prayed.

"Mari, yur papi no tink. He good fater and hosban to us. Yez, Mari, I OK. Yu hurt?" Sara said as she touched Mari and checked her to make sure she was physically well. She noticed some very bright red spots on Mari's face near her hairline and cheek. She also noticed some bruising on her arms.

"Mami, I'm OK. So, officer, what else is going to happen to my family? When will everyone go away? What is going to happen to my dad?" Mari asked Officer Williams.

"She is really scared, Pearlie, but she is just doing it. She made sure her mom didn't sugarcoat the incident. Man, it must be so hard for Mari right now, and her mom is so scared too. I sense Mari's fear because she is worried her family is going to get broken up because of her. She just wants her family to be happy and everyone to go away. She wants a normal life away from here. I can sense how her guilt is just digging so deep into her soul. I will need to really whisper to her hard and hope I get through to her. I feel as though I did not help her enough," I told Pearlie with a heavy heart.

"Little one, you did and are doing what you can. Yes, she is hurting. She's confused and she doesn't know what to do. She thinks she's weak and she is not sure how life will turn out because she thinks she shouldn't have gone over to Scott's house. We both know she didn't do anything wrong. Benjy has some demons he must get rid of. We can talk about that later. Right now, I want you to know you have done nothing wrong with Mari. She is stronger than she thinks she is. You just need to continue being there with her and whispering conversations that will give her that inside strength she holds and needs to release." Pearlie turned to me and responded to my insecurities.

"But, Pearlie, maybe I told her to do something wrong. Maybe she sensed what I was saying, did what I suggested, and now she is in this mess. Maybe it's my fault, Pearlie." I fretted as I told Pearlie my concerns. This is so weird, I am a Spiritual Guide and I am insecure. Weird! "Stop, Candace. You did not do anything wrong. You came into this case knowing lots of unknowns were going to happen. Situations are in motion. Mari is very strong. She does not realize it, and it is up to you to let her know this. She understands more than you are giving her credit for."

"I know, Pearlie, I just do not want to steer her toward the wrong direction. I do not want her to go through what I went through if there is a way to avoid it. Also, I do not want her to end up like me."

"I know you do. That is what I have come to love about you. It is your heart and desire to help—"

Just as Pearl was going to continue speaking to me, we heard a deep moan coming from Sara.

"No, I no have my hosban go to jail. I talk to judge and tell him Benjy no mean to hit me or Mari. Wat are we going to do witout im? How I feed my children and pay rent for apartment? No, I no wan not'ing to happin to him."

"Mrs. Santiago, I realize this is a difficult situation. How did this happen, Mrs. Santiago?"

"Mami, stop. Tell him. Enough! Papi hits you and he puts you in the closet for days. We cannot take you out of there or we will be put in the closet too and makes it longer for you and us to get out. I am scared for you and us. What if he comes back and is angrier? This is all my fault. I should have never gone to Scott's house. This is all because of me."

"No, it is not, Mari," Detective Williams interrupted. "You did not make your father drag your mother into the closet. You did not cause him to hurt you by putting you into a dark closet full of this stink of life. This is about an illness or an issue your father has. So, Sara and Mari, what do you want to do? Would you like some time to think about it in your home and have Mr. Santiago come back to you in a couple of hours when he has had time to cool off? Or would you like to press charges against Mr. Santiago for assault?"

"Oh no, no jail for my Benjy," Sara mumbled.

"Mrs. Santiago, I understand this is a lot for you to take, and my biggest concern is keeping you and your family safe. We will be able to talk to Mr. Santiago and he will understand we intend to keep him for a number of hours tonight in jail. My big concern is that he will continue to hurt you all because he does not understand what is making him do this. Maybe he will get better or maybe he will not. It is your choice," Detective Williams said as he closed his notebook and looked at both Sara and Mari, hoping they would do the right thing. He knew deep inside that Mr. Santiago was not going to change by going back home. He had seen this same scenario workout too many times. He had seen wives and partners give the abusive person a chance, only to see the wives and partners several weeks later, again in the same situation with much more severe wounds both physically and emotionally. What he wanted to tell Mrs. Santiago was to look at her daughter and think of her son and ask herself if she wanted them to walk in her footsteps and his footsteps when they got into relationships. Yet he knew that there was a certain fine line that he could not cross even though he wanted to. He wanted to help them so much but he had to do it by the book and ensure the prevention of domestic violence advocate could get through to them, especially Mrs. Santiago. Detective Williams had to hold on to hope that Sara and Mari would make a choice that would keep them safe.

"OK, I tink I do not wan to say not'in' about my hosban." Sara stated very sternly as she stared at Mari ignoring the detective, wishing he would disappear.

"Mami, what are you doing? What are you saying? Papi punches you, he spits at you, and you just spent a weekend inside a closet. I know, I was with you! Do you not remember I pissed in my pants because I did not have room to pull down my pants to pee in the small pot he put in the closet. *Mami, ayudame.* Mami, help me understand. I love Papi too, but I do not like living like this. He held us in a closet. He gave us water and bread as if we were prisoners. No, it has to stop!" Mari screeched at the top of her lungs. She felt as if she was having an out-of-body experience. She wanted to shut up so badly so she wouldn't rock the boat or wish this whole horrible situation away. Why did her stupid self have to go to Scott's house? It's all my fault again, she thought as she stared out into space.

"Mrs. Santiago, Mari is correct. It is not your fault and it is not his fault. The fact is that your husband put you and your daughter in a closet and held you hostages in your own house. Do you think that is the right thing to do to a wife and daughter? However, again, this is your choice," Detective Williams asked Sara while he tried to bring her eyes from the floor to his.

"Wha yu wan me to do? Where do I go? Where I go wit my kids? I no have money. How I take care of my kids wit no money? I no be able to feed them. I love my children and I love my hosban. I wan my family together." Sara wept into her hands as she slowly walked backward until she reached the wall and slid downward onto the floor into a fetal position and simply cried. Mari ran to her mother and cried with her until she was sobbing dry tears. No one approached them. Detective William walked into the kitchen and called on his phone to the officer holding Benjy in the back of his cruiser.

"Pete, this is Detective Williams. Let Mr. Santiago go. It seems Mrs. Santiago does not want to press charges. We'll have to let go of another one. Good ole family love fest. This fucking sucks!"

"I feel you. It's not right. We come out and can even get our asses killed not knowing if these domestic-violence perps have guns or knives. They can get us while we are trying to help them. No prob, I will let this scumbag go. I'll be inside in a minute," Patrolman Jackson responded and roughly pulled Benjy out of the backseat of his cruiser. They walked back inside the Santiago residence.

"Pete, hold him in the hall a minute," Detective Williams yelled out so Benjy was not brought into the kitchen where Sara was nonresponsive. He pulled open his notebook folder and pulled out two cards with a pamphlet.

"Mari, please put this in a safe place in your room, and when your mom is ready, maybe tomorrow, make sure she takes these business cards and pamphlet. Tell her to put them in a safe place you and she will know about. This is a business card with my contact information in case you need to call me. It doesn't have to be if your dad is trying to hit you or you are in danger. You can just call me to talk about resources. I will do what I can to make sure you and your mom, brother, and dad will be OK. It might be kinda tough at first but things can turn around. If you don't want to talk to me, I'm giving you a card of a really great agency that helps families that are going through some really hard times. I am sorry your mother did not want to speak with the prevention of domestic violence agency advocate. The name on the other card is of another advocate or friend in that agency that you can call if you want to talk or if you want more information for your mom or you about restraining orders, which means your father cannot come one hundred yards or less from this apartment or your family. They can also give you information about places you and your family can go to so your father cannot come near you or know where you are. They can also help you get account floor that will help you sort all of this stuff out. Many times, these situations just stick in your head. I am also giving you a pamphlet for you both to read. It talks about domestic violence. It is not something you want to ignore. If you ignore it, you can get trapped in what is called the circle of violence. Life just goes around and around in the same way and nothing good ever comes out of it. But the advocate of the agency can explain more to you than I can now. Mari, just know there is real help out there if you reach out. Sara, I promise you, you will find a hand and you will not be alone," Detective Williams whispered as he put both cards and pamphlet and placed them in Mari's hand. Mari felt the pamphlet and slid it inside her blouse. She reached over and held her mom and slowly continued rocking her.

"Once again, the child takes care of the parent," I whispered to Pearl. Pearl did not say anything to me as she guided me toward Mari. I gently placed my hand on Mari's shoulder and leaned forward to her and spoke directly in her ear. "This is not your fault. Please do not put this burden on your shoulders. I've been where you are and you do not deserve to be in this position. You are a kid and should be loved and not pushed into a closet as a piece of trash. You are worth so much more. You all are. Listen and reach out to someone. Open your heart to trust. I know it's hard to believe me, but you have many people around that truly love you and care for you. Also, I will always be by your side. Just call out to me, Candace, if you ever just need to talk or need some strength. You have a ton of it, but it is nice to lean on someone too when you get tired," I whispered softly to Candace.

Mari looked up and saw nothing except for Detective Williams writing in his notebook. She reached over to Sara and stroked her face softly, brushing any hair that was stuck to her face because of the tears.

Mari looked up and whispered, "Candace, if you haven't noticed, this is not a fairy-tale ending like Cinderella. There is a beautiful princess, but she is not being hauled off to a castle by a kind and handsome prince, just a wannabe prince being hauled off to jail while his beautiful gentle princess is left in shambles."

I leaned into Pearl and watched Mari hug her mother quietly while my own tears washed my face.

CHAPTER 31

Detective Williams finally finished his paperwork and slammed close his notebook. He saw Mari hugging her mother. He went over and kneeled down next to Sara.

"Mrs. Santiago, since you are not going to charge your husband, we are going to release him to your home. We can hold him overnight so he can cool off if you feel you and your children are in danger. Do you want me to do that or do you want to have Mr. Santiago come back inside your home?" He looked at them, already knowing what the answer to the question would be. He had handled too many of these cases!

"Detetiv Wiliams, I wan my hosban to stay in his house. My children and me be OK. Tank yu for coming to my house. I take care of my hosban. He be OK here. Tank yu," Sara said as she lifted her head off of Mari and struggled to stand upright.

"Mrs. Santiago, I gave Mari my card and some information that you may find very useful. Please read them or have Mari talk to you about it. Just know I am here for you. Also, the lady from the Prevention of Domestic Violence who spoke to you, please keep her card. She is still here speaking with your sister. Our business cards are very important to have. Just call us if you need us," Detective Williams said as he slowly lifted his hand to shake both Sara's and Mari's hands.

"Tank yu, Detetiv Williams. We be OK," Sara said as she looked stoically to the wall in front of her, behind Detective Williams.

"OK, Mrs. Santiago, just know I am only a phone call away. Also, we will have a car patrol this area tonight if possible. Do you understand?"

"Yez, tank yu," Sara responded, looking at Detective Williams.

Gail from the PVD walked over slowly as she saw the detective finishing with Sara. She knew that Sara would not listen, but she would still attempt to talk with her for at least a moment.

"*Sra. Santiago, le puede hablar sobre su situacion y las opciones y recursos que usted tiene? Nosotros les podemos ayudar lo mas posible para su familia y usted?*" Gail asked Sara if she could speak with her regarding the options and resources available to her and her family.

"*No, muchisimas gracias y desculpe que tuvo que venir para nada,*" Sara responded to Gail, informing her that she apologized for Gail having to come out for nothing.

"*Esta bien, Sra. Santiago. Yo me comunico con usted or Mari luego en la semana para hablar con usted sobre un hogar en cual usted y su familia puede colocarse si a caso su situacion con el Sr. Santiago sucede de nuevo. La dejo con este comentario, como se va a sentir usted si esta situacion sucede de nuevo con su hija. No deje que su esposo las ponga en un hospital con el amor que el siente para su familia. Es peligroso. Por favor llamame. Podemos hablar mas.*" Gail turned to Sara and spoke about another place they could go to for shelter should another situation occur.

"*Gracias.* Tank yu," Sara said.

"Mari, I let your mom know that I will call later this week to follow up with you guys. I want to make sure everyone is doing well and is safe. I also let her know that we have a safe house in the event another one of these situations occurs, which I hope not, but we currently have space available for your mom, you, and your brother. I also left her with this comment, do not let your father love you so much that one or both of you will end up in a hospital or worse. It is dangerous," Gail spoke softly to Mari as she had risen and was standing by Sara.

"No, I stay here. I and my familia stay here! Tank yu!" Sara interrupted as Mari was going to say something to Gail. Sara was very firm as she stared at the floor. It was too much for her to take in right now. Sara had never had anyone aside from her family come into her home. Now she had the police and this lady from another organization, who were all complete strangers to her and her family. People had already gathered outside as she went to her bedroom window to get some air. She quickly looked away and shut the blinds so no one could see her. She felt so embarrassed and ashamed that she could not keep things away from others. Now Ana and Pablo knew what was going on in her family. It was shameful. She did not want her secret of being beaten by Benjy to become public. Now her own daughter has been thrown into the despicable closet and she would know how disgusting her father can be. Sara had to figure out a way to protect her family from Benjy so they would not be joined in her shame. She was a terrible wife and mother for having others come into her home like this.

"Pete, why don't you bring Mr. Santiago over to me," Detective Williams bellowed, trying to control his voice since he was still watching Mari sitting on the floor, hovering toward the wall her mother just finished warming up a few seconds ago. She looked so vulnerable and Detective Williams hoped she would be one of the fortunate ones that would break those chains that hold so many children in their parents' footsteps be they good or bad.

As Benjy approached Detective Williams, he just looked at him, not knowing what to expect next. All he knew was that soon Sara would get her due diligence by his hand. He would wait until the right time as not to bring the cops around again.

"Mr. Santiago, you are free to go without any charges pressed against you by Mrs. Santiago. I will tell you that if I hear one loud sound from this apartment or anywhere that you are with anyone else, to include Mrs. Santiago or any other family member or friend, I will personally be here to take you downtown to jail. Do you understand me, Mr. Santiago? Do I need an interpreter to ensure you understand what I am saying?" Detective Williams loudly enunciated every word to ensure Mr. Santiago understood.

"I understand. No problema. No loud noise from me or anyone, offizer," Benjy meekly said as he looked straight into Detective Williams's eyes.

"My name is Detective Williams. Good! Mrs. Santiago, please do not hesitate to call me or 911 if you need help." Detective Williams knew the look Benjy had. It had another side to it. He had seen it before so many times and it sickened him that he could not help. He did not know how this case would end, but he hoped it would end on a much better note than others he had seen. He slammed his notebook shut, trying to get rid of the sick feeling in his stomach, knowing that he would be back. He just did not know under what circumstance.

All Sara would think about was her daughter and son. How could she send her husband to jail when she had her daughter and son to think about? She would not go back to Puerto Rico to her parents' house or even her sister Ana's house with her children. Sara had to take care of her children and not bother someone else. She would accept whatever Benjy had in his arsenal against her. She would deal with Benjy as long as he would not hurt her children.

"Detective Williams, what about my family, Ana and Pablo? I do not want any trouble from my hosban and them. I no wan no more trouble," Sara said.

"Mrs. Santiago, I will go speak with them. I will have them go home and if you want to call them, that is OK, but we do not want you to ignite any problems too. Understand?" Detective Williams clearly stated to Sara as though she would talk to Ana and make them pissed off about what happened. Then Ana and Pablo would come over and fight Mr. Santiago.

"Detective Williams, I sure all be calm between my hosban and my familia. No one go to jail," Sara replied.

"Yo, what the hell is going on over here? Hey, you with the badge, why are there so many NYPD Blues out here, to include yourself? The whole neighborhood is lit up with the cop lights," Jonathan asked Detective Williams.

"What is your name, son?" Detective Williams asked.

"First off, I ain't your son. Second of all, I am the resident's son. My name is Jonathan Santiago. So, again I ask what's going on?" Jonathan asks a little more softly.

"Your parents had a scuffle with each other and we came out to make sure everyone was OK. Do you know about the *special closet*?" Detective Williams asked, to see if the son was a conspirator or with his father against his mother and sister.

"Whatcha talking about? I know nothing about no closet! What are you talking about a special closet?"

"Well, it seems your father had put your mother and sister into the closet with just a small pail for them to do their business when it was necessary. You understand?" Detective Williams continued to probe to ensure if Jonathan was or was not involved with Benjy's domestic violence.

"What did mom and my sis do to piss off my dad?" Jonathan asked.

"Oh, so it might have been your mother and sister's fault that caused your father to put them both in the closet? Are you kidding me? Your mother and sister did nothing as far as I can see to initiate your father getting *pissed off* and incite your father to treat them like animals. You get me?" Detective Williams asked as he got really close to Jonathan and could feel his breath. "That is not what I meant, officer. I mean sometimes my mom gets to nagging and hollering at my dad and you know, he has to shut her up," Jonathan said very slowly and articulately.

"Well, let me tell you, Mr. Jonathan Santiago. I have gone to too many domestic violence scenes and this one is definitely no different. Your dad has no right to shut your mom up by putting her in a closet or giving her a black eye. That is number one. Secondly, your dad has no right to bring in his daughter into a domestic violence scene that he created that is absolutely crazy! A situation in which your sister could have really gotten hurt. This is domestic violence at its worst and it needs to stop. Smacking a person around is not the answer. Nor is it violence. I am here to help you and your family be safe, you feel me?" Detective Williams said as he started to give Jonathan some time to breathe in what is going on in his home and decide whether he would help his mother or his father.

"Yeah, I dig. Are my mom and sis OK?" Jonathan asked.

"Yes, they are physically OK but are not emotionally OK. They, especially your mom, are going to need your support and your sister support for a while," Detective Williams stated.

"I ain't gonna go against my dad. I love my mom and sis, but you know, I don't know the whole story. I gots to hear it from my pops," Jonathan told Detective Williams.

"I hear you. You love your father and want to hear about. I get it. But it does not give him or anyone else the right to hurt and abuse anyone in the way that he did. Without the proper ventilation and food, your mother and sister would've died. Do you get what I am saying? Your mother did not ask to be put and kept in that closet, nor did she deserve to be punched. Your sister did not deserve to be thrown in that closet either."

"Yeah, I get you," Jonathan replied.

"What you need to say is 'Yeah, I get you, Detective Williams.' You feel me?" Detective Williams said as he got in front of Jonathan, ensuring he was looking at Detective Williams's face. Detective Williams wanted Jonathan to understand the severity of his home's situation. He understood how Jonathan wanted to have his father's back but Detective Williams also wanted Jonathan not to inherit his father's way of handling a domestic argument.

"Yeah, I feel you, Detective Williams. I don't want my mom or sis to be hurt," Jonathan said softly as he looked down.

"Jonathan, here is my card. If you need someone to talk to, call me, text, or e-mail me. I will do my best to quickly connect back with you and if I can't answer what you are asking me, I will do my very best to find you an answer or someone else that can answer any questions you may have. Just know you do not have to have this burden on your shoulders. There are many professionals who are around that can help you and your family."

Pearl and I just stood next to Mari and Sara, also hearing what Detective Williams was telling Jonathan. We also understood Jonathan's emotions and all he was trying to unravel. Pearl had felt this way too and had seen too many cases that she did not care to remember since they did not always end very happily. I, being a newcomer, felt sick to my stomach. I wanted to shake Mari yet I knew I could not. I felt so helpless since I knew deep in my heart that Mari did not want to stay here with her father and mother together. Mari also did not want to go to some type of safe house where she would not know anyone and would have to share her life with strangers. She wanted to stay home with her parents, taking out the fighting part of course. It's right now, she just wanted to get through this night. Her aunt and uncle were sent home to avoid any type of altercations with Benjy that might start another incident visit from Detective Williams and his police buddies.

Mari was grateful for Detective Williams coming to rescue them from that hellhole of the closet. Mari could not stand the smell and could not believe her father had put her mother in there several times, plus shoved her too into the "get right" closet. The worst part was knowing her mom had spent time in this closet in the past without her knowing about it. Mari would have definitely done her best to get her mom out of there. It was a damn closet. It was big enough for clothes and not for a human being, especially two human beings. There isn't a bathroom in the closet. There was a bucket for her mom to do her number one and number two businesses. The smell was horrible, yet her mom had to clean it to the point no odor would ever come out of there except for a good fragrance. She would definitely not forget it. This just creeped her out.

"I keep saying the same thing but I have to repeat it. Mari and Sara should never have been put in that stench-filled closet. What was Benjy thinking? I know he was not thinking. His hate was simply coming out," I said as I retreated toward Pearlie.

"Hold on there, little one. Benjy is infected with knowledge passed down onto him. His father, his father's father were all like that. Does it make it right? *No, it does not!* But, it is what it is. It is up to you to get through to Mari and help her help Sara. It's a tall order. I know this, but I also know you, you can make it happen. Sara absolutely loves her children. She cannot see anyone else telling her kids what to do. Where's she going to go? Will she go back to Puerto Rico to her parents' house that is already filled with family? No, she is not going to put her kids through that. She wants her children to grow up with a father. I know her husband is really screwed up, but Sara feels she can change him. You know what that spells—disaster. A husband or wife will *not* be changed unless they want to be. So definitely you have one heck of an assignment," Pearl said as she stroked my hair away from my face.

"Pearl, abuse has many faces and voices. I just hope Mari will listen when these faces and voices meet hers. It is going to be rough to say no to her own blood. I hope she can recognize the truth from the lies."

CHAPTER 32

"Mari, hey you, hold up," Scott yelled out to Mari as he ran up behind her in the school corridor.

"I really enjoyed you being over to my home and all. Did you have a good time? Want to try to get together again this weekend?"

"Ummm, I don't know about this weekend. I really had a good time too. I just don't know about this weekend. You know, family stuff," Mari said without looking at Scott, knowing she would melt at his amazingly gorgeous hazel eyes. She did not want to let him know what a loser her family is. She would be mortified if he knew the cops were over because of her father going ballistic about her going over to his house. She had enough on her plate. She couldn't let anyone else know what happened in her house.

"Oh OK, got it. Glad you had a 'good' time at my house. I was hoping you would have had a better time. Honestly, I hoped we could continue to do this on a regular basis. I thought you were into me, well, like I am into you. I guess I'm wrong," Scott poured out to Mari as they walked on to their next class. Scott had liked Mari for long time but never had had the courage to say anything until now.

"OK, awkward. Look Scott, I do really like you. I just can't see this going anywhere. I mean, I got things to do. I don't know what I will be doing on the weekends or whatever. Sorry, it would have been nice but life is not always 'nice,' you know?" Mari whispered as she continued to look down after she made the quotation marks with her hands when she said the word nice. She continued to look down at the floor as they walked.

"Hey, I really understand what tough is even if you don't believe me. I would just like to know if we can continue to hang out. Be friends and honestly, see . . . if maybe . . . there might, ummm, see if there is anything else that might, you know . . . happen. It would be cool to go to your place and you come to mine so the parents don't freak out about who we are hanging out with. Ya know. No stress and just play some video games or see movies or whatever else we may want to do. You know, out there is a lot of crap. Maybe, just maybe we can get away from it for a while," Scott whispered back to Mari, moving closer to her and staring at her as he spoke so he could ensure he didn't miss any facial expression that might show him that he may have said something wrong or right. He really wanted to hang with Mari and see what happened next, no pressure on anyone. He knew it would be a tough try, but he wasn't planning on giving up anytime soon.

"You know, Pearlie, Scott may just be what Mari needs. A distraction and he seems to check out from what I have seen. What do you think? I know that this Scott outing was what got Sara and Mari stuck in a closet by Benjy, but Benjy was wrong! The kids did not do anything except have some teenager fun. That's it," I mused, hoping Pearlie could pick up on my wanting to help the kids out with some mild interference that would not expose who I am and my mission at hand.

"Hmmm, so you just want me to help out the kids?" Pearlie quietly asked me as she walked along with me behind Mari and Scott.

"Yes, just want to help out the kids," I whispered back.

"Well, right now this situation with the kids is not what your focus is, unless it will help Mari with her dysfunctional homelife. We are here to help Mari. Now, with all that said, if your helping Mari involves Scott in a positive way, and keep in mind again—free will. This is all about Mari's free will to choose what she sees and hopefully gets to actually hear what you have to say to her that will help her in her home situation, then will it be OK to involve Scott."

"OK, I will ensure Mari's best welfare will be foremost in my dealings with her. I just pray that Mari will hear me. That she will actually see what is happening around her and who the good and bad guys are."

"So, what are you thinking, Mari? Did I just jam too much stuff down on you? I did not mean to do that. I am just being honest as to what I hope happens," Scott mentioned to Mari, hoping she will understand him.

"Yeah, I get it. I wanna, you know, thank you for thinking of me that way. A lot of guys wouldn't do that. They would just take advantage, you know. So thanks!" Mari softly said as she continued to look at the floor the whole time although that wasn't what she wanted to tell Scott. She wanted to hug him. Tell him how much she thanked him for not seeing her exterior but seeing her interior self. She wanted to hug and kiss him until she could not believe. Yes, she had a huge crush on him especially now, but how would he care for her knowing what a freaking crazy family she had? He would run for the hills if there were any in New York. He would probably despise her and would ignore her if she tried to talk to him. He would probably go to someone who was so much cuter than she was and had less headaches than she had with her family. She couldn't deal with that. She could not have anyone know about her insane family-DQ time, *drama queen time*! Who in his right mind would lock his wife and then his daughter in a closet for not just one day but more than that, with just a pot for pooping. That was just crazy. Scott deserved better, not her but a beauty queen and someone without craziness.

I mean, I am the one that was happy to have my perverted father hug me and tell me I was beautiful when I knew he was nuts. How weird is that?

"Mari, it is not weird. Many times, victims cling to their captor's views because victims do not know any reason to disagree. Just know I am here for you. I am whispering my thoughts to you because I cannot do anything else. Know I want to scream to you that you do not have to take what is being said to you from your mother or father. Understand firsthand the world of dysfunction that dismembered your innocence and drew you into its depraved thrall does not have to continue. You have a God-given free will," I whispered to Mari. I vowed to end the domestic violence and sexual abuse Mari and her family had to endure despite having all that a girl in her particular living situation had. I wanted to shove down my encouragement and guidance from my whispers and could not stop hoping that Mari could escape the miserable demise many others go through. I thought for Mari the following:

"My throat feels constricted, I feel asphyxiated.
I cannot speak, yet I know I have a voice and know my course.
Why can I not talk? Is it fear? Me, naw! I know my heart's source.
I love my Mami and Papi. I can talk.
Then why don't I speak and walk the walk?
I guess I feel alone with no one that will really talk. I just want to walk and walk
and walk."

"Candace honey, do you know why you did not think Mari would mind your words in whisper?" Pearlie leaned into me and whispered these words.

"Why, because I was not a real hero like you and working over a century with cases?" I asked nonchalantly as if I were going to be fired on the spot for not bringing Mari to Pearl on a platter. Yet in reality, I wanted to reach out to Mari and just wring her neck since I had been through what Mari had just gone through, in a different manner and different era. I knew no one would understand the disgust, humility, and non-love she just felt.

Yet I felt a huge heat source from Scott, signifying that he indeed cared for Mari. I never dealt with boys nor what they could bring to a relationship like this, so my first reaction was to kick Scott out of the equation. Yet Jethro, Scott's guardian angel as Scott prayed to the Heavenly God, was getting into my way. Pearlie could not see Jethro for some reason. Somehow, I and Jethro could see each other. Jethro looked like an Ivy League athlete from the 1960s. Jethro simply sneered at me as I stared him down.

"Look, Mari, I am here to be your friend if that is all that I can have right now. I am cool with it. Yet, I want to help you since I sense you are going through more than a person could handle. I mean, I am sure you are cool with all that is happening with you, but I just want you to know that I really had a cool time with you and I want you to know that I am here for you. I'm not trying to be corny, just being honest," Scott said as he leaned into Mari.

"OK, OK. I gotcha. I will definitely call you if I find myself in a major jam, which I am not in right now. Oh, but guess what, Scott—I don't have your phone number!" Mari smiled at Scott as she stepped back and tried to make a joke of this very serious situation. In reality, Mari wished she could just lean into him, and he would pick her up and hug her while he kissed her and time would move forward into a world where medieval carriages with horses were still in style. She would be dressed as the most stylish princess in the kingdom. Scott would twirl her in the air, and everyone would recognize she was someone worthy of someone like Scott.

"Yo, Cinderella. You there? Here is my phone number. I don't always give it out, but for you, I will break that rule. You know how it is." Scott smiled as he gave her his phone number and made her stop so she would input his number into her cell phone. He did not want her to lose his number.

"OK, Scott, I now have you in my treasured phone list. This is a very special phone list. Just know that not anyone can simply be put into my list. Just VIPs get in there." Mari playfully pushed him so she could shake the nervousness she was experiencing at this moment.

"Geez, I am impressed with myself now. I already have you in my phone list without you asking me to do so. You have always been a VIP in my phone list," Scott coyly said to Mari as he stared at her with wanting eyes.

"Whoa, you better have me in your VIP list since I am a VIP," Mari softly mentioned shyly as she continued walking, avoiding Scott's heated glance at her. Luckily, she reached her class and waved at Scott good-bye.

"I will talk at you later. Take it easy," Mari told Scott as she quickly walked into her class. All she could think about was Scott as she took her seat, but nothing could happen with them due to her family's insane situation.

"Hey, you," Jethro called out to me as this scene with Mari and Scott played out in front of him. His role was to protect Scott and he felt a really lousy pit in his stomach as Scott gave Mari his phone number. Jethro knew not what Scott was getting himself into with Mari, but he knew he would have to be on guard as he felt Scott's heart resonating heat as he stared after Mari.

"What? Who are you?" I asked as I approached Jethro. "What do you want?"

"Candace honey, who are you speaking to?" Pearl asked as she followed me curiously.

"What do you mean, Pearlie? Can't you see this guy? He is following Scott as he speaks to Mari," I asked as I looked at Pearl as if she was nuts.

"Candace, the only one I see is you talking to air. So what is going on?"

"Pearlie, I don't get it. I don't get why you don't see this dude who is hanging all over Mari's friend."

"OK, so I guess your name is Candace. Mine is Jethro, the reason your pal cannot see me is because I am the new guy on the block. Not many people can see me nor hear me since I am a guardian angel in training. You know, we have the same big guy in the sky to look at and speak to if we mess up our case subjects," Jethro said as he looked down to the floor very bashfully.

"Wow, I did not know there were other angels out there. I mean, I thought there was just one God and, you know, the angels, supervising angels, and all the other staff. He ran everything in Earth and all over the universe," I spoke very softly as I was amazed there were other angels aside from me and my buddies from Spiritual Guide's Course 101 and Pearlie. This was huge! This was yet another part of the world I did not know about. Jethro seemed a little stiff but I got it. I mean, you have to care about your case subject. I sure cared about Mari and felt as though I loved Mari as a sister. How weird was that? I barely knew Mari, yet she felt such an intense bond with her that I could not imagine anyone breaking.

"Yeah, I get where you are coming from. I felt that way once I got to really know Scott. I felt as though no one could get to him unless they came through me and then they had to really be OK. You know? What is that all about right? Yet I got really close to him. So I am protecting Scott from Mari, if you know what I mean. No disrespect but Scott is my responsibility," Jethro said as he squared off in front of me.

"OK, I get it. You are Scott's big protector. Got it! Yet you have to understand that I am here for Mari and she is really, really special. She is going through a really tough time and I need to make sure she can handle it and handle Scott's situation regarding her. You understand, Jethro?"

"Yes, of course I get it. Scott is an absolutely amazing guy with an impeccable reputation."

"OK, glad you can vouch for him, but I do not know him and I am going to be on guard. I know that Mari likes him, but her situation is making her a closed closet since she is scared she will scare him away if he knew what is really going on with her and her family. She is very embarrassed and I will not let her get further embarrassed with someone that will not care about her."

"Yep, I get it. That is how I feel about Scott, so we are both on the same sheet of music. So, now that we have wasted so much time on how much we care about our subjects and do not want them to be hurt, what do you think Mari is going to do about Scott? He is a great catch, and if I may say, Scott can get any girl in his school to go out with him," Jethro mentioned as he fixed his jacket and brushed his jacket straight with his fingers.

"Oh, I see what you are getting at. You think Mari can't get another guy to care about her. Well, you are so wrong there, dork. She is a major catch."

"Candace, although I cannot see Jethro and get 100 percent scenario on you and Jethro, I can see you are both gathering muscle on both your turfs. There is no need for that. What there is a need for is to figure out what Mari wants and what is going to be best for her while her parents are dealing with all of this. Plus, we have not even dealt with her brother and her family. You have a lot on your plate. Therefore, the last thing on your plate is worrying about another guardian angel interfering with Mari. Get it?" Pearl indicated as she placed her hands on her hips and put her feet together, indicating she would not expect an argument from me.

"Oh, OK, Pearlie. I hear you. I just do not want this baby angel to dictate how Mari will end up with her home situation if Scott gets involved in her life. Personally, I think he would be great for Mari, but Mari does not seem to want anyone to know about her mom and dad's situation, which is affecting her directly. I feel horrible for her. I know what that is like. I mean, my mother opted for pills and alcohol so it would knock her out at night while my father decided to use me as his lover instead of my mother. It made me sick! I do not want Mari to go through that if I can help it. I have a bad feeling about this family situation. I have a bad feeling Mari's father is going to make a really stupid move and I may not be able to help Mari. So, yes, I am concerned about her and who she hangs with. Yet I cannot do anything except whisper to her my thoughts. That totally bites! How am I expected to do my job if she cannot see me and hear me out?"

"Are you done, Candace? I understand how you feel. It really is difficult but this is what is given to us. It is given to us because God believes you can make it happen. If he did not have faith in you, he would not have given you this case."

"What if I mess up, Pearlie? Does that mean I cannot get my wings? Or even worse, does that mean I cannot get into heaven?"

"Candace, you are given situations in which you are expected to react in a certain way, yet it is up to you. Ultimately, is it about you? No. It is about your case subject. God does not dictate what you do or say. It does not work that way. Remember this term, free will, well, it is a pretty strong meaning for a purpose. It not only gives a subject the ability to listen or reject what you whisper to her or him, but it also allows you to do what you believe will be the very best solution for your case subject. It seems harsh but it seems the reality of life. I want you to know that I am here to help you along with your journey. I want you to know that Mari is nothing but that trauma she felt at seeing her mother in that urine- and feces-infected closet as she was also shoved in there by her own father. Not only is it hard to understand anyone shoving a person into a closet, but a closet with urine and feces. Plus, it is even harder knowing that your own flesh and blood shoved someone you love into a place like that and then shoves you, his daughter, in there too. There is a lot of processing right now for Mari. So she may not be thinking of what you are trying to whisper to her. Just be there for her. She can feel your aura and know you are one with her. Love her through this," Pearl said to me as she placed her arm on my shoulders. I slowly reached up and held on to my mentor's hands as I thought about Mari's torment. She is indeed a princess with a potential prince, but her carriage has not arrived at her home. Perhaps I can help Mari—if she will accept my help. Right now, it's a waiting period. Not only is it a waiting period for Mari to reach out and have someone help her, but now I had to deal with Jethro, who is Scott's guardian angel. I mean, so what that he already has his wings? I am protecting Mari, and Scott may be a great guy with a guardian angel following her around to ensure Scott does not get hurt, but I am around to make sure no one does any hurt to Mari. We are both doing the same thing, but we are each in each other's space. Ugh, this truly sucks! I need to make sure Mari, Sara, and Jonathan are OK and that they get the right help. Hopefully, Benjy will get the right type of help too, although I am not thinking too much about him at this point. Then the pitch yell "Here we go."

CHAPTER 33

Sara had gotten up extra early so she had time to put on her makeup, making sure to cover up the bruises on her face, arms, and legs from this past weekend. She went along her normal way of life as if nothing had occurred. She told herself everything would be all right. Benjy had apologized to her and told her how very sorry he was to put her and their family through such a traumatic situation and he hated himself for being a big part of that. Sara remembered the beautiful roses he brought her and an amazing card of apology with a handwritten note within the card, expressing his hard-felt sentiments regarding all of the commotion that occurred because of the misunderstanding they had. Benjy held Sara in his arms, held her tight, and looked straight into her eyes, swearing on his mother's grave that he would never do that to her again. He only asked that she would forgive him for his stupidity. She prepared breakfast, packed Benjy's and her lunch as normal, plus ensured Mari and Jonathan had their lunches ready for their school day. Sara wanted so hard to believe Benjy, and in her heart, she forgave him. Sara hugged Benjy back and told him she forgave him, but this was the last time she would go through something like that. She did not want her children to ever see police lights in front of their home and have Benjy or her in handcuffs. It was scary and she could not deal with that ever again. Benjy had taken her hands and placed them both on his heart. He stared at Sara hard and told her he loved her and their children. He would never ever do anything to bring the police to their home. He swore on his mother's grave again. Sara stared into his eyes and told him she forgave him.

Mari stood quietly by her bedroom door and almost puked at the intimate exchange between her parents. Mari did not believe her father would stop his womanizing and hitting her mom. She so wished it would be true and even felt guilty for feeling that her father was lying to her mom. Mari just felt she would see her mother inside the closet again. This time though, Mari felt she would force herself to be stronger and call the police, especially Detective Williams. Somehow, Mari felt he would understand their dilemmas. She just hated her parents fighting and seeing how terrible this fighting made her family feel and how separated it made her family become.

When Jonathan finally got home that famous evening after the NYPD visited their home, he just asked what Sara had done to piss off their father. Mari could not believe that he asked that. She could not believe that he had automatically assumed their mother had fault for the police coming into their home and dealing where their own parents' issues. It was embarrassing and hopeless. Mari just stared at Jonathan and asked him if he was for real. Of course, he avoided Mari's question and headed to his personal haven for a while—his bedroom. Mari knocked on his door loudly and asked him to come out and stop being such a coward. Jonathan simply ignored Mari and placed his headset on, erasing his homelife for a while. That was the only way he would deal with such insanity—lights out and music on. Tomorrow would be a new day.

Sara had everything done by 6:30 a.m. and had another hour until Benjy and she would drive out to the factory they both worked at. She went to her nightstand and pulled out her Bible. Sara had not read much of it but always pulled it out when she was having a hard time. She figured God was helping others, and her situation was not as important as other persons' might be. Why would God listen to her? She only had to deal with a slap in the face or a punch here or there, while others might not have food or might be dealing with soldiers invading their homes in war-torn countries. How could her situation be as important as that?

"Pearl, my heart aches so much for Sara and I wish I could help her too even though Mari is not listening to me at this time. So how can I help Sara when I cannot even help Mari when she has so many questions and stresses? Pearlie, what do I do? I want to help so much and at least Sara wants to help her family and not stick her head in the sand like my mother did. What do I do?"

"Well, Candace, the first thing you need to understand is that Mari is not you. You had your own horrific issues but these issues are Sara's and Mari's. You need to focus on her needs and how you felt when you were being violated. What would you have wanted someone to do to help you? Think about that and hopefully you will come up with the remedy that Mari needs at this time. You may need to come up with something different as time continues to move on, but for now, there is help for her to cope with her hurt. It has been a very traumatic time for her. It will continue to be so as time continues. She has friends, and she does not want anyone to know of the chaos she has to deal with in her own home. Make sense, little one?" Pearl asked as she looked at me and realized this scenario may be hitting me in a personal way too. As a new Spiritual Guide, I still remembered some of my most heartfelt memories, be they good or bad. I had to allow what I wished to be retained in my memory bank. Ideally, those memories would stay joyous.

"Yes, Pearlie. I understand. I just wanted someone to beat my father to a pulp and dunk my mother in a tub of full cold water so she would wake up and face reality as it was occurring in her home. Yet I know in my heart I would not want my father hurt. I simply wanted it all to stop. I wanted my mother to stop hiding from reality. I wanted her to be my mom and protect me from the world even if the demon was my own father. That's all. I wanted it all to stop," I told Pearl as I had tears streaming down my red cheeks.

"Well, little one, I cannot do much about your past, but I can help you with what is at hand. I would sneak on over to Mari and check out how she is. Right now, she is so confused, angry, hurt, and wanting to talk to Scott, but she is scared about losing him too. She is more nervous about her mom being hurt again. Help calm Mari down, Candace. She needs you to whisper to her realities and hope. She needs you, Candace. I know you can help her," Pearl told me softly as she gently wiped away my tears.

In the meantime, Sara wiped off the dust from her Bible and started reading Ephesians 5:22-28, "Wives submit to your husbands, as to the Lord. For the husband is the head of the wife as Christ is the head of the church, his body, of which he is the Savior. Now as the church submits to Christ so also wives should submit to their husbands in everything.

"Husbands, love your wives just as Christ loved the church and gave himself for her to make her holy, cleansing her by the washing with water through the word, to present himself as a radiant church, without stain or wrinkle or any other blemish, but holy and blameless. In this same way, husbands ought to love their wives as their own bodies. He who loves his wife loves himself." Sara softly wept as she realized how much she loved Benjy, that awkward skinny kid that went to her father and strongly asked him for his daughter's hand even though his knees knocked so hard Sara swore she heard them upstairs in her room.

"Pearl, I just hope Sara does not love Benjy so much that she does not see he can love her to death, literally to death," I told Pearl as Sara read the Bible verses over and over, and I prayed Benjy and Sara would abide by those words.

CHAPTER 34

"Yo, dude, what's been going on with your parents? I have been hearing some stuff about the police being out at your place. You OK? Is your dad at your place or is he in jail? Do you need to talk?" Jonathan's best friend Frankie asked as Frankie slid into step with Jonathan as he was going up the step to their school's front entrance.

"Hey, man, all is cool. Nothing happened except the cops came over to check out a couple of things at our place. No biggie," Jonathan answered as if nothing had happened at all at his home. He learned all about his parent's insanity and how his dad threw his mom and even his sister into that dirty closet. He just wanted to forget everything, but everyone wanted to talk to him—his mom, dad, sister, even that Detective Williams, and now his best friend Frankie. Ugh, couldn't this day be over already?

"Man, I just want to go to class and leave the past in the past," Jonathan responded to Frankie, keeping in step with him but knowing he was going to be brought back to that topic. It was off base to anyone who wanted to talk about it with him. He just wanted to forget about her. He really loved his papi. His papi had taught him how to become a man. No one understood that except for Jonathan. Jonathan remembered his papi teaching him how to pick out his clothes, comb his hair, and even tie his shoes. He learned from his dad how to flirt with teenage daughters. His father really got into it. His papi, his dad, even went into the pharmacy and picked up some condoms so that he wouldn't get into any type of problems with getting chicks pregnant. Couldn't anyone understand what a great guy he was? Even though his papi, his dad, made a really bad mistake. Lately, teenage girls didn't seem to attract his attention as much as teenage guys, but right now, he could not go there with that topic.

"Yo, dude, got you back. I was just curious to find out if all is good at your place. Not trying to rag on you," Frankie mentioned as he headed to his class and was not going to ditch it today. Jonathan was also going to class and doing a mental "mirage" with his ninety-year-old social studies teacher having everyone in class read from their books that were written centuries ago. "Yes, invest in your child's public schools!" Jonathan thought sarcastically.

"Cool, dude. Thanks. I'm not trying to ditch you or anything. Just need to get my head straight too. Only one place to do that and that's in my art class. All we do is just paint *whatever we feel motivates us* per Mr. Hensen. He is such a weirdo," Frankie said as Jonathan laughed for the first time since all went down in his place with his family.

"Yeah, he's strange," Frankie said as he chuckled along with Jonathan. Frankie had Mr. Hensen before and knew what it felt like to be in this class again.

"Hey, Jon, if you ever need to rap, let me know. I get it. I have had that happen in my place too. That is why my pops lives by himself, and I live with my mom in her own place with my other two younger sisters."

Jonathan nodded at Frankie as he turned into his class, and Frankie went on ahead to his. Jonathan knew Frankie had gone through some crazy stuff with his parents. Frankie had told him he had gotten in his father's face one time when he had smacked his mother so hard that she was hospitalized for a fractured cheekbone and jaw. When Frankie saw how hard his father had smacked his mom and how Frankie could not wake her, he picked up the phone to call 911, and his father took the phone from his hand and smashed it against the wall. Frankie asked his father why he hit his mom so hard since he was concerned about her, since she did not open her eyes. His father simply replied that women who talk back to their husbands need to learn a lesson. He taught his mother a lesson. That was that.

Frankie could not believe what his father had said and told his father that his wife was his mother and he could not treat her like that. She should be respected and he needed to respect her. All she did was work, clean house, and take care of the kids and even him—her husband. That was the thanks she gets for being faithful and good. She gets a smack in the face from someone who thinks he is a man because he can hit a defenseless woman. Wow, his father was really a big deal. Frankie's father got so angry at him that he picked up Frankie with his left hand to where Frankie's head touched the ceiling and, with his right hand, smacked him across the face. Frankie's father then released Frankie onto the floor. As Frankie slammed into the floor, he felt his elbow bone crack. That did not deter Frankie from standing in front of his father and demanding his father to apologize to his mother. As his father was about to reach out to Frankie, there were several knocks on the door by the police and an ambulance was outside their apartment. The 911 operator was able to connect with Frankie's home, and since she could not reconnect, she contacted the patrol cars in that area and the fire department to check on the family. The police came in and noticed a body on the floor. Before the police could handcuff his father, he returned to Frankie, who was leaning over his mother, and spit into his face, claiming Frankie could not be his son.

Frankie in disbelief simply wiped his face with his shirt and ignored his father's rants as the police put handcuffs on him. All Frankie wanted to do was wish his life away and hope he did not have to see nor live in such an environment again.

Husband and wife beating each other did not make much sense in Frankie's mind. Jonathan, on the other hand, had understood Frankie's father's rage since he had been brought up in that same environment. The man works hard and has the right to expect a correct dinner on the table when he gets home from work. Also, going out during the week or weekend with his friends is the option the husband has available all the time. The wife needs to understand these needs. Simple! There is man and then there is woman. Simple!

Frankie was an ace in school and helped his younger sisters with their schoolwork since his mother had to work in the *bodega*, grocery store, and she would usually come home pretty worn out after dinnertime, typically around 4:30 p.m. Frankie would check out what his mom had put out to thaw. He and his sisters would then form an assembly line to help with the dinner cooking chores. No one complained since their father was usually home sleeping after his night shift. In their home, it was a great night when there was no screaming or shattering dishes. Then there was divorce, and Frankie and his sisters went to live with his mom. He saw his father every other weekend and never complained. His father seemed to change. He was nicer to Frankie. His father asked Frankie how his mother was, and his sisters, but never pried. Frankie noticed a Bible on his father's night table by his bed. He noticed his father would read it every night when he was at his house.

Frankie definitely understood what Jonathan was going through, even though they both approached the home situations in a different way. Jonathan was obsessed with his hair and his looks. He always kept an eye out for any new high school student that wore a skirt or was female. Jonathan always made it his mission to learn who the newbie was. He always tried to teach them the ways of the school as it was known in Jonathan's life. He always tried to learn the carnal side of his high school newbie. He wanted to learn whether the newbie would be part of his cool group or the nerd group, as he referred to the newbies that did not go the extra step to be part of his cool group.

Frankie was cool with Jonathan. Yet Jonathan knew where Frankie stood. Frankie was cool if the available girl would enjoy a time out to the diner and chat about school and what made her happy. What were her goals in life? Frankie had one goal—get out of his neighborhood! He was going to take his mom and sisters out of the neighborhood and buy them a house in the suburbs, where his mom would not have to worry about a mortgage payment since he would pay the bills. She could just stay home and be a mom to his sisters. He loved all of them so much it hurt. He kept pictures of prominent homes in his bedroom and pictures of his idol—Larry Ellison, who owned Oracle Corp. Frankie wanted to own a technologically based company that computed what areas had available petroleum to help all countries' petroleum challenges. He wanted to keep the innovative spirit he saw in Mr. Ellison. Frankie wanted to monitor the petroleum locations and to whom it would go to so that gas prices would not be dominated by one source. Frankie wanted to ensure the citizens would pay appropriate prices for gas so they could see extra after they receive their paychecks. He wanted to have people recognize his efforts simply by the efforts projected by his company. That was Frankie's dream. He planned on making it a reality. No more apartment living for his family or himself. No more! Life brought you a situation yet you had to bring out your A-game if you wanted to leave the inner-city way of life. But at this time, that dream was put on hold. He snapped out of dreamland when the apartment door was opened by his father. His mom was still on the floor. She had regained some consciousness as she started to sit up. There were firemen next to him along with EMTs trying to lay his mom down on the floor so they could check her out. He saw his mom's face twisted with anguish as the police men but handcuffs on his father. Frankie felt bad for his father and thought maybe it might have been his fault that his father was so screwed up. Maybe if Frankie did not ask so much stuff for school or he tried to talk with his father more, maybe, just maybe, his father would've stopped hitting his mom. Maybe Frankie could fix things going on in his father's head and his father's attitude.

To this day, his father still stayed at his home and did not go out as far as Frankie could tell. Maybe things would change for his father. He hoped so. One day, his family would be OK and get out of the hellhole they lived in. Someday, his family would use their minds in the right way and help others instead of destroying others.

CHAPTER 35

Benjy was hugging Sara when both Jonathan and Mari came out of their rooms for dinner. Mari noticed there were some pretty red roses in a clear vase on top of a table setting that her mom only used for special occasions. Mari felt her stomach churn as the acids created fire in the pit of her being. All she could think about was the closet journeys that were sure to come, along with some face and body punches that would make it easier to scrunch into the tight quarters of the closet. Mari could not believe this was happening and that her mom, her mami would actually fall for all this crap. Unbelievable! Why was he not in jail? How could they let him get out so soon? Mari knew it would just be an overnight in jail for her father if her mom had told the police to take him away. Her mami did not want to do that, so the police just took her papi for a drive and some time at the station to call him off. Mari had decided to just go to bed as her brother did. She knew it would not do much except make it worse for her mother when he got angry at her and them, his children, for sending him there. Oh well, nothing she could do except be on her best behavior so her father, Papi, would not forget her and love her in a way that he would not push her into the closet.

"Pearl, look, I know what this is like. Mari's father will hit them again, and this time it may even be fatal. You know, it may be that he loves her to eternity! I truly hope this is not happening, but I know that my father never stopped. It's a roller-coaster ride. The monsters are monsters unless they get major help from the right type of professionals. This will not work!" I said as I sat down and covered my head, not wanting to hear or see what Benjy would have to say. I knew this was not what I was supposed to do, but it was just an automatic response.

"Ahhh, Candace, you sweet, sweet child. I understand your pain, yet you are pain-free here. There is nothing that can hurt you except yourself. Remember, Mari is your case. You need to be there for her. Remember not all cases have horrible endings! I know, I have been around for a couple of thousand years. I have heard and seen it all. Kindly get up and go to Mari. She needs you now, more than ever." Pearl picked me up gently and smoothed off my hoodie. Pearl knew that I would do the right thing—eventually.

"Yes, you are right, Pearlie. I need to keep it together. Thank you," I answered as I looked at Pearl with her head held high and walked to Mari so I could whisper to her words that I truly hoped would keep her strong.

"Mari, you are such a strong young woman. I know how tough it can be to keep it together when everything around you is just so damn crazy, girlfriend. Just know I am here for you. I will do my best to keep it together for you. Please smile and keep yourself alert. Take out that detective's business card plus that prevention of domestic violence advocate's card and keep it near you or on you at all times. You just never know what can happen. But know that your mother is doing the best she can for you and Jonathan. You can choose a different path. Make your own destiny!"

"Yes, I know. I will do my best for not only myself but for Mami and Jonathan," Mari whispered back, not realizing she was talking to no one that was around her. Mari thought it was so weird she kept hearing things from a female but was never able to see anyone. Oh well, such is life. She would just have to work harder at school so she could get a scholarship to go to college. Maybe even a grant. She had heard her teachers talking about grants that college students do not have to pay back. Mari felt so strong she had to do something to help her family get out of this mess. She also wanted her mother to know she had the strength to get rid of her father, would have him go somewhere he could get his head together and be the papi he used to be. Ugh, she would just have to continue praying and hope that God would eventually hear her if he had some time on his hands to hear her cries.

"Jonathan y Mari, yur Papi is come back hom. He and I be happy. Yu will be happy too." Sara looked at her children, hoping and praying they would understand that their father, their papi would be good to her and them. He would not hit her or put her in that disgusting closet. She just had to make sure she could help Benjy more and not complain as much. He was right, she did yell at him too much. OK, he go out with the guys. She needed to be better to her Benjy. She would try harder to make him happy.

"*Hola, hijos.* Hello, children. I be back and all be good again. Look those beautiful roses I buy for your mami. Your mother luvs them. Look at my beautiful Sara, yur mami, she is beautiful and good. Yur Mami Sara told me she no call no policia to our house. OK? We don't have trouble here. All good again. Yur mami will be better to me. Tonight, I go out with my friends so yu and yur mami will know what I need to make everyone happy," Benjy said as he headed to the bedroom to get his underwear and clothes to bring to the bathroom so he could get ready for his night out with the guys.

"This is such crap! He just got back with our mami and he is already going out. I know how this is going to end. Mami will get angry since he will be out late and she does not know who he is with. Papi will try to ignore her but then he will manhandle her and she will end up with a black eye or weekend in paradise in the *closet,* Jonathan thought. He had always looked up to his papi all his life and now he was utterly confused. He had learned everything from his papi, his dad. His papi had taught him everything like baseball, how not to take any bullshit especially women's, how to treat a woman so that she knows she is special and a guy's time is not wasted, and lastly, how to ride a bike as long as Jonathan was not riding it in the street and Benjy was around to supervise his son. Yet right now, he didn't want to think about his homelife, and he knew he could not ignore his mother's black eyes or her weekends locked up like an animal. Now his sister was being locked up too. His sister was a pain in the butt, but he had to protect her. That was what big brothers did, at least that was what both his father and mother had taught him when he was younger. Jonathan could not ignore all of that, yet his father was his idol and his father always knew how to act like a man and not be punked by any guy and, least of all, by a woman. It was time to stand up and have a man-to-man talk with his father. Shit, this was not going to be easy! He had mentally written a detailed script in his head in his last class today. Yet it seemed to be all scrambled up in his mind now that he had to face his dad.

Benjy shaved, took his shower, put on his Friday night clothes and his cologne. He was ready to go out and rock this Friday night with his friends. He wanted to tell them how he got out of jail because he taught his wife right. He figured he would have a great time and then come home and catch up on some sleep with his woman, Sara. She really was a wonderful mother, worker at the factory, and she really did try to be a great wife. She had much to learn in the wife department since she nagged so much and could not understand he needed *his time* to function. That is why he designed that closet for Sara. He needed her to understand who was really in charge at home and everywhere else. He saw how other men looked at her at the factory with eyes of desire. Sara was petite but she was indeed very beautiful. But he needed her beauty for himself and only for himself. No one else! He also saw how beautiful his daughter was growing up to be. She was growing up, and he could see her supple curves that moved him every time she walked into her room. He needed to ignore his feelings. He had to let it go since that was his daughter, yet . . .

"Sara, I go now. I be back. No call me. I be wit my friends. Yu embarrass me when yu call me. Yu hear?" Benjy bellowed to Sara as he was in the hallway headed toward the apartment door and she was in the kitchen serving dinner to his children.

"Benjy, yu no wan to eat wit yur familia? I make yur favorite food." Sara ran out to the hallway as Benjy was opening the apartment's front door.

"Sarita, I eat wit the guys, OK? Yu an thee children eat. I be OK. See yu later tonigh," Benjy said as he slammed the door on his way out.

"Papi, I want to talk to you. Can you wait a minute? Can I go with you?" Jonathan yelled out at his father as he ran past Sara in the hallway and down the project's stairwell. Benjy stopped at the bottom of the stairwell to look at his son.

"Papi, where you going tonight? You wanna play some cards or dominoes?" Jonathan asked.

"No, hijo, not tonight. I go with my work friends to talk and have some fun," Benjy responded, feeling a tad guilty for not staying home but feeling the exhilaration of going out with his friends and what could be out there overpowering his will to stay home.

"OK, I talk to you tomorrow. OK, Papi, you and me!"

"Oh yez, hijo, yu and me. Tomorrow," Benjy replied as he continued going down the stairs to the entrance of the building.

"Yeah, OK," Jonathan said as he walked back to their apartment.

"Hijo, let's go inside and eat food. OK?" Sara said in a happy tone as Jonathan came into the kitchen, hoping her son would get his spirits raised after his father most likely bashed his feelings.

"Yeah, OK, Mami. Let's eat dinner and then we can see TV," Jonathan replied, asking you his mother was trying hard to help and right now his feelings were all over the board.

"OK, hijo, we be OK, I rite? We be OK," Sara reassured her son as she felt his hurt in her heart. Things had to change in her home. She could not continue to see hurt in her children's eyes. No more hurt.

"I hope you are right, Sara," I responded as I read and rechecked her case assignment folder.

"Ahhh, everything the same as I left it. The woman, ohhh soo good to look at. Tis is the good time Papi needs. Rite, *muchachos*?" Benjy said as he turned to his friends and entered his neighborhood bar.

"Oh yez, we work very hard and as they say in *Ingles*, we play hard," Joaquin said as he motioned to the bartender the need for five beers and found a table right next to some friends he had not seen in a couple of weeks.

Time passed quickly and Benjy needed to go home, although he was quite busy trying to get a phone number from a hot woman he had danced with all night. He knew he had to get home, but the smell of her perfume stopped him from doing what was right. He did not care. It was his free time and he wanted this time for himself. Who cared if he had some outside fun from his family? It would make him a better husband and father, right? But this woman was not budging, and he did not feel like buying her any more drinks if she was not going to his car with him.

"Well, muchachos, I go now, it be 3:00 a.m. Ohhh, my Sara be angry. See yu at the factory, rite?" Benjy hollered at his three friends that were still at the bar. As he finally got home, he went to the bedroom and saw his beautiful Sara.

"Ahhh, I hear Mamacita. Yu want to have fun wit me?" Benjy summoned to Sara as he took off his clothes and slithered into his bed while Sara was hugging her side of the bed.

"No, Benjy. Yu smell of woman. I no wan yu now. I thought yu come home early and not do tis no more. You hurt my heart. Yu bring me flowers. Wa is tha for? Not for me? Yu wit other woman. Go from my bed, yu no good for me," Sara softly said as she knew what she must do and what her husband Benjy was about to do since she was disobeying his requests and rules. She had to remember that he might want to have her body after he came home late while being out with the boys. Yet tonight, that would be different. She had no desire and knew she had to deal with his punishment—the closet.

"*Mujer*, yu no good for mee," Benjy said as he grabbed Sara by the hair and threw her off the bed.

"Why yu no wan mee? You been wit some other man?" Benjy yelled at her as he climbed on her as she struggled to get off the floor.

"Yu no good for mee!" Benjy yelled as he cocked back his arm and threw a hard blow at her left cheek. He then picks up an unconscious Sara and throws her as a rag doll inside his special closet for her.

"Ahhh, I know who I hav an be good for me," Benjy said and sneered as he went toward Mari's room.

"Mari, open the door," Benjy said softly but with force as he knocked on her door very strongly.

"Mari, open. I need to talk to yu," Benjy said as he heard his daughter stir in her bed.

"*Mari, abre la puerta ahora.* Mari, open door now!" Benjy said in a stronger and deeper voice, in hopes his daughter heard him.

"Papi, what is wrong? Is Mami OK?" Mari said as she opened the latch on her bedroom door so she could look at her father yet hide behind her door since she was wearing a nightgown. Her nightgown was cotton with bows and frill on the top but did little to hide her breasts exposure since the cotton was thin.

"Ahhh, hija, yur mami is good. She be in a plaz she can learn how to be a good wife. Wha yu tink, hija? How yu be a good wife? Yu be there for yur husband when he need yu, rite?" Benjy screamed at Mari.

"Papi, what are you talking about? I do not need how to be a wife for a long time since I am not married or plan on marrying anyone soon? What is wrong with you, Papi, you are talking crazy. Where is Mami? Did you put her in that closet again? You smell of alcohol," Mari said loudly, hoping to wake her brother and maybe get some help from him if he did not have his dang headset on.

"Papi, we talk in the morning whatever you want to talk about. It is too late right now. You need to rest, Papi, and sleep, OK?" Mari said softly as she gently but firmly tried to close the door and hopefully latch the door shut before he could step inside her bedroom. As Mari tried to calm her father down and keep him from coming into her bedroom, he pushed the door in, like a bull, knocking Mari backward onto her bed. Before Mari could get off the bed, Benjy had his hand clamped down on her mouth while he reached under her nightgown. Mari was so stunned and could not believe what was happening and was voiceless while her father tried to rape her.

"Mari, kick him off of you," I screamed at Mari, feeling her emotions. I must get through to Mari. She may be my case study, but Mari felt like my friend, someone who could become a best friend forever.

"Mari, you can do it. Fight back. Do not think of him as a father right now. Just do your best to kick, bite, and scream as if your life depended on it," I yell at Mari, hoping that she will somehow hear my voice or my higher being's voice. There is a God. Believe it, and he will help you, I think as my stomach hurts, feeling the fear and hurt Mari is feeling.

"Ahhh, hija, yu know yu wan me. I vill teach yu how to become a woman a man wants," Benjy said as he tore her underwear off her skin with his right hand and plunged onto Mari as a volcano exploding its lava into her.

At that very moment, she felt Benjy fall onto her as a limp rag doll, so she took that very opportunity to push him off her and kick him in the groin as she screamed for help.

"Mami, Jonathan, someone, *help me!*" Mari screamed as she continued to push Benjy out of her room and lock her bedroom door latch closed.

"Oh my precious God, what is happening? What just happened? Am I going crazy?" Mari thought as she ran for the business card Detective Williams had left for her. As she went into her closet, she reached into an old running shoe, pulled the corridor from inside of the shoe and retrieved the detective's business card. As she ran to her backpack for her cell phone, she dialed the number and actually hoped that Detective Williams would answer. Unfortunately, Mari reached Detective Williams's voice mail and left a message for him to contact her. She indicated in the voice mail she really needed help now. She thought her family was in real danger.

As Mari finished the voice mail to Detective Williams, she heard what she thought was a chair being thrown against the wall and her brother's voice.

"Oh my gosh, please do not let my brother and father be added. It's all my fault! I should have kept quiet. Now my brother will get in trouble with my father and mother," Mari thought as she grabbed her flannel robe and opened her door cautiously.

"Papi, how could you do something like this? Do you not know that is wrong to go into Mari's room and you try to hurt her? Where is Mami? Where is Mami?" Jonathan yelled as he grabbed his father's white T-shirt and held him up toward the kitchen ceiling, limp as a rag doll. "Did you not know I'd looked up to you? You mean everything to me. Where is Mami? Where did you put her? Is she in your crazy closet? Come on, show me where she is!" Jonathan yelled at Benjy as he dropped Benjy onto the floor, pushing him toward his parents' bedroom.

"Jonathan, don't hurt him. I think he is hurt more than we can imagine. We just need to find Mami so we can make sure she is OK and safe," Mari told him as she searched his face for some type of compassion toward their father. Mari cannot continue to blame Jonathan at all for exerting all of his emotions toward their father. She was still in shock as to what her father did to her, but right now, what was important was finding out where their mother was.

Benjy opened the heavy drapes that separated the living room from their parents' bedroom. He then faced the closet that he had used to throw his wife to center her attention and respect to him, the husband and head of the household. He needed the closet to set boundaries and control for his needs. As he faced the closet, he turned to his children and coldly turned toward the closet door while reaching in his trousers for the key to open the closet. As he inserted the key into the closet and opened the door, both Jonathan and Mari leaped on the closet to help their mother out of the box that held their family's secrets.

Sara was partially dehydrated and quickly fell toward Jonathan and Mari, who were right in front of her. As Sara fell onto her children's hands, the doorbell rang, and Mari left Sara so she could rush toward the door to open it. Detective Williams rushed into the apartment and saw Sara on her knees as Jonathan smoothed her hair and Benjy was staring at the key while faintly hearing the policeman talking to his family. Benjy quietly kneeled and put both his hands behind his head, understanding what was ahead of him. Detective Williams put his handcuffs on Benjy and took him into custody. He motioned to another officer and told her to move Benjy out to the police car while he finished talking to Sara and her family.

"Mami, are you OK? Do you need any water or anything at all?" Mari asked her mother as she placed Sara onto the floor. Sara lay on the floor for a few minutes with eyes open and suddenly sat up and stared at both Jonathan and Mari. By this time, the paramedics were surrounding Sara. She pushed them away and looked directly at her children.

"Enough is enough. I done. I try hard and help put food on the table for long time for yu two and yur father. Do no hate yur father. He good man. He sick in thee head. Yur father be sick in his head an heart. But I wan to know if you wan to go wit me live a different life? I no live like this no more. Yu understand?"

"Mami, I think Mari and me be OK going where you go. We your family. I will be the man of the house and make sure nothing bad happens to you and Mari. That is what I will do. Just tell me where we will go." Jonathan quickly stepped to Sara and kneeled down to her level so he could hug his mother. He had never noticed how tiny and frail she was. Yet he would not let anything bad happen to her ever again. Never!

"Mami, Jonathan is right. We will go wherever you go. No more silence, we have to move forward and live. No more secrets, right? We have a voice," Mari added.

"Oh wow, Pearlie. Do you think Mari will tell Sara about the rape that occurred?" I asked Pearlie as she put a star in her case subject folder. Hope, faith, and happiness.

"Well, let's see what happens. You may be surprised," Pearlie responded as she frowned toward the scene in front of her. She prayed I was right and Mari tells Sara. It will be difficult, but it was something Sara had to know before she embarked on a new life with just her and her children. It will be difficult at times, but it will be fulfilling to be free of violence imposed by Sara's husband to her and her children.

"Mami, I need to tell you something that is hard for me to tell you, especially now. But I have to tell you so you understand why I cannot stay in our home," Mari said as she looked at Detective Williams, and he pulled Jonathan by the shoulder toward the kitchen and pulled out his portfolio with his right hand to open it to some type of form.

"Mami . . . Papi came into my bedroom—"

"Wha yu say, hija?" Sara asked as she pushed herself away from Mari so she could look at her daughter's face clearly and not just hear her words. Mari, afraid of a bad reaction, retreated into her introversion and faced the floor. Yet she talked and hoped her voice was heard.

"Uhmmm, Papi came into my bedroom after knocking on my door and telling me he needed to talk to me. Just as I opened the door, Papi pushed the door open and jumped on me on the bed. He pushed the door so hard that it knocked me on the bed. Then he . . . then he . . ." Mari whispered.

"Go ahead, Mari. Say it. Tell your mother the truth so she can make good decisions about your future and hers. Be honest with her. Tell her," I whispered back to Mari as I tried to surround my arms around Mari but realize I cannot touch her and am holding air.

"Hija, tell me wha happened wit your papi? *Estas bien?* It is good. *No problema,*" Sara said as she realized Mari was going through her own trauma. Sara was terrified of what she would hear, but she needed to know if her intuition was correct.

"Mami, I tried to get Papi off of me!" Mari blurted out. "But he held me tight on the bed and then he . . . then he . . . then he entered me," Mari said as she fell onto the floor and cried on Sara's legs.

"I did not want him to do this. I think Papi is out of his mind and did not know what he was doing. I mean, he would not hurt me intentionally. I think he might have been on something that got him crazy. I am so sorry, Mami. I tried to fight him off me but he was too strong. I tried to scream but I was so scared. I am so sorry, Mami," Mari bellowed as she drank her own tears as she spoke to her mami, her mother.

"Hija, it no be yur fault. It no be yur fault. *Comprendes?* Do yu understan? It no be yur fault, hija. Yu no do not'in' to make this happen," Sara said softly as she kneeled down to the floor and hugged her daughter as she caressed her face. Sara softly moved Mari's hair off her face and held it, looking directly into her eyes.

"This no be yur fault. Yur papi *loco.* Yur papi crazy! We go someplace he no see us or he go someplace he get better. OK? He no hurt yu no more. I promise yu! *Te lo prometo!* I promise yu until I die," Sara softly said as she realized she will need to make a new home for her children and herself. She will not allow her husband to hurt her daughter or son again! No more! She will not be silent about her past tortures from her husband. She will bare all to the police and that lady from the prevention of domestic violence agency. Her husband crossed the sacred line. Although sickened by what she heard from Mari, Sara had to be strong and ensure her daughter did not take on the guilt. It was Sara's fault this had happened to Mari and she would never forgive herself for it. If Sara had left Benjy earlier, nothing would have happened to Mari. But Sara did not know where to go and who to go to. Now it does not matter, Sara had to protect her children by any means necessary. Sara approached Detective Williams to get answers.

"Officer Williams, I needa talka to yu," Sara said as she slipped in between Jonathan and Detective Williams so she could move Jonathan toward the hallway. Sara needed to speak with Detective Williams privately.

"Mrs. Santiago, are you feeling OK? Are you hurt and need medical attention? What can I do for you?" Detective Williams said as he moved toward Sara and motioned to one of his other officers in the apartment to take over for him with Jonathan's form while the paramedics were still following Sara to take care of any wounds she might have.

"I needa yur help. My hosban, he hurt my daughter," Sara said quietly as she looked down at the floor.

"I needa Mari go to doctor for checkup down there. Yu know. I needa make a sure she OK? Yu know?" Sara looked up at Detective Williams hoping and praying he understood what she meant.

"Yes, Mrs. Santiago, we can do that. I need to ask you if you want to stay in your home or would you like to go to a safer place?" Detective Williams asked Sara.

"No, we be OK here. I needa tink wha we needa do. Yu know?" Sara asked Detective Williams as if he could see through her and see how much her heart hurt. She was beyond herself in misery, but she would not let her children see her weak. She had to be strong for her children.

"OK, Mrs. Santiago," Detective Williams said as he saw Sara so tired and broken. Yet, he could sense a source of fire in her that he did not see in some victims of crime. Mrs. Santiago seemed very strong indeed, even though her stature was so petite.

"Mrs. Santiago, the paramedics will take Mari and you to the hospital," he said as he motioned to the paramedics and nodded that she was ready.

"Yez, tank yu. Jonathan, yu be good? OK? I go to the hospital wit Mari and we then come home. OK? We be home soon," Sara told Jonathan as he was approaching her when he saw the paramedics guide her toward the apartment hallway.

"OK, Mami. No problem. I take care of everything here. You take care of Mari," Jonathan said in the most confident voice he could muster up and having his life turned upside down.

"OK, hijo, *te quiero*. I luv yu," Sara said as she closed the door behind her.

"I love you too, Mami!" Jonathan said as he stared down and continued to answer questions for the officer that was left behind.

CHAPTER 36

After many, many months of going to court and therapists, Sara and the kids were finally free of Benjy. The judge found Benjy guilty of numerous domestic violence offenses to include attempted statutory rape of a minor, Mari, and imprisonment. I continued to follow Mari everywhere she went and whispered to her words of encouragement that she was accepting.

A couple of months after court sessions that felt like years had gone by and family counseling sessions, Sara, Mari, and Jonathan seemed happier than I had ever seen them. Additionally, Mari found out that her favorite Aunt Candi was coming over for a visit. Mari was ecstatic since Candi seemed to make everything feel better. Mari later pulled a book from her bookshelf and lost herself in it.

"Hi, Titi Candi," Mari yelled as she came into the kitchen from her bedroom to greet her favorite aunt.

"Hola, Mari. How are you?" Titi Candi said to Mari as she checked her out to make sure Mari was indeed well from all the craziness that had occurred in her world lately.

"Hi, Titi Candi. I am so happy you are here. Please tell me you are staying for a while," Mari blurted out as she hugged her aunt.

"Yes, I will stay here for a week or two. If you do not throw me out of your home, I will stay," Candi responded as she pulled Mari off her to look her straight in her eyes.

"That is great, Titi Candi. I am so happy."

"Good, I stay then," Candi told Mari as Mari had already taken her overnight bag into her room.

Candi, Sara, Mari, and Jonathan spent most of the day catching up and avoiding all the negative situations that had occurred in their lives. Sara believed she would simply chat with Candi privately and discuss the details if necessary so Candi was up to date on all the family business. More importantly, Sara wanted to make sure Candi was doing well. Yet, Sara was competing with Mari, who wanted her Aunt Candi's undivided attention. Sara conceded and let Mari take over Candi's time and attention.

As dinner came and went, Sara, Mari, Jonathan, and Candi got into a serious game of Monopoly that claimed Sara as the winner. The rest of the team moved forward, toward the sink and stove to clean up the dinner dishes and pots. This was new to Sara. She was so used to having to clean up immediately after dinner per Benjy's desires that she never knew the concept of relaxing and having a few moments to chat with her children and family instead of always being a host and servant to all that came to her home. This was all new and exhilarating for her. She absolutely loved the idea of her not having to do cleanup immediately after dinner but sit there and see the happiness in her children's faces while they kidded with each other and their aunt. It was beautiful to see their children being what was seen as *normal* in a family. It was so wonderful to see Mari and Jonathan smiling and playing with each other. It had been a long hard road to get to where they were now.

Sara went to the Center for Prevention of Domestic Violence and Sexual Assault in her area while all the lawyers and court schedules were in her life, but she knew it would help her. She spoke to a Spanish-speaking advocate who helped her throughout the trial process, and therapy was available for her and her children. She got more hours at her job to help pay for her visits, but it was well worth the money. It was tough having to see her husband in chains and having to speak against him, but she did it for her children and herself. She realized that if she had not gotten strong and stood up for not only herself, she had to get strong for her children. She did not want to see Jonathan act like her husband and her daughter choose a husband like she did. They deserved better. She also realized that her husband would have continued to beat her and her children. She could not let that happen. Plus, Benjy too needed help. She was one of the lucky ones. The company where she worked allowed her time to deal with her personal baggage even if she had to endure gossip about her husband. The company did not dock her pay.

Sara had put into the legal system divorce forms. She would be the first woman in her family and her husband's family ever to seek a divorce. She spoke to her parents and they were not agreeable with the divorce but supported her and allowed her to do what she thought would be best for her and her children. The advocate at the center helped her obtain the forms and showed her how to fill them out. After the forms were filled out, they both put the forms through the system. Her husband would receive Sara's petition for dissolution of marriage while in jail. Benjy would not like it, but he would be in jail for a while for imprisonment, statutory rape, and domestic violence. It was so very difficult to lose someone to such impulses, but Sara had to be strong and she was. She did not realize how strong she was until she had to deal with all of this and ensure she was a loving mother to her children, trying really hard not to bash their father. Sara tried very hard to be there for Mari and Jonathan to help them through their journey in all of this, but she knew she had a strong spirit within and that would help her make it through this chapter in her life.

As all the evening's activities came to an end, everyone went to their rooms for some rest and to enjoy an additional day off due to a federal holiday. Yay! They could use all the rest, Sara thought. Everyone crashed without any effort. Even Mari told her aunt they could chat the next day since she was off from school.

Candi was the first one to wake up to head over to the bathroom. Next was Mari who could not wait another moment to head over to the bathroom as well. She was doing the pee-pee dance all the way to the door when she realized the door was locked.

"Hello, Aunt Candi, is that you in the bathroom? I really got to go now," Mari tried to softly yet loudly enough be heard from inside the bathroom. She did not want anyone else waking up and pushing their way in front of her, even if it was a game. Not today, this was a real pee moment for her, as Mari continued doing her pee-pee dance.

"Si, Mari, I am here. I will open the door but shut it behind you very fast so I can jump into the shower. OK? Promise?" Candi whispered back, trying to make it a game.

"OK, OK, just open the door," Mari responded.

As Candi opened the door, Mari quickly locked the door and ran to the toilet to urinate but realized her aunt was simply sitting on the bathtub's edge, staring at a white tubular item. As Candi was about to take off her robe, she heard Mari exhale really hard.

"Mari, are you OK?" Candi asked her niece as she saw Mari's face extremely pale and about to faint.

Mari turned toward Candi and asked, "Did Papi do that?" as she pointed toward Candi's protruded abdomen.

"Yes, he did. How did you know?" Candi asked.

"I just knew," Mari answered, feeling sick to her stomach.

"All will be OK. Trust me, Mari. I will make sure all is OK. I just do not know how to tell Sara. I will do so, but it may must take some time in explaining everything so she will be as OK with this situation as possible." Candi tried to reassure Mari as she hugged her niece with all her might.

"Oh no, this is not right, little one. We have a new journey with Mari and her family. This will be a tough one," Pearl stated as she moved closer to me and hugged me as both Mari and Candi were doing.

"It is not right, but just remember when it rains, the sun has to come out at some point," Pearl reminded me as I tried not to bump my new wings into hers.

"Yeah, I know. A new day, a new case, and hopefully some more wings," I told Pearlie as we just stood and watched Mari and Candi.

I whisper to you soothing words when pleas resound within the canyons of your mind.

> I whisper to you when outstretched arms embrace barren air.
> I whisper to you when rivers of tears flow and no one is near.
> I whisper yet desire to scream.

I beseech you, I beseech you come to my side.

Don't lie down and ignore my cry.

I hear your voice oh imperceptible one,

Although evil torments my life, breaking me down to my bones.

I reach toward your whisper that brings hope to my soul.

I will whisper forever to your soul,

Knowing you have the strength to overcome strife in your life.

Reach out to me and I will embrace you.

I will now scream words of joy and be by your side,

As the ocean will always have a tide.

—*Nilsa L. Cleland*